MELODY
OF
MANA

✦ BOOK 3 ✦

MELODY OF MANA

✦ BOOK 3 ✦

WANDERING AGENT

Podium

Podium

MELODY
OF
MANA

✦ BOOK 3 ✦

CHAPTER 1

✦

CATCHING UP

I was quickly moved to the headquarters for Dad's army. It was a large governmental building they'd taken over some time ago. They'd chosen this one because of the nearby prison (for captured soldiers, mages, etc.), the thick walls, and the ready-made offices. I, of course, didn't get to see much of it, due to the fact that I was rushed in, taken to an office, sat down, and given a list of places and names to memorize by Mystien.

His safehouse and contact list was about a page long, and Dad told me, in no uncertain terms, that I wouldn't be allowed to leave until I could recite the whole thing backward. I later learned that this was an exercise that I'd be doing for several weeks, so that I wouldn't ever forget where to go if things ever hit the fan again.

"Please tell me you're not actually going to make this a daily thing," I said when Dad finally returned to test me late that evening.

"It's in case you ever run away again, and yes, I am."

"I did not *run away*, I was *kidnapped*," I retorted.

"You were, and you smartly made it to a nearby, safe location. From which you ran away halfway across the country to stay with a bartender you'd never met."

"Well, when you put it like that it sounds stupid."

"It sure does, and so you will be given to memorize a list of places to go and people to see should things ever go wrong again."

"Fine, not like there's too much else for me to do right now anyway. The academy is shut down, you don't want me out and in the town, and you and John are both busy out of your minds."

"You could spin. You love spinning."

"I loved spinning when I was six, Dad, and most of that was spending time with people while doing it."

He gave me a very sad look. "It's been too long, far, far too long. I'm sorry that I had to leave, and even more so for all that happened afterward."

Now it was my turn to feel bad. "You didn't have much of a choice from what I understand, and I'm not even mad that you didn't tell me where you were going. I know that I was too young then and you couldn't trust me, but what happened to the village wasn't your fault. That all lies squarely at the feet of Lord Hazelwood."

"Lay squarely, he's dead."

"Did you . . . ?"

"Yes. You don't need more details than that. I don't want you to have nightmares."

"Oh, Dad, nightmares are my normal state. I saw the town slowly starve while I tried my hardest and failed to stop it. I gutted Malke. I was kidnapped, threatened, fought a massive iron golem and a mana eater. I was hit with a lightning bomb and left barely able to move in a field. I . . . I saw Rod . . . after what they did to him. Good dreams are a rare gift for me, and knowing that you skinned that bastard or something wouldn't bother me a bit."

He sat down near me, finding one of the office chairs. "Alana, that shouldn't have happened. I wanted you and your brothers to have a peaceful life, not . . . not the one you've had."

I rose, heading over to him and kissing his cheek. "Things happen, Dad; it's not your fault. Now, can we go get some food? I've been in here all day."

"That sounds good actually; let's go. Also, where in the world did you run into a mana eater or an iron golem for that matter?"

As we rose and moved to the door, I looked at him. "Do you want the story of how I met the crown prince first? Or the one where I was at a party that turned into a bloodbath?"

"Alana, do me a favor."

"Hmm?"

"Don't dump all of this on your mother at once. Who knows how she'll react?"

"I think I'm going to gloss over the worst parts. She is a bit prone to overreacting. Anyway, since you didn't answer . . . It all started after we went to see the exams for the academy . . ."

* * *

I slept in late the next morning, not realizing how much I missed that luxury that students seldom got. When I woke up in the room assigned to me, I found that it was still a bit depressingly empty. I didn't have many of my meager possessions on me, and those I did were mostly functional.

There was a bowl of fruit for breakfast, along with some bread and water. It was plain, but good, and that was something that I missed a bit as well. Not everything had to be formal, my hair didn't need to be put up in braids, and I didn't need lots of layers that I couldn't hope to put on without either help or magic. It was relaxed. Well, there was a guard just outside the door who informed me, "The general said to stay here and memorize your list," but I could live with that.

Mystien came by around noon.

"All right, Alana, the reports about you from your teachers say that you had an unusual magic item. There are perhaps other things too?"

"Um? The lamp?"

"Indeed, let's see it." I shrugged and brought over my lamp, which was still hovering around a full charge. "What's it do?" Mystien asked as he gave it the same odd look everyone did when they first saw it.

"It's a lamp."

"What's it actually do?"

"It's a lamp."

"Seriously?"

"Yup."

"Why does it feel . . . sort of too right?"

"I'm not completely sure on that."

"Best guess."

"Three-point-one-four-one-five-nine-two-six-five-three-five-nine," I sang. Translating the song was a bit clunky, but it still kind of worked.

"I . . . Is that pi!?" Interestingly pi was pronounced the same here. I suspected that some, or many, other people from Earth had seen to that.

"Well, some of it. Pi isn't really a number that you can just say . . . I think? Regardless, that is way more accurate than what everyone normally uses. I think that's why it looks . . . wonky, or part of it at least. I was also humming when I made the thing, so there may be some bardic nonsense going on too." I knew for a fact that pi was irrational, but there was no reason to go into detail there, or to tell him I knew a hundred digits of it.

"Okay . . . very well. That is something I'll want to experiment with later, but for now let's go over the spells you can do."

I spent the next hour or so going through most of the variations of what I could do for him, and giving basic, if not completely accurate explanations.

"I see why the capture team had a hard time with you. Lucien taught you illusions, I'm guessing?" At my nod, he continued. "The fire and lightning are particularly impressive. Most bards never manage something like either of those. I'm also personally amused by the sugar spell, not because it's magically impressive or anything, but rather that you spent that much time and mana learning to make sweets."

"Sweets are important! What can a girl do if she cannot bake cakes or make her tea tasty? The best parts of life are enjoying sweet things." I raised my fist in an overly dramatic pose. "Long live sweets!"

The old man groaned, tossing a ball of cold water at me with a lazy flick. "Try to take this seriously."

As I dried myself, I glared at him. "You're still a grumpy old fart."

"And you're still childish."

"Being childish is an art form, Mystien. You should engage in it more often. It's fun."

"I'm well aware, but there's a time for everything."

"Fair enough, anything else?" I'd shown him my spells now. I was a bit surprised that he hadn't asked about the sky-metal. But if he wasn't asking, I wasn't volunteering it; when I got used to things and knew everyone was on the up-and-up, perhaps.

"How exactly did you manage to keep casting after the capture team silenced you?"

"Oh, I cast through dance."

"Interesting. I knew there were elves who did that sometimes. Did you discover that on your own?"

"What? No, I've been taking Atali Dance at the academy for like a year."

"Oh. When your father sees you doing that, I'm sure he'll be . . . surprised." He barely held back his laugh. "I don't know if he's ever seen Elven dances before. I wonder what he'll say."

I leaned in close. "Yes, good, embrace the laughter." Eventually, he gave in.

I was informed that Mom was somewhere safe and would be told of my "rescue" as quickly as possible. Messengers had been dispatched, but they were notoriously slow, particularly now, as the snow had finally begun to fall in earnest.

I was locked up and mostly bored for about a week. I'd spent my time alone working on my core for the most part and doing some self-assigned work on item creation, all theoretical, in the last part, but it was fun. I spent my afternoons doing some dance practice, good for if I got silenced again and excellent exercise. The fact that my dad was never around in the afternoons may have had something to do with the time slot. I'd also taken to wearing my earpiece as a decoration, hoping for some information on Dras.

As I came out of my evening session of core improvement, I heard a noise in my ear.

"How should I know? She just said to use this thing if it got bad and to try and be outside . . . No, I don't know what it does, no, no. Yes, I did try it when we evacuated, but nothing happened. Just relax, I'll only be a . . ."

"Who's there?"

"Alana? Where are you? Are you invisible again?"

"No, it's the earpiece. Who am I talking to?"

"Oh, sorry. Yeah, it's me, Dras. You haven't forgotten me, have you?" His voice on the last bit was a bit cheeky.

"No, you idiot. I was just slammed for a few days there. I'm glad you're okay. What's the news?"

"Yeah . . . yeah, I understand. We need help, Alana. It looks like the palace fell a few days ago and the city is overrun with soldiers. Are you still in the city?"

"Um . . . yeah, so . . ." This was going to be an awkward conversation; there was no doubt in my mind about that.

CHAPTER 2

✦

A QUICK OUTING
AND IRRITATED MENTOR

Right, right, Dras, first I need to know what you need." It took me a few moments to put all my thoughts together, then into words.

"Well, help mostly." He seemed to think it was obvious.

"Duh, what I mean is what specifically do you need? Are you trying to leave, get food, what?"

"Looking for information, and any info on where kingdom's army is."

"Well, the army is gone, Dras; the kingdom is gone. Looks like the government has changed, at least here. Not sure what else there is to say about that. Where are you?"

"Shit, and I can't say."

"Yeah, so, new regime. What do you need now?"

"I don't know."

"I don't either, Dras. If you want to surrender to the new soldiers, that's probably easy enough, and you'll be safe."

"We'll be safe? Alana, they invaded the capital. They took the city! Do you know how many people died?"

"I do, and I also know that no more need to perish. You could also go to the temple district and stay there for the time being, but you'd have to swear not to get involved in the fighting anymore, and they'd hold you to it. That's what I did with Kala. I'm sorry that I couldn't bring you along on that, but there was no time. A lot of things happened." I opted for the moment not to tell him that my family was with the new owners of this city, mostly because I was afraid of how he'd react.

I knew that Dras would eventually learn about my family, but there was no need to rush that. I hoped that he would forgive me, but first I needed him, and whoever he was with, to be safe. Was that a bit hypocritical? Yes. I was not going to force him or trick him too much though.

"I don't suppose you could help us get there?" Dras asked on the other end.

"How many of you are there?"

"Fifteen."

"Dras, I can't make that many people invisible, and I don't know the undercity as well as you do. I'm afraid that I am not too much help here. I also did promise not to get involved in the fighting anymore for now. I doubt the temples will look kindly on me helping you that way."

"Can you at least let people know we're coming? I'd rather not show up unexpected."

"That I can do."

It was decidedly something I wasn't supposed to be doing, but I took a bit of time after lunch the following day to write a note explaining to my dad that I was fine and would be back shortly. Hopefully, he wouldn't find it while I was out. I was more than tired of his overprotectiveness and decided to do what every decent bard would have and go for a bit of a break.

As I was setting up all the spells I would need for this, I wondered briefly if the propensity for making a break for it was from being a bard, or if that propensity is what made you a bard. It really did seem to be a running theme among the lot of us, and there had to be something more to it. I'd also noticed that all the priests tended to fall into the same basic mold, same with wizards. Someone surely had asked these questions before, and I'd have to look up the prevailing theories if and when I ever got back to school.

I opened my door a few minutes later and began a brief discussion with the guard. It was mostly on the timetable for my family getting home, which I knew he didn't have, and requesting that dinner be pushed back just a bit, so I'd have more time to get back to my room. I walked down the hall as my illusion finished up, closing the door with a simple movement spell.

Once I was well out of the vicinity of my room, I dropped the invisibility. They certainly had some form of defense against that, and I was known to at least some of the people here. It might be hard to come up with an explanation if any were too curious about what I was doing, but that seemed unlikely as long as I kept my head up and looked like I was going where I was supposed to be.

Of course, I ran into a small snag. A man whom I didn't really recognize stopped me in the hall.

"Hey, you're the girl General Verren sent us after. Alana, right?"

"Yes, sir, did you need something?" I smiled lightly and looked him straight on.

"Yeah, he told us who you were a couple of days ago. Don't worry. We'll keep it secret. That said, me and the boys were wondering how you managed to keep casting after the silence spell?"

"Oh, you don't have to make noise to cast, just perform. As soon as you hit me with that spell, I started dancing."

"Dancing? I've heard of elves doing some dance magic, but that's an odd one."

"Yeah, they taught us Atali Dance. Our professor talked about the basics a few times. I was also nearly done with the spell."

"Regardless, you caught us all right off guard on that one. Mind running us through some of the info on it later?"

"Not at all, just send a letter to the general or Mystien." I almost asked him to send it to me, but if he did that too soon, it would cause issues. Better to punt the problem on to Dad.

"Thanks, see you later."

Once I was past him, it was a straight shot to the exit. In pretty much every place I'd ever been on either world, public buildings like this seemed to follow the same design: labyrinthine back areas, which I only knew because of a few outings; numbered doors; and big, open, obvious public doors.

Security was minimal since I was leaving, not coming in, another oversight on somebody's part that I was not going to complain about. Those coming in were thoroughly checked and identified. There was no chance of me entering as easily as I was leaving, but I'd burn that bridge when I came to it.

The streets were, unfortunately, packed to the brim with snow. I'd been inside so much I hadn't even thought about it being winter right now. The main roads had at least been cleared, and a spell kept me from getting warm. I did stick out a bit in my "sit around the house" outfit, as I'd neglected any of the thicker clothes or shawls that most women were wearing right now. There was also almost nobody around, which didn't help either.

About halfway there, I heard a crunch of snow beside me. Turning around, I saw Charles, who seemed to be just about everywhere in the lower city nowadays.

"Hi." He was wearing a newer-looking outfit, a dark gray tunic and pants with matching cloak.

"Hi, Charles, did you need something?"

"Is everything okay? I got the feeling you were being kept like a caged bird there."

"I broke out. Don't tell anyone." I made a *shh* motion with my finger, which got a smile.

"I see. Mind if I join you? The old man asked me to keep an eye out."

"Sure, I'm just going down to the temple district for a bit though."

"Not planning on running away then?" He asked as we began walking again.

"Nah, just going for a walk. Dad means well, but he can be suffocating sometimes."

"That I understand. When I first got back, my mom hardly let me out of her sight for a while." He had the same calm, quiet voice, but this had to be the most words I'd ever heard him speak.

"What did you do?" Perhaps he had some advice to help with my own problems.

"I made it clear that I could take care of myself and that she needed to stop."

"You make it sound so simple."

"It is simple, but simple isn't always easy."

I spent some time going over that last statement in my mind. I kind of understood why Dad was being the way he was, but clearly needed to put my foot down. I'd lived on my own for several years and just putting me in a room was not going to work for long. He'd know that I'd left when I came back, so hopefully that would put an end to this house arrest.

Soon enough, we made it to the entrance of the temple district, and while I wanted to go in, I was now very connected to one of the forces in this city. I could enter, of course, but I felt that it would send a bit of a mixed message, and I doubted Charles would be able to follow. He seemed to be staying out of the fighting, but that didn't mean that he didn't prefer one side.

Once there, letting them know that a group of fifteen was coming, and likely had multiple casters, was trivial. I also asked for a note to be sent to Kala telling her to use the thing I gave her (specifically unspecific) if and when she got time. We could at least have phone calls if I wasn't going to be seeing her.

On our way back, Kala came on the radio.

"Hey, didn't you say not to use these around people?"

"It's probably fine, and if it isn't, you can heal any damage it does." She laughed, and from there we chatted until another voice joined the call.

"How does this thing . . . wait, I hear someone. Alana, is that you?"

"Mystien? Where did *you* get an earpiece?"

"Lucien gave me his, obviously. The better questions are who are you talking to and why did you neglect to tell me about these?"

"Hi, I'm Kala."

"Um . . . one second." I put a silence bubble over the receiver and looked at Charles. "Didn't you have Lucien's earpiece?"

"I gave it back after we found you."

"Great." He smiled at my obvious sarcasm.

"Um, well, Mystien, it slipped my mind."

"Oh, is that so? Well, we need to have a chat. I'll be up there to see you in a moment."

"Up where?"

"Your room, obviously." At this point, I noticed that Kala had decided to sit this one out, probably for the best.

"Oh . . . I'm not there right now . . ."

"Alana, where are you?" I could feel the displeasure through the very sound of his voice.

"I . . . went for a walk."

"A walk? You went for a walk?"

"Yup. Wanted to deliver a message personally . . ."

"Hey, Alana, we're nearly there. Is everything good?" Dras could not have possibly had worse timing.

I could hear the sigh from the other end. "Why, hello there, newcomer, nearly where?"

"The temple district . . ." Dras seemed to hesitate as he, too, was picking up on the frustration.

"Alana."

"Yes, Mystien?"

"How many of these exactly did you make?"

"Four."

"Are you sure?"

"Yup."

"Good, come back immediately. We need to have a talk."

After that declaration, the conversation between everyone died. Dras seemed to smartly decide that he should shut up and be quiet. Kala grasped the same situation earlier, and both said goodbye quickly, which I guessed meant they took out their earpieces. I did the same only a few moments later, if for no other reason than not wanting to get into any more trouble.

"You know, Charles, I'm reconsidering running away," I said to my quiet companion.

"I'd rather you not." That seemed sincere and caused me to look at him briefly. Honestly, I'd been a really terrible friend to him over the years. I should change that.

"Fine then, I'll go back. I think Mystien is going to skin me though."

He quirked an eyebrow but said nothing. I was a bit surprised when he followed me all the way to the headquarters, even more so, when the guards there recognized him. He had to go through checks, but so did I. They were also expecting me and were even so generous as to send an escort along to make sure I made it back to my room with no chance of getting lost. How helpful!

CHAPTER 3

✦

ANGRY GUARDIANS
AND MY TUTOR

I was hesitant to return to my room actually; getting chewed out was never fun. When we arrived, I just opened the door. The guard looked at me with a frown, as I imagine he'd been told off as well.

My former teacher had a look of near rage on his face. "Alana, why did you leave without telling anyone?" He didn't even comment on Charles, who'd followed me in.

"Because you would have stopped me or asked questions that I didn't care to answer."

"Well . . . at least you're truthful. Do you know why we were keeping you here?"

"Because my dad is insane and overprotective? I've lived on my own for years now. I hardly need someone looking after me every moment."

He got up and flicked me in the head, then set up a silence bubble around the two of us. His was not as complete feeling as mine, but it did feature a shade that prevented anyone from seeing us. I noticed that he'd even set it so that Charles was just outside.

"Alana, you are still dense, and it might get you killed. You are a military asset to whatever side you're on."

"I'm a sixteen-year-old girl who isn't even fully trained."

"Who taught me something about water I didn't know. That increase in power alone allowed us to sweep away a number of forces that would have otherwise posed a much larger issue. Now, you have instantaneous communication over distance. Do you have any clue how valuable these little items you made are? What if I gave them to generals in different regions and we coordinated like that? That is only one small thing you could do with them."

"I don't think they'll work over more than about a city or so of distance . . . I haven't checked, but I'm pretty sure that they can't use them to communicate that far. And it's not quite instant."

"That is absolutely beyond the point! I don't think that our enemies have found out about you yet, but if they do, you are in real danger! Good grief, just think for a second. You are the child of a general in a city that was invaded *less than a season ago*! That alone makes you a target."

"I'm DENSE? Mystien, I've lived on my own for YEARS! If you expect me to stay locked in a room because you think it's best, you've lost your mind! You say that I'm capable and then treat me like a glass ornament that will break. I won't! I can take care of myself, and I can decide who I need to trust with important things. As for those communicators, I only gave them to people who I knew were safe. I haven't even told anyone else about the water thing, or any of the other stuff I've been working on—except you with the whole pi bit."

He sat down and buried his face in his hands. "Alana, this is dangerous. Obviously, we won't keep you here forever, but you do need to be more careful. At the very least, don't go running off alone out into the city where we can't help if things go wrong for now. If you get hurt or killed . . ."

"I don't really have much of anywhere to go, except the temple district, and even then, they're busy. And it's winter and basically sucks outside. That said, I need to be trusted to take care of myself, to move about when I feel like it, and get rid of the damn guard outside of my door. I think I've demonstrated just how useful that is."

"Fine, I'll speak to your father tonight. Will you remain in place until then?"

"All right. But tell him that if he thinks he can lock me in my room forever, he's lost his mind too." I pouted a bit, feeling like this wasn't a complete win.

"Good, now, before we have any more surprises, kindly tell me what you've been working on. The things you left out, too, please. If I know, I can possibly obscure their source, or at the least tell you how much you absolutely can't tell anyone about them."

"Um, so I learned some things about sky-metal."

"The mythical, non-real substance that mages of the past claimed to have?" he asked with the I-wouldn't-believe-anything-you-said-if-you-weren't-someone-who-gave-me-crazy-things look.

"Oh, it's super real. Want to know how to make it?"

I told him about everything, except the hundred digits of pi and being able to read the core. The orb still weirded me out a bit, and I didn't want more of them floating around. He didn't ask where I'd learned some of it, and I didn't volunteer information. If he did, I would explain to him that I cracked the core's internal language and got it from there. That was at least plausible and possible, but I didn't really want to lie to him, unless it was necessary.

Mystien didn't take any notes; he just looked at me as I told him how to break down matter. It was a hard thing to explain, so I just told him that I focused on the thing, trying to take out every different bit, kind of like sorting grains of sand.

He didn't seem to believe me about the communicators and how they were basically a mix of a lamp and light detection script, but he'd test it and find it to be true, so I had no issues. He did ask for a lot of specifics on the frequency and the like. It seemed that wizards knew that light could be put at those levels, but nobody bothered because it seemed useless.

When he'd finished, he dropped the dome. Charles was still sitting quietly by the door, waiting for us.

"Thank you for bringing her back. We talked and I think we will be okay now," Mystien said to him, nodding.

"Of course, you did tell me to keep an eye out."

"Wait," I interjected. "You said Lucien told you to do that."

He smiled as I glared at him. "I said the old man, you never asked which one."

"How do you two even know each other?" They were getting along far too well for my taste. The last thing I needed was for all my friends to be arrayed against me.

"Lucien," they said in unison. It seemed I was going to have to go have a chat with the old bartender some other time.

Mystien did talk to my father, who was not angry. He was furious, enraged . . . really, really mad. He didn't yell or scream though; he just showed up at my room and told me exactly how irresponsible he thought I'd been. I might have guessed he was calm had his aura not betrayed him. But he'd completely lost focus, and it was an angry black cloud filling up the doorway. He did take away the guard and told me that we'd speak in the morning. All in all, I felt that that was about as good as it could have turned out.

* * *

The next morning, both Dad and John showed up. I hadn't seen my brother in a few days, but he looked smug, perhaps because brothers are like that when their younger siblings get in trouble.

"Mystien seems to think that me trying to keep you locked in is a bad idea, so I've got good news."

"You're going to let me go as I please?"

"No, but I won't try to restrict you to your room. I will ask that if you want to go outside you take someone responsible with you."

"I am responsible," I pouted, probably not the best time, but I could take good care of myself.

"Your actions yesterday strongly disagree, someone responsible who is strong enough as well. Your brother, or me, or Mystien, or . . . we'll think of some others. As for now, I've got something to cheer you up a bit and keep you busy."

"Oh?" One did not normally expect presents for irritating their parents, but what did I know?

"Yes, we managed to capture one of the professors, who I understand taught you. I'm also as certain as I reasonably can be that she has no loyalty at all to the former nobility, and she agreed to tutor you. This way, you can keep up with your education as well as we can manage until we get the academy back up and running."

That last part piqued my interest. "Wait, you're reopening it?"

"Yes, there will be some changes, but young mages still need guidance." He looked a bit smug at that. "And you are going to be attending. I'm staying here for the foreseeable future and not having you go would not look good."

"Hooray!"

"Good, I'll go and prep your tutor. Come down to the training area in a bit." With that, he left us.

"You really managed to tick him off, you know that?" John offered after Dad had made his exit.

"He'll get over it, or he won't, either way I'm not five anymore and he can't just keep me locked up."

"Oh, he totally could. If he wanted it, you'd be in a locked and really warded room. You might eventually escape, but it would be a good long time. From what I hear, Mystien talked him down from that though."

"Because Mystien has some sense."

John just shook his head for a few moments, seeming to not believe that I could, or definitely would, find some dumb way out of whatever prison Dad might have been envisioning. I hadn't experimented with a whole load of things that were on the list, but I just didn't have time for it, yet. Locking me up would have been a surefire way to see me poof like smoke at a magician's show.

"So, who's the professor he found?" I asked, hoping it was someone fun.

"No idea."

"Seriously? You didn't even ask?"

"Nope."

"Come on then, let's go find out." I turned and left, heading down the hall. We made it all the way to the end before John told me I was going the wrong way.

After a few times of my trying to lead the way, my brother took over. I was hoping he would after my first wrong turn, but he seemed to think that he had years of teasing to make up for. Eventually though, we did arrive at the training area.

"You took long enough," Dad said a bit gruffly as we came in.

"We got a bit lost," John responded, chuckling.

"Right then, I believe you've already met?"

I looked past him to see Professor Etia standing there, looking pleased as punch. "Good morning, Alana, I'm so happy you're all right. Is this charming young man your brother then?"

My dad gave her a brief look. "John, you are not to sleep with your sister's tutor." He seemed to have at least some sense of what Professor Etia might try.

She looked a bit scandalized but recovered her smile quickly.

"I agree completely, Father." Two could play John's game. "It would be completely inappropriate."

"Thank you," my father said.

"I mean, while she may be an excellent dancer and would probably blow his mind, it's just wrong. I mean, while those hips may not lie, it's just unacceptable."

"Where in the world did you learn that song, Alana? It's classical. I haven't even heard it in years." Professor Etia gave me a look as she asked.

It took me a full moment to process that. It would seem someone was a fan of 2000s music. Interdimensional copyright infringement aside, I had work to do.

"Uh . . . a book, I think. Anyway, my brother definitely shouldn't try to end up with you."

"Whose side are you on?" Dad asked as he turned back to us.

"Whichever one lets me tease John more, of course." That got a lovely chuckle from my professor; she at least understood.

CHAPTER 4

TEAMING UP WITH PROFESSOR ETIA

Professor Etia was as interested in our lessons as I was. I'd not had a chance to talk to her since I'd managed to pull off lighting with her techniques, but now I had all the time I needed. She was thrilled that I'd managed such an advanced bit of magic with dance, even in part, and insisted on making that the focus of our lessons. That was not particularly surprising, but it did at least give me something fun and physical to do.

She had managed to not be locked up because she was an elf. The good professor was quite clear, even before the war, that she didn't really feel any loyalty to the kingdom, as it was for and run by humans, and was only here for her own reasons. That had not won her many friends in the elites of society, but everyone could easily tell that she was quite good at what she did. Her skill had landed her a teaching position, even with her blasé attitude about governance.

Therefore, when the group of students she'd been leading out of the school got caught, it was easy for her to prove that she cared about the welfare of her charges, but not who was in charge, because it was common knowledge. She'd been held for a time and interviewed but could honestly care less about opposing the new regime as well, since they didn't seem that much different in her eyes from the previous. Not caring and having no connections had meant that she didn't pose a threat. She was still watched and knew that if she tried anything, they'd be on her, but I didn't think she would.

I now *could* go out into the city if I took someone with me as a body-guard, but that wasn't horridly appealing at the moment. Everything was deep in snow and mostly shut down. The places that were still open were limited in number, and they tended to be filled with those who were just trying to get by with the destruction in the city. Said destruction wasn't too terrible overall, but many houses had been destroyed in the fighting, so there were more refugees than were easy to handle.

Which is why one afternoon I found myself going to a dinner meeting with my dad and Mystien. It was of the informal sort as I wasn't really involved in their official work, but I thought it still counted.

"How are things progressing?" Dad asked, looking up from his food. We all ate pretty simple fare here, it being a military installation and all, and he seemed to prefer that.

"Good, I'm learning a lot about dance casting. There are some tricks to it, so it's slow-going, but it's at least fun."

"Excellent, I'm glad to hear you've found something safe that you enjoy."

"I've been thinking." Both heads turned toward me, and Mystien set up a privacy barrier. "Good grief, nothing that serious."

"And yet it does seem to become that serious when you start acting." Mystien was far more paranoid about me trying new things now.

"Is there any way we can help those who lost their homes in the fighting? Even food and stuff."

Both men let out a breath. "Alana," Dad began, "we are doing things for them. There are a number of shelters set up, and food is being brought in from the eastern part of the empire where it's more stable. Some of them aren't accepting it, but some are. Things will repair in time, but it's hard to do in winter, for now we're just trying to make sure everyone makes it through okay."

"But a lot of homes are gone, and I've heard some of the men in the training hall talking about how people are still grabbing up all the food they can." That was true enough. I spent a lot of time there, and some of the guards did talk to me. Many of them were a bit tired of the duties guarding supply locations and distribution points. It was apparently hectic most of the time.

Dad looked at me with very tired eyes. "Alana, John told me about what you went through in the village. About . . . about how the people starved. That isn't what's happening here though. Please believe me that between us and the various temples, there is no chance of that kind of starvation. Even housing isn't as bad. While a lot is gone, we can set people up in the undercity in the worst cases; it's not great, but it will serve."

He'd hit the nail on the head there. I knew that things were not great right after the siege and thought that they would certainly struggle through the winter. I was even prepared to go full on bakery mode again if it helped. His words did ease some of my fears, but apparently enough showed through on my face.

"Oh, good grief." Mystien shook his head. "Why don't you just go and look around a bit. In fact, I'm heading down to the border of the temple district in a couple of days to have a meeting with Bishop Theodore and hopefully young Dras. You can come along; it might even help."

"What? What do you want with Dras?"

"Well, we want him on our side obviously since you went and gave him a military secret. Barring that, we want your little communicator back. If he's loyal to the crown, then him having it would be an issue, particularly if he tells anyone where he got it. What is your opinion?"

I considered. "Dras is a commoner, and while he's skilled, I don't think he's all that into the old royal family. We both had a pretty good interaction with Prince Lief though, so that might affect him. But overall, I think he could be convinced at the very least to stay out of it."

Dad added in, "I can't believe you just handed something like that out like candy."

I huffed, "Not like candy. I gave one to my only trusted adult guardian, one to my best friend, and one to my years-long friend that I've been dating." I honestly hadn't gotten to see Kala much, but we had managed a few conversations via communicator.

My father stiffened a bit. "I see, then you should definitely go. If that's the case, you probably can get this young man on our side. When you do though, I'd like to have a chat with him, so he knows the things about you he should."

"I'd also like to talk to Miss Kala. We can't get her on our end militarily, but if she understands things, her order will make sure she keeps them quiet. I doubt they'll be willing to make her hand over the communicator, but we can ask for it." Mystien seemed a bit more pragmatic. Dad was just being weird.

"Why do you want them back so bad?" I asked.

"Because we don't want anyone else listening in on our conversations." Mystien seemed to think this was obvious.

"Just change the settings."

"What?'

"If you want one on a different grouping, just change the light settings." There wasn't an easy way to talk about light frequency in our language. It was baked into the core, but that was all in faux English and so not really useful.

"Is that workable? Can we actually have multiple different lines for communications that won't overlap?" I often forgot that a lot of things that seemed rather obvious to me would be new ideas to others.

"Sure. Why not? I mean, obviously there are limits, but you could have a bunch if you really wanted." Mystien sighed and pulled out a piece of paper, on which he began to write furiously. "What's that for?" I asked.

"I'm writing up the requisitions I'll need for protecting a private workshop with some wards, so we can explore the capabilities of these in actual privacy."

I just frowned. "There are a few I'd like to add if you really want to get into this too deeply." I was not going to be exposing myself to lots and lots of potentially high-energy radio waves without some protection.

He gave me another look. "Once I've done my setup, we can add what you think we'll need."

Conversation after that was rather mundane. Dad asked about my day and how I was liking Etia. I really was enjoying our lessons and was learning tons. He even said that he'd come to see some of our training against the team that had come to the school, which was scheduled for the next day.

They still did want to go up against me again. I think the failure had hit them a bit hard with all of their previous success, and they needed to prove something. That didn't seem all that important to me, but if it helped them, I was fine with it. They were polite enough about it all anyway.

Professor Etia had volunteered to join me since she wanted to know where my skills in that avenue had progressed and show me some of her own. I'd never seen her fight, so I was excited to get a look at how Elven bards did things. It was a chance that was rather uncommon in our lands and one I didn't plan to miss.

The next morning, I joined my teacher. While I'd chosen my normal armor, which had been kindly dyed black, she showed up in her full dancing regalia.

The men assembled just gawked like idiots for a few moments. The whole capture team seemed stunned; my brother, who'd somehow inserted himself into this, was absolutely slack-jawed. The only small mercy was that my dad hadn't shown up just quite yet.

"So, what are we doing exactly? Knowing the rules of the exercise are important," Professor Etia declared as she approached both me and the capture team.

"Um . . . so this is a standard practice session. The goal is to disable your opponent, with minimal or ideally no harm from us. We'd appreciate it if you didn't bring in any magic that is too injurious, and a simple light ball or intentionally weakened spell to signal an attack is more than sufficient."

"Very well, what about weapons?"

"Right, right. We don't normally use standard weapons, but we do use these." He produced one of their small needle-like tubes. "These are filled with a sedative and are generally thrown by one of our wizards. Since we don't actually want to knock anyone out, we'll be substituting some small padded sticks instead. If you need an actual practice weapon, we can ask some of the soldiers. I'm sure they'd be happy to loan you one."

"I don't think that will be needed. What about area constraints?"

The man briefly explained that we'd be using one half of the training room. They'd brought in a few small columns and the like to place here and there for cover, to imitate the things that were normally in a given space. There was even an old beat-up table that had been taken from somewhere and a few ratty chairs. He told us that they liked using stuff like this when possible because real fights were almost never in wide-open areas.

She seemed happy with that and nodded after a few more questions to me about how exactly my barriers worked. "All right, I'm ready then."

Both sides moved to designated parts of the training area to prepare. We were planning on waiting for my father. We didn't have to wait long though, as within a few moments he entered the room. Then he did a double take upon seeing Professor Etia.

My guess was that dad had never actually seen Atali Dance or any of its costuming. He'd been busy and never come down when she was teaching me, so I knew he hadn't seen me dance. John was certainly in that boat, too, and based on how he was full-on ogling Etia, I suspected that he would really enjoy what was about to happen.

"Very well then, let's get this started," Dad declared after taking a moment to compose himself.

CHAPTER 5

MOCK BATTLE

As soon as Dad's words left his mouth, chaos erupted. Professor Etia didn't hesitate for even a second and began casting, with me only a beat behind her. While I started with singing, we both also launched into dance. It was immediately obvious how far beyond me in that skill she was.

To their credit, the capture team didn't miss a trick, either, and began their spread. A few of them even prepped their darts to launch at us as soon as they thought us ready. Meanwhile, their other wizards began a series of small spells, which they launched like machine-gun fire. It seemed they were beginning much as they had before.

For my part, as soon as I got my shields up to a manageable level, I started spinning out duplicates of myself and Professor Etia. I thought that perhaps someone like Charles would be able to tell the difference, but their wizards should not be able to in a short time. Each of the illusions mimicked our moves nearly perfectly, and within seconds one side was filled with girls spinning in unison.

It was as I was getting those set up that we were hit with the sound cancellation magic. Since I knew it was coming—and we'd practiced dance casting pretty thoroughly in the past few days—this was no big deal.

Several of the darts launched at a mix of us and my illusions. Some passed through fake dancers; some hit my shields and came to a stop before starting to fall. They only started to fall though, and I understood why Professor Etia had been asking about my shield. Those that missed were being deflected into the air harmlessly and turning in wide circles.

My kinetic blocking shield basically just dispersed the energy; that was how most shields tended to work. This meant that the little projectiles either bounced away lightly, deflected, or just sort of stopped. All of these were fine in that they wouldn't actually break any of the little darts until they hit the ground.

My professor was taking them, all of the launched ones started to circle. The faster ones began to go in wide arcs around the room and toward the capture team. Those that had hit my shield simply floated over to her where they circled around her wrists and waist, getting those to split everywhere was a bit of a pain, but I managed it. There was little power involved there, but there didn't honestly need to be that much; they were small and light.

One of the mages holding the silence spell had eyes go wide as one of their projectiles came back and hit him. Two others followed and the last one maintaining it faltered as he had to dodge.

As it dropped, my teacher began humming loudly, her fingers snapping to the beat. I recognized it as one of the practice songs, a simple tune that worked well on drums and flute. With hardly a thought, I fell into rhythm with her. That was the moment the fight changed.

One bard was not much of a threat. Two not working together was not too much more. Now though, each of us was feeding off the resonance of the other. They were still having trouble tracking the real us from my illusions and had lost three of their number.

Professor Etia went on the attack, firing back dart after dart in waves of twos and threes. They didn't stop if they missed, however; those simply started to turn, arcing around us in a circle. I noted that she seemed to be circling them in predominately clockwise rotations and added a bit of wind to help speed them along.

Our fight continued much like that. I eventually managed to get a storm up to send light bolts at anyone who looked like they were making shields while Professor Etia kept the team pinned down with their own weapons. At that point, it was pretty much over, and we all knew it. As our last opponent ducked out after getting a light shock from me, there was silence.

The gathered soldiers didn't seem to know exactly what to think, and to be honest, neither did I. I thought we'd done well, and perhaps even taken down most of them, but I did not expect us to actually defeat their entire team.

Professor Etia smiled at me. "I did not get my job just because of my good looks."

"What in the world was that spell you were using?" I asked. "It wasn't like anything I'd seen before."

"Oh, it's used in later forms of dance to make ribbons, little torches, or stuff fly around. Some bards will make swords dance back in Atali, but it's really difficult to do. Most of them end up spending so much time mastering that one trick that they never learn anything else. They make great gladiators and all, but lousy actual combatants."

"Will you show it to me later?"

"Of course, Alana dear."

I doubted that I'd ever use it for swords, but it was a neat trick, and really useful for something like darts. That and the way she'd quickly established a way for us to work together had been huge in winning.

"My, my, that was something," the leader of the capture team said as he massaged a spot on his arm where he'd been hit.

"Yeah, it certainly was; you two did a magnificent job." John had wandered over, ostensibly to get a better view of my teacher's outfit. This was at least my guess since he wasn't looking at me at all.

Dad looked . . . stunned. He came over to join us rather slowly, watching me as he did so.

"Alana."

"Mmm."

"Did they . . . teach you that at school."

"Yes? Mostly at least, I've learned a bit since Professor Etia started tutoring me too."

"And the dancing, they taught that at the academy." He seemed genuinely confused.

"Yeah, it was fairly popular with girls."

"I can imagine it was popular with boys too."

"Actually, I didn't end up with any male students. A bit of a shame, some of the forms for men are quite nice," Professor Etia added, looking a bit disappointed.

"That isn't exactly what I meant." Dad seemed a bit flustered by her comment.

"I know what you meant, but regardless we had all females for the year I was there. I suppose if it had continued, we might have gotten one or two boys who were curious before long though."

I didn't think my dad really knew what to make of Professor Etia. She both understood their respective positions and didn't seem to really give a damn. I thought he wasn't really into being treated all high and mighty, even if he often was, but for her to just show that sort of attitude must have been jarring. Most of the men here wouldn't have given him even a bit of sass, but she seemed to think that he was unlikely to hurt her. If I was to place money on it though, she was probably right. My dad was a dangerous man, to be sure, but he didn't seem prone to harm people just for being mouthy.

"Anyway, Alana, kindly don't show your mother that kind of dancing immediately when she gets here, or let her know that you've done it in public. She'll likely have some opinions on it. If she's eased into the idea, I think she'll take it better."

"Fine, I'll give her some time to adjust. Anything else?"

"Yes, while I'm thinking about it, perhaps it's best not to mention that the tavern you stayed at serves so many brothels, to avoid misunderstandings. Also, if you have one of those outfits like your teacher, you should make sure she doesn't see it."

"I don't."

"Oh, you should get one though. They're quite comfortable and they look excellent!" My tutor had lots of ideas, and I knew that eventually I probably would end up in one.

"I don't right now to avoid misunderstandings. I do have a tailor picked out for the future . . ."

"Alana, please. I love her, but your mother is from a very small village and will not be able to handle so many new and . . . different things too quickly. I think she still sees you as you were when you were kidnapped." Dad was looking increasingly worried. I suspected for good reason.

"You still see me as I was when you left, Dad. Or at least you did." I knew that that comment would sting a bit, but it was true. He had consistently treated me like I was about five and it was getting old.

Dad didn't seem to have anything to say to that, so John put his arm around his shoulders. The other soldiers had moved off a bit by now, seeming to know that this was a more private conversation. It didn't do well to have your boss think you were listening in on him.

"Hey, Dad, don't stress too much. It's not too bad, I'm sure it'll be fine." John was wildly optimistic about how Mom was likely to behave, but then he'd also spent a ton of time with her after I'd been separated too.

After my big brother led off my dad, Professor Etia turned to me. "You know, I don't really understand you humans all that well."

That was a rich statement. "What exactly are you referring to, Professor? There's a lot going on here."

"Well, if someone from another land had ended up teaching me some new form of magic when I was your age, my parents would have been absolutely thrilled. You also seem very . . . pent-up. It's kind of strange to me."

"Oh, I think it's because we get pregnant so much easier. A child too young can cause a lot of issues in the family."

"Perhaps, but aren't many children good? Even if you didn't want one at a time, there is magic for preventing that."

"Yes and no. A child when the family isn't ready for it can be very difficult. And there is certainly magic to stop it, but most humans don't have access to magic, do they? Because of that, many who don't will have strong opinions about those who do things that might lead to what they think will damage the family and society."

"That makes sense, I suppose." She seemed to think on that for a bit before asking another question. "Your Atali is going quite well. Do you think you'll ever visit our lands?"

"Hmm, probably not, but it might be interesting. Is there anything I should keep an eye out for if I do?"

"There are a number of things, but if you do, I think you should visit my home. My family would get a real kick out of your illusions and weather magic." She was smiling lightly, looking kind of far off.

"Do elves not do those?"

"We do, but I'll admit that you seem to be using the illusions to a much higher level than most. Your lightning is also quite good, even by our standards."

"What's it like there?" I asked, hoping she might expand on what general things I knew.

"Oh, it's lovely. The forests are warm and comfortable year-round. We don't get snow there except high in the mountains. The cities are also lovely, molded by priests as many of them are from the trees themselves . . ." She went on for quite a while about the plants and the architecture. Which sounded like it was far more intricate than we had in most places.

I learned that many elves revel in the idea of art. They take a long, long time to practice and perfect whatever art they resonate most with until they master it. Etia, of course, loved dance and had mastered as many different forms as she could, even weaving the best magical tricks she could find into her art. While she had her choice, others would focus on things like sculpture, painting, or writing beautifully. Still others would seek perfection in the form of combat, training their bodies and minds into honed blades to fight the many magical beasts that roamed the Elven lands. It did sound like a very interesting place.

CHAPTER 6

✦

TERMS OF AMNESTY

Bishop Theodore

I leaned back in my chair for a brief bit of rest. The last couple of weeks had been exhausting. The city was already fully taken by the time I'd managed to get back, but as soon as I had, the chaos started. That girl, the walking headache that she was, had wandered off almost as soon as things were declared "safe" to go and help her friend at his bar. While I hated that she didn't seem to think to consult anyone about it, I couldn't actually fault her for trying to help those who'd been displaced, which she'd certainly been doing both in the temple district and without.

My problem was that I was hoping to immediately have her delivered to her father's men and she'd left no information with any of my subordinates as to where she was headed. By the time I'd gotten messengers to the various orders to look for her, then for anyone who'd seen her, I was a bit miffed. The fact that she'd left where I knew she would be protected had me truly irritated, and that didn't even account for the loss of handing her over to her father and getting both his gratitude and the look on her face.

I had to admit to myself that I rather disliked the girl. It wasn't truly her fault, but the way she acted still grated on me to no end. The poor priest who had taken care of her in Istlan had deserved more than a note if she were planning to leave. He might have tried to stop her, perhaps even hold her with force for a while, but every caster knew that doing so long-term just wouldn't work. In all truth, had he been made aware of her plans to come to the now former capital, he'd probably have arranged safe travel.

I also had to admit that going to that particular tavern wasn't the worst of ideas. At the time, I hadn't known enough about the situation to judge, but from what I heard from her mother, her teacher, this Mystien, had spoken at length about his friend in the cap . . . no in Lithere, we were no longer the capital of anything. Going to see someone known to be trustworthy and likely to establish contact again wasn't the worst idea, I simply would have liked her to stay with us. That man's tavern was in a . . . part of the city not quite appropriate for a young girl.

Anyway, she was no longer my problem. I also had a number of things to take care of today. The most bothersome of which was a request by this Mystien to speak to the people who'd taken shelter in the temple district. Normally, he wouldn't be allowed in until everything was settled, and while things were technically done, Lord Durin had graciously offered to let us keep the zone for refugees only for a hundred days.

I didn't trust the Lord of Shadows any further than I could throw him, but he knew how to deal with people. He'd ordered that all accused of criminal behavior in the war be given a fair hearing before justice fell upon them. His soldiers were under strict discipline against the worst predations as well, and those few who were identified with any evidence had been dealt with harshly.

That said, many of the terrorist incidents had just been too convenient for him. There had been many attacks against different factions within the kingdom; many of the most dangerous had seemed to be targeted, or had their families and assets targeted. It bothered me, but I had no proof of any wrongdoing, and there was much proof of the good he'd done.

So, I approved the request from his subordinate. He would be allowed to enter and meet with several of those he'd requested. I'd asked to be present to make sure that nothing inappropriate happened, which he'd quickly complied to therefore, it seemed he had legitimate business. What that was I hadn't been told, but I suspected he wanted some of them to join the new regime properly.

When the appointed time arrived, so did the wizard. He was older than I'd thought he'd be and walked with an air of confidence. His robes were dark blue and black, and while they did not project the normal look of purity so many strived for, they did cut a striking image.

I nearly cringed when I saw that he'd brought Alana along with him. I'd hoped to not see the girl for several years, and yet here she was, as if to taunt me. Her clothes were obviously newer, too, a dress of deep black with red pleats and ornamentation. I nearly cringed when I saw her aura; it had been some time since we'd come face-to-face, and the little monster was probably close now to a battle-mage in raw strength than anything else.

"Greetings," I offered. Dras and his mother were here, along with one Professor Klien, who was representing the other members of their particular group. The boy had been requested, though I wasn't sure why, yet.

"Greetings," Mystien answered with a nod of his head. "We're here to discuss the possibility of your group and you, in particular, young man, of returning to society at large from this camp."

The poor boy was taking a bit of time to process things, while his mother's face got more and more sour. "Alana?" he finally said.

"Hi, Dras. Mystien is right. We do want you to join up." She seemed a bit embarrassed for once, speaking politely and keeping back a bit.

"I have questions," the professor began. "Why Dras, and what exactly is one of our students doing sitting there with you?" His eyes were narrowed, and he looked between the two with hard suspicion.

"I can answer that one easily enough. Alana here learned magic under me, and it is by her recommendation that I've come to ask the young man to see sense." The old man kept his face neutral as he answered, but it was clear that he felt that this professor, in particular, was of no importance.

"Learned magic under . . ." Suddenly, the man was on his feet, teeth bared. "You little bitch! You sat there day after day doing what? Planning our downfall? Making roads for your friends to come in and slaughter and destroy so they could take over? Wanted power that badly, huh?"

"I didn't . . ." she began, seeming genuinely afraid.

"There will be no violence in this place." I allowed my own voice to take on the steel that I'd had to use too many times over the years, that threat of death to those who would violate the protection the Shield offered. That alone was enough to stop the enraged professor from doing anything stupid. We were in the very temple of the Shield, and I would not tolerate any attack here from either side.

"She neither knew what I was doing, nor where my loyalties lie during her time in Lithere. Nor did she, to my knowledge, aid Lord Durin's plans in any way. She was barely a child when I joined him and didn't know that I was doing so."

"Did you?" Dras asked, looking a bit stunned.

"No, of course not."

I didn't know the truth here, but I suspected she really might not. Even if I couldn't stand the girl, that much at least seemed likely. It didn't matter though. She'd now been firmly entrenched in one side of the conflict, and there was no going back for her.

"So . . . what are you offering then?" the teacher continued, sneering and not bothering to take his seat. "Let us all come back and be good little pawns for your new master?"

"We are offering to allow you to resume your lives peacefully, well, most of you. Lord Durin has no need to persecute children and those who are willing to live in peace, but those who cannot adjust will be exiled from his lands. The latter group includes many who will be unable to come to terms with the loss of their status. Of course, the combatants are being dealt with slightly differently, but that is not part of this discussion." His message was clear. Most of them can come back, and you can screw off far from here. There was no way this man would be allowed to stick around with that display.

"What would we have to do?" Dras asked, his voice a bit broken.

"Nothing odious, a simple oath that you've no plan to rebel against Lord Durin and you will be permitted to continue your life. If you wish to join in his service once you are of age, that can, of course, be arranged. Until then, you would be encouraged to return to school and finish your studies. We're planning to reopen it come spring, and we will honor the paid tuition of those who wish to return." His eyes flicked briefly to the professor. "There will be some . . . changes, needless to say, but again, nothing that should cause you any issues."

"We're uninterested," Klien huffed. "That is a waste of a deal, and we won't be working with you or your little traitoress." The boy's mother seemed to have some opinions as well but was smart enough to keep quiet for the moment.

"I gathered that you were, but I doubt you speak for your entire group. Since you seem to not desire to at least hear us out, should another not explain to them our offer? Young Dras perhaps? He's a caster, on the cusp of adulthood, and at the very least isn't dismissing things out of hand."

"Are they decent? What do you think?" He looked at Alana as he asked, seeming to consider.

"They seem good, and I don't think Mystien or Dad would work for anyone who was a monster. That said, it's still new to me too."

Dras rubbed the bridge of his nose for a bit while the professor, now effectively dismissed, glared. "I'll tell everyone what you said, and . . . I'll take the oath afterward."

"I can't believe this. Is there no loyalty anymore? After all our kingdom did for you, even letting you into the academy, you're willing to abandon it?" The professor looked at the boy with cold eyes.

"Professor Klien, you're mistaken. The kingdom treated me and my family like disposable trash until Alana managed to get me good enough to pass your exam. She's the one who taught me day after day without asking for so much as paltry reward so I could have a chance. The way I see it, if she thinks these folks are okay, they're probably okay."

He was apoplectic, but the scorned teacher left, closing the door behind him as he did so. I'd have to send someone to keep an eye on him later; his attitude had been out of line. I knew that some of those who'd been nobles in the kingdom were making louder and louder noises about the current state of things, but I wasn't sure if he was in that group. Many of them seemed to want to go back to fighting, or rather, seemed to want someone else to go back to fighting.

There was a bit of back and forth between the young mage and the older wizard, who seemed to treat him like he might be a potential ally. Eventually though, he did have to leave.

"Well, Dras, I look forward to seeing you again some time. I don't often get to chat like this anymore, and it has been refreshing. Oh, and about that item Alana gave you, could I get it back? We need to do a bit of testing on it to make sure everything is in order."

I had been a bit suspicious earlier, but this was just too much. It seemed obvious that this was important, perhaps even the reason he came here himself.

"Um, sure. That's no problem at all." I watched the boy hand over some small carrying case on a necklace. Every instinct I had was to scream at him, but that would violate my neutrality here, and that I couldn't do.

"Thank you so much," Mystien said as he turned to leave.

"See you soon." His student waved as she moved to follow.

The rest of us went in short order. From the look on her face, this young man would either have to cast some spell to silence his mother, or deal with an angry tirade soon enough. I didn't envy him. We came to the doors in silence, and I looked down.

Alana and her master were going down the steps when it happened. Klien must have been waiting for them there, and as they descended, he strode forward, raising his hand. I could see the spell before I could react and before him an incredible torrent of water formed, speeding at the pair like a boulder falling from a mountain. If nothing else, the academy had always hired very skilled mages, and this spell was one that could easily shatter a stone column.

It flew forward at unimaginable speed, a blur as if rushed at them and . . . did nothing. The old man hadn't made a gesture or spoken a word, but it seemed he'd cast something in that split second. His eyes moved over to his attacker, and I heard a disdainful "pathetic."

I was glad that he at least didn't respond, fighting him as well would have been a disaster. Sadly for the attacker, he had forced my hand. He had sought to kill in a place where all were given safety. While he was still stunned at his own failure, I made a wave of my hand. The small silver projectile that issued forth hit the would-be killer square in the gut. His eyes went wide as he looked down before falling dead on the spot.

"I have kept my word, Bishop, and will continue to do so." Mystien looked at me as he spoke.

"You have. Though it might be wise to go now."

Alana looked stunned as well I noticed, freezing in place. Eventually, her escort guided her off with a firm but gentle hand.

CHAPTER 7

✦

RETURN

Mystien basically pushed me back to the small carriage we'd come in, as I was having a hard time moving on my own.

"I . . . don't understand, didn't he know he'd die?"

"Probably suspected it, might have thought he could get away after he killed us."

"But why? I knew him. I was in his class. He never acted like that."

Mystien sighed. "Alana, Klien was one of those we knew we'd have to send out of the country, at best. His family was one of the higher ranked ones, and he was a known supporter of the former king. He lost though. He lost his home, his status, a fair bit of his family, and now he knew he would lose everything else except his life. He chose to try and take us out. Desperate men do desperate things."

"He always seemed so nice, all the same."

"He probably was. You were no threat and no real issue to him. At the end though, you were the traitor who brought him low, at least in his eyes. I hated that you had to see that, but it is better that you did now, when you could be protected rather than see it later, when you cannot."

I was quiet for the rest of the ride. We had one more place we had to go, and I'd been the one to ask to go there anyway. Mystien took me over to where the army was handing out goods to those who needed them. They had a system whereby a household could sign up to receive some basic food and fuel aid. It would be temporary, but the people waiting in line there didn't seem to be in any distress.

I watched as a woman and her children were given several packages of food and a small bit of oil. They thanked the guard and went on their way. It was easy enough to ask to see what was in one of those, and since I was with an officer in the army, I would be allowed. Each contained a few pounds of tubers of various kinds, some grain, and a bit of dried fruit. I knew about what someone needed to live from long and harrowing experience and that, along with the oil, would certainly be enough.

In the end, I had to concede that my getting involved wasn't really needed. These people were getting taken care of at least as well as those in the temple district, and they also had the chance to take care of their homes and try to make things better there. Someone had even organized to clean out the main roads of snow, something still very important to keep on top of.

"Satisfied?" Mystien asked after I finished looking around.

"Is he like this to everyone everywhere?"

"Lord Durin?" Mystien asked, and I nodded. "Mostly, he understands the value of keeping the populace happy and of seeing to their basic needs. Keep in mind that what we're doing here is a temporary measure, one designed to keep further issues at bay. It will end, and when it does, things will return to . . . well, not how they were before, but a form of normal."

"I'm a bit surprised; from what I've seen I'd think the common people would be ignored in favor of keeping the remaining nobility from causing further issues."

"Lord Durin is abolishing the nobility."

That came as news. To be fair, I knew little about his policies so far, but I imagined that it would cause some problems. "Really? But doesn't he need magic?"

"Are you a noble now, Alana? Or do you think I am? What about your friend Dras, Lucien, or Kala? There are plenty of other casters than just the nobility. We will be recruiting as many as we can and even some of the lesser-ranked nobility who didn't participate. It will be made clear to everyone that those who can excel will be given power, and those who cannot will have it removed."

"All right then. I'll just have to wait and see what Lord Durin does."

"Indeed, your father and I have known him for a long time, and his plans do have a tendency to work out well for us."

In a couple of weeks, Kala was finally able to come and see me again. It had been miserable without her, and we spent a lot of time catching up. The temple district was still a mess with all of the people there who were afraid that Lord Durin would just kill them, particularly the fallen nobles. They were managing though, and she hoped it would all be over soon.

I told her all about my time and the continuing training I was getting. Having a tutor on hand to help me polish up some magic had been wonderfully useful. I'd even learned the spell she used to move the dart things around during our practice battle. It was a variation on a standard movement spell, but there were some little tricks here and there that worked very well with moving objects. It helped them maintain speed while allowing you to alter their direction.

It was during one of our afternoon meetings that she brought along Dras. I was thrilled to see him, and the reverse seemed to be true as well.

He greeted me, saying, "Hey there, long time."

"Indeed, how is everything?"

"Mostly good. Our house is gone and my mother still hates your guts, but that was kind of expected."

"If she didn't, I'd be more worried. Where are you living?"

"Oh, I found us a place to rent for the time being. Mana is at a premium these days, so money isn't a huge issue."

"That's good. Anything else happen recently?"

"Not too much, some personal stuff, trying to get things in order. You?"

"Just training mostly, not like there's too much to do until the snow melts."

Around that time, my father showed up. He was in and out most days dealing with many aspects of administration that he had to take care of personally. From my understanding, he left all the paperwork to Mystien while he took on the business of expelling all those on their list who were trying to hide in the city. I'd only been taken to his office once or twice, but it was mostly empty except the desk piled high with reports.

"Good evening, Kala."

"Good evening, sir." The two of them were getting along swimmingly. Dad seemed to think that Kala was a polite young woman who was having a good influence on me, and the fact was that I didn't spend time with many people.

His eyes narrowed as he turned to Dras, focusing on him with harsh intent. "And you must be young mister Dras. It's a shame that we haven't been able to meet before now."

"Oh, uh . . . yes, sir. The paperwork so that I could come into the complex just went through. Even if it's only this area, the security is quite thorough, sir."

"Oh, I see, I see. I didn't know you were trying to get on the list, or I might have stepped in to handle things personally. Actually, while you're here, let's go and check on everything, so there are no problems in the future. I'm sure the girls won't mind me borrowing you for a bit." With that, he practically pushed Dras out of the room, taking him along to . . . somewhere.

"Be nice!" I piped up as he moved to close the door. It only got me a lazy wave of his hand back.

"Does your father think you're dating Dras?" Kala asked after they'd left.

"Probably."

"Haven't you told him about us though?"

"No . . . not yet."

"You should."

I grumbled a bit before settling down with her. "I don't like to talk about that kind of thing, and I don't really think my family would get it."

"Mmm, still." I could tell she was a bit irritated that I hadn't divulged that tidbit to my dad, even after all this time, but it just never seemed like the right time. Anyway, she was here as much as she could be, and he knew we were basically sitting in each other's laps the whole time.

"Can I at least wait until my mom makes it here, so I don't have to go over everything several times?"

"Fine." Oof, that was decidedly irritation.

She let the subject drop, and we sat silently, each afraid to begin the discussion again. That was until Dras came back, looking pale and a bit shaken.

"Good grief, he wasn't nice, was he?"

"Alana, did I do something to piss off your dad? I don't think I've ever had my life subtly threatened so many times and in such a short span, particularly not by someone I think would actually kill me."

"I think he's just being overbearing," I answered.

"Do you now? My mother is overbearing, Alana. She, however, has never tried to intimidate my friends."

"Now, Dras, that is flagrantly untrue, and we both know it. I remember her little screaming fit at The Sky, and how she tried to have the Shield toss me in an orphanage. If Dad does anything like that though, let me know, and I'll straighten him out." I made a little punching gesture with a *UWAH!* at the end. The fact that he was about three times my mass and a monstrously powerful physical magic user just made it funnier.

Both of them left well before dark. It wasn't because the city was dangerous to them, that would have been a real joke, but that the ice would be worse at night, and it would also just generally suck more outside with the snow and all.

Our visits continued apace well past midwinter. It was at this point that I was told that Dad had a surprise for me, and we'd need to spend a day together. At our meeting time, he appeared, and we walked toward one of the covered areas in this complex. This one was set up with large doors out to the street, a place for the wealthy to come and go without having to walk out in the rain or snow.

His personal carriage was there. It was a plainer affair but seemed well-made. He didn't use it much but rather had it for when some personal goods needed to be moved from place to place or on the rare occasion I wanted to visit some shop or other. He'd asked that I use it for that kind of thing, since I was being discouraged from walking and could not as easily ride a horse in a dress. There were methods, sure, but I didn't know them, and I didn't have one of the special saddles ladies tended to prefer when riding.

As we plodded down the road, I kept an eye on things. We were definitely headed to what used to be the nobles' district and went by the different mansions. There was rather little that I knew up here, having only come by carriage a couple of times and one walk back from it when I first met Kala.

Soon we neared a mansion that I recognized. Rooke's home loomed tall over us, still looking massively impressive. Then the slowing carriage pulled into the drive opposite, slowly advancing up toward the house.

"What do you think?" Dad asked as he helped me step down.

"It's massive and lovely. Whose is it?"

"Ours."

"What?"

"I've been told that I need a home to match my new station. The former owner of this one was killed in the fighting, and he had no clear heirs, so it's been given to me."

"Dad, this place is huge. What would we even do with it?"

"I don't rightly know, Alana, but I'm hoping to get ideas on that soon."

The gravel crunched under our feet as he led me up to the doors. "So you brought me out here to see this new place?"

"Oh, the real surprise is just inside." He smirked a bit as we came to the door and he pulled it open.

Inside was an impressive entry. There were statues and decorations all over the walls and a floor of some stone I couldn't identify, black with gold streaks through it. I wasn't much for ostentatious, but it was pretty. More importantly, as we entered, my mother turned around to look at us. She'd been talking to some people who I guessed must be staff but dropped that as soon as we came in.

Mom walked right up to me. She looked almost the same as she always had. Her clothes were much nicer, sure, and she'd aged a bit, but it was still her. Silently, she wrapped her arms around me, pulling me close, and I felt a few hot tears form as I buried my head in her shoulder. We didn't need words for now, just a feeling of finally being home again.

CHAPTER 8

✦

FAMILY LEARNING TIME

Mom spent hours doting and having me tell her what all had happened, and then doting more. There were a few things I glossed over a bit, leaving out most of the details. The fact that I'd been present for so many attacks had been a particular sticking point with her, where she'd pushed to get more information. I simply acted like I was a bit less involved, saying that I'd gone to hide before everything got sorted during the attack on the party, or that our team had taken cover in a creek bed during the attack in the copse. I also left out how injured I'd been during a few of those outings, so as not to cause her any further stress. It all became "yeah, and there was an attack, so we mostly tried to hide," rather than the whole story.

She asked about friends, and I told her all about Dras, Kala, and Pinea, how I'd met each one and what they were like. It occurred to me that I'd not heard about the last of those, and I made a note to ask Dad about it. She insisted that she wanted to meet Dras as soon as possible. My guess was that she'd made the same assumption as Dad had, which I'd have to correct whenever it came up.

Eventually, I was shown to my new room, which had a huge window. Said window looked out toward Rooke's house. Dad had left Mom and me to have our time but had returned now, and he watched me, smiling as I looked about.

"What do you think?" he asked when I'd finished, and then he looked out the window again.

"Um . . . do you know what happened to the man who lived across the road?"

"What? No, why?"

"He was one of my teachers and helped me a lot. I wondered if he was okay."

"Give me his name and I'll see what I can find," Dad replied with a sigh. "What about the room?"

"Oh, it's lovely! Kind of big to say the least. I'm not sure what I could put in it."

The room was, in fact, both massive and beautiful. It was easily as large as our house had been back in Orsken, and even more ridiculous than my room at the academy. I looked around to find the multiple closets, and even a small washroom attached to the side. It was fairly empty, except for furniture though. There was a bed and desk, of course, along with a small table and a vanity over near the windows.

I assumed that the noble family that had previously owned this mansion had had daughters and the like, at some point, and that all the furniture was appropriated from their rooms. That was a bit odd. It felt like I was some kind of thief, moving into someone's home where I had no business being.

Dad ran off again, determined to get a lot of other things in order. Mom, on the other hand, stayed, and watched me check out the room before joining me on the bed.

"It's a bit odd, isn't it, dear?" she asked as I ran my fingers over the carefully embroidered covers.

"Yeah, I feel like an intruder or something."

"I felt the same way when we first got to Lord Durin's estate. The rooms we were given there were lovely, more than anything I'd really ever expected to get in my life. Like someone else had let me into their home, and I'd just taken over everything. I wasn't prepared for it at all and I still don't really think I'm there."

"It's not just that it's opulent. It feels like we came in and killed these people, then took their stuff. I don't really know how to process that."

She wrapped her arms around me, holding me close. "That isn't completely different from what your father and John did. If it helps, I'm told the man who owned this previously was rather cruel."

"It doesn't really."

"Hmm, well what would we do with it otherwise? The man who owned it died, and it doesn't seem that anyone else had a true claim to it. We could just let the place rot, but that seems silly."

"I guess. What is Lord Durin's home like?" I decided to change the subject, not really feeling comforted at all by her words.

"It's quite different. Not opulent in the same way that places in Lithere or his new capital are, but it is lovely. Perhaps he'll invite you to that estate for some function or other one day."

She eventually left me to acclimate, something I appreciated very much. Unpacking didn't take all that long, as I still had little in the way of personal possessions, and soon I was as settled in as I could be.

Our dinner that night was something else. The dining room was too big, and we all wanted to be close and chat, so we ended up sitting next to one another with huge amounts of table taking up space in the room. John joined us, since he would be taking up several rooms here until he was either assigned somewhere else with the army or found his own place.

The food was also a bit odd. Because of Dad's status, Mom and Uncle Barro, who was still living at Lord Durin's estate, were afforded some measure, and Mom had gained several servants to help out. These were hired from people of the former empire who had been willing to join up with Lord Durin, and the food the chef made was tilted slightly more toward more eastern flavors than we were used to. It wasn't too different, but some of the herbs that were used were weighted more strongly in one way or the other. A sage-like plant made far more appearances than I would have wanted, while the rosemary that was endemic to most parts of the kingdom was almost totally absent.

As an aside, most of the plants in this world were exactly the same as in my previous, barring magical plants and a few that might have been there, but I didn't know them. Those we ate would be intimately familiar to most people of a western persuasion, with things like potatoes, beans, grain, and the like very common. Herbs were much beloved and used in most dishes, which was a bit odd coming from where I did, but they were refreshing. Those, too, were either exactly the same, or something very close, which might have well been a different cultivar.

After dinner, we retired to a sitting room where Dad and John chatted while Mom began to work on some light embroidery. I joined with a bit of sewing, one of my dresses had a small rip from something or other, and it was easier to repair it now than later. My mother was horrified at the current state of my sewing skills. She watched me for only a few moments before she came over to check my work.

"Alana, what is all this supposed to be?"

"It's a rip. I'm fixing it."

"Poorly. Goodness, look at these." She took the piece from me and began undoing what I'd stitched, which was a little frustrating, but I knew for a fact that she could do it better.

"Admittedly, but it still needs fixing."

"Why are you being so sloppy? The work on your dress is quite good." She took a brief look to confirm that the stitching on it was extremely good.

"Well, I didn't make my dress, Mother. I don't think I've made any of my clothes since Orsken."

That seemed to make her freeze in her tracks. "Have you not been keeping up with your handiwork at all?"

"Er . . . I spin a bit sometimes, and do a little embroidery here and there . . ."

"What will you do when your children are born? What will this Dras boy you are dating think when he learns you can't even make basic things like children's clothing." This seemed to her the highest form of possible failure.

"I'm not dating Dras, Mother. He's just a friend."

"What?" both Mom and Dad said at once.

"Now hold on, Alana, you told me you were dating him," Dad said as he looked over.

"No, I didn't."

"Yes, you did. You said you gave one of those items to your long-time friend and the other to the person you'd been . . ." I could almost see the gears turning, then clicking into place. "Kala . . ." There it was.

"Mmm-hmm."

"Wait a moment. Alana, are you . . ."

"Yup."

"How do you . . ." my brother, always helpful in his foolish words began.

"We don't, at all. I'm not really into girls like that, but we're still going out."

"Alana," my mother began as she rubbed her head. "You know this can't last, don't you? With your father now in the position he's in, you will have to get married at some point, and regardless of what you think of it, you cannot marry another woman."

"We both know that, Mother. Kala knows she'll have to do much the same. The Lovers are apparently pretty heavy in their encouragement of experiencing every kind of love, so this is more . . . romantic, but not physical."

She looked like she was having a headache right then. "We'll discuss this later, Alana."

"I'd really rather not."

"Well," Dad said, seeming a bit off-kilter as he looked at me, "I may have to have another conversation with young Dras. I believe I may have taken a few years off of his life in our last one." He shrugged. "Good news is at least, I don't have to worry about you coming home pregnant or something like that."

"Oh, Dad, you wouldn't have had to, anyway." If I was going to be honest, I might as well shock them all at once.

"Why?" He narrowed his eyes as he looked back to me.

"I have a Lovers' Mark."

While they froze, John looked at me, smiled, and said, "And here I thought I was the problem child. Well, I'll leave you three to it." He then made a hasty exit.

You would think that my relationship with another girl would be the big deal, but it wasn't quite on the same level. Both of my parents were up in arms about my acquisition of a Lovers' Mark. Both wanted to know who I'd been with at my age that made me make that decision. I considered telling them that I had it for years, but that seemed like a worse idea than any other. I did let my mom have her breakdown for a few moments so she could get it all out before I could get a word in.

"You know that most of the girls who were at the academy have one, right?"

"IS THAT SORT OF BEHAVIOR THAT RAMPANT AMONG THE NOBILITY?" Mom had started yelling a while ago and didn't seem inclined to stop.

"Stop screaming and listen. When Lord Durin's armies started taking out cities, everyone who wanted one was offered it. They didn't know, and nor did we that he would take such a violently oppositional view to . . . mishandling captured women and girls. So pretty much everyone who didn't already have one got one at that time."

Mom sat back down, breathing a sigh of relief. "So that's when you got it."

"No, Mother, I got mine some time before, for basically the same reasons. I didn't know if I'd have to flee again and thought it was a good preparation to make, just in case, and before you ask, no, it has never actually been relevant that I have one."

"Oh, well then, that was very smart of you, dear." Mom was now trying to catch her breath. "If you ever have anything like that, you need to tell me again I'll try not to yell."

Dad looked a bit contemplative and saddened. "It's horrid that you had to think about things like that. I'm glad you took precautions, but . . . none of Lord Durin's men would do something like that, none who wanted to live for long." He sighed. "I'll admit that there have been a few incidents, but every man found to have done that was either executed or handed over to the Lovers for whatever justice they would enact. I even saw Lord Durin beat a man to death personally after it was proven that he'd abused several girls in the camp."

"He killed the man himself?" That was a bit stunning.

"Yes, publicly, and it sent a powerful message. Afterward, he gave a speech to the men about how we were to observe the forms of proper war. Lord Durin may be a conqueror, but he's a civilized one."

"That is good to hear. Now, if you'll excuse me, it is getting late." Neither of them spoke, so I followed in my brother's footsteps.

CHAPTER 9

◆

RETURNING TO THE ACADEMY

Following all of my admissions to my family, things were a bit . . . strained. Mom was still concerned about a number of things but seemed to at least be contenting herself for the moment with badgering me about my poor handicraft skills. I didn't really care to learn much more about those, but she was insistent, and so we ended up having a bit of time every evening where I was cajoled into practicing with her while we talked.

She had a point that they were considered the proper thing for most young women to know. I didn't like them, but I did have to admit at least that much. According to her research, lace making was also considered something important to have a base level of skill at for high-status women. Lace was expensive as it could be and being able to make small bits of it yourself would save your family lots of money. In the end, we alternated between different things during our after-dinner time.

Kala visited a few times and marveled at my new place, giving me a few jibes about it. She also got the suspicious looks from my mother and knew what had happened.

"At least they don't seem to care at your temple," I said one evening after her third or so visit.

"Oh, they do, in some ways, but are also bound by our own beliefs. As long as I am pursuing some form of love, they will not interfere unless things get dangerous."

"Like what?"

"Obsession, abuse, that kind of thing."

"Huh. Any news from other parts of the city?"

"Well, most of those who took refuge in the temple district are returning home. There are a few that are still afraid or were nobles before everything happened and are trying to figure out what to do now, but it looks like Lord Durin's people are trying to make inroads with them."

"Dad hasn't told me much about what happened to the nobility now that the kingdom has been replaced."

"Well, I've not gotten too much information on that front, but I can tell you that a good few died. Some turned during the city's invasion, understanding that we would lose. Some surrendered or were captured. It seems that they're being treated differently based on that kind of thing."

I looked over at a big pile of packed things that had been left here just the other day. Between the invasion, checking over, and general confusion, my stuff from school hadn't gotten to me until just now, and I was nearly ready to go back. There was also a note from my now former maid Dora, explaining whose they were and how it was all put together. I'd left a note with Dad asking him to check in on her as well. If she'd been captured, I wanted her treated well for all her good work.

"I wonder how many of our classmates will be returning," I idly mused.

"I suppose we'll just have to wait and find out. On a more fun subject, are you excited about tomorrow?"

"Of course, who doesn't love new clothes?"

A lot of the details of the new academy roster and the like were being kept really quiet, as a surprise or something, but we did know that there would be new uniforms. That was all fine with me as my last one was getting both a bit short and a bit tight in a few spots, and it would have to be adjusted or replaced in short order. I still had it, as the cloth was lovely and it would be a real shame to waste, but I hadn't decided on a purpose for it just yet.

Marcus was the same as always, a bit grumpy, a bit crass, and the best tailor available. He had us come in with a few others for our fittings and made all the needed changes to get the uniforms just right.

A copy of the new design was on display, of course, and it was lovely. The primary color was a deep black, with wine-colored accents and silver buttons. Most of the former design elements had remained, though the skirt was a bit longer. If I had to be honest, I did think this one was better, if just a bit.

My brother had come along with us today and stood to the side as we were measured. Some of the other girls who had at first sent me light glares had straightened right up as he filled the area around him with an angry silver flame. He did otherwise pretend not to notice them. Seemed he had learned some tricks from Dad over the years.

As Marcus finished up, I watched him work on a piece carefully. In that moment, I had an idea.

"Marcus."

"Yes?" He sounded like he knew I was about to be a thorn in his side.

"If I wanted to learn a bit of the kind of magic you use, how would I?"

"Thinking of becoming a tailor?" He did not sound amused; most people didn't want competition in their industry.

"No, but if I could learn just a bit to make my sewing better, my mother might stop berating me about it." That comment got me a deep chuckle.

"So . . . you want me to teach you to sew using magic, because you can't be bothered to learn without it?"

"Because I'm better at magic than I am at sewing, and I'm told that I'm completely unacceptable at the latter."

"Afraid that I will have to decline giving you lessons. Though I will tell you that learning to do it by hand will help you understand what you need the magic to do."

I groaned a bit, but he'd at least given me a hint. It had been some time since I'd really begun work on anything truly new, and this might be a good project. As I left the shop, I made a note to see what I could do with some scraps of cloth later on. Not that my mom would be able to do much complaining to me once school started again.

The day to move back to the academy came. I hadn't even unpacked my things, so there wasn't too much for me to do. My new maid, a slip of a girl whose name I hadn't even had time to learn, accompanied us on our way. Normally, I'd have taken the time to speak with her, but my parents were so busy fussing that there really was no time.

"Make sure you write, keep us informed, and come to visit on your days off." Mom was having a fit. You'd think she had a child go off to a school before by the way she was going, but no, it seemed it was just one of those things that everyone did.

Dad spent his time telling me to be careful and to not cause any more problems. There were a bunch of new security measures, but he was still weary of having me out of sight. I was also informed that there would be a few students who came from rather trusted families who'd be keeping an eye on things, as I should do as well.

I met with Kala at the gates and left my parents. We were told that there would be an assembly on our first day, so we headed to the given location, which was the arena where the entrance exams and a few classes were sometimes held. Oddly, it seemed more busy than usual, and there were more faces that I didn't recognize than I did. The school hadn't been that big, so that was really odd.

When we came into the arena and found our seats, the answer as to why was immediately obvious. It was packed, there were at least half again as many students here today as there had been in the past, and a number of those we knew were quietly chatting about it. The teachers from where they stood also seemed a bit irritated. I was happy to see that a number of faces I knew were in that booth, though Rooke was absent.

Once we'd found our seats, a man with long black hair and midnight blue robes walked into the center of the arena. There was a buzz of conversation until—with a motion of his hand—a wave of water covered all the sand, leaving him standing in a shallow, but placid pool.

There were gasps. All the wizards sit up straighter; everyone else just sort of gawked. That amount of water in that short of a spell was pretty much unheard of, as was his fine-tuning and control. In an instant, he'd properly demonstrated that he was strong enough to put us in our place, and once we'd settled, he spoke.

"Greetings, everyone, I am your new dean, you may call me Sectanius. We have a few announcements." He paused for effect, looking around at all of us. "As you may have noticed, we have quite a few more students than last year. This is due to several reasons. Firstly, those who have proven themselves in other schools in the empire are now being moved here to study, since this is the site of the most advanced magical academy. Secondly, for our incoming students, the exam is now open to all, with scholarships being given to those who perform but cannot afford tuition. It is my sincere hope that we will have no issues integrating everyone together. I am sure that you will all work with me."

"I think we'll do best if we try to keep our heads down," Kala whispered.

"Yeah, good luck on that," I returned.

"There are also a few small changes in the class scheduling, as I'm sure you'll soon see. I think the majority of you will find it to your liking that Etiquette has been removed from our curriculum . . ." That statement was greeted by a wave of cheers, which he waved off with a smile. "And replaced with Civics, a new class designed to teach everyone their rights, place, and duties to our noble empire."

While most people sighed, I felt my eyebrows rise quickly. That sounded like an entire class of propaganda. It might be important to change some minds, but from the sound of it, we'd be getting a full helping of whatever Lord Durin was selling. I could at least hope that I was wrong.

"Ah, and one final announcement. Since there is no longer a kingdom of Bergond, we shall have to give our noble institution a new title. Thus, I am proud to have you all as the first class to the new Academy of Shadows!" There was a good bit of cheering at that, and I joined in lightly. I had a feeling that I'd get to see exactly what Lord Durin was like even if I'd yet to meet him.

CHAPTER 10

◆

PROPAGANDA
AND AN UGLY CRY

It took me several days to wrap my head around the current factions in the school. Because oh boy, there were now factions, who did not like one another at all. We'd always been a bit divided between nobles and commoners, but with the invasion, and the influx of new students that was on a whole other level now.

First, we should cover the former nobles of Bergond. They were, in a word, pissed. They were also not stupid enough to let that slip out. They'd been beaten, stripped of their titles, and now reduced in status to those commoners who they'd at the very least looked down their noses at just a bit. They were also now the outsiders. They wanted to think they still had something on everyone else, but everyone else knew they didn't. There also weren't all that many of them, for obvious reasons.

Next came those former commoner students who were still attending. This group had friends in the former nobles but were always a bit looked down on. They knew the school, some of the teachers, and most were trying to get along with everyone. Dras was finding himself ever more popular nowadays, and I wished him the best with it. He also seemed to be hanging around Clarissa a lot less, but he didn't tell me, and I didn't pry.

Thirdly, we had the newcomer students from Bergond. This group was a big mix that most fell in with the former commoner students, but they didn't have the prestige of knowing the place already. Since they were all in their first year, they were all being watched to see where they'd go.

We also had those who'd come from the former empire of Ermath. This faction was trying to be friendly where they could, but there were some oddities about them. The biggest was that they all thought Lord Durin was the absolute best. I hadn't had too many deep talks with them yet, but from the way they acted, you'd think he'd personally walked into their town and saved them all—which he really might have done in some cases. From what I understood, Ermath had made our country look like a day care in the way it handled people of the lower classes. I was still keeping my distance for the time being since I was trying to figure out if they'd been brainwashed.

Then we had my faction. We were the ones who didn't really fit too neatly into any of the groups, and I was the queen bee. Well, sort of, all of us were sort of out of the various factions for the moment since it wasn't completely obvious where we fit. Lots of loners and those who'd not gotten too involved or were too hot of an asset to really be taken in without consideration.

The priests might have been a faction, but if they were, they seemed to think that the best move was not to play. I had to admit they really might have a point there. It was sometimes too bad that I didn't really fit into their little group, being a bard.

I did not like this division at all, particularly because it put too much attention on me. The nobles seemed to think I was a traitor. The old commoners also thought that I was probably a traitor but seemed to care a lot less. The formerly Ermathi students thought they should get to know me but were a bit worried. I got the vibe that Dad and John had done some big things, but I didn't know what yet. The exiles and the priests tended to be friendly enough, but that didn't really help too much.

I mused on all of this as I sat in Civics. It was full of propaganda, but the way it was presented wasn't too bad. There were a lot of lessons on philosophy and how we should all strive to uplift, rather than to degrade. That isn't to say that there weren't parts of the lecture where we were just flat-out told what was right, and that Lord Durin had been doing his best for everyone, because that was there, but it was subtle. I wasn't sure if that was more or less insidious, but I was leaning toward more.

At the moment, we were going over questions about how a change in farming technique should be handled. It was a high cost in the short term, with large long-term benefits. All the numbers were from real villages, showing how the method had increased yields and the rate at which it had done so. The math was easy enough, and I'd worked out the answer a bit ago.

"What do you think, Alana? What choice should we make? To remain with the current way, or to change?" The professor looked at me expectantly as she began this part of the lesson.

"I believe we should change, Professor," I said with confidence.

"Counter opinions?"

One of the former noble boys raised his hand. With a nod, the teacher gave him the floor.

"I disagree strongly. The investment in changing the crops would be stifling to the community. It would cost a fortune to switch over." He looked like the idea of spending that money was horrid. "As it stands, the current yields are within acceptable levels for those working the land to live and pay their taxes."

"There is the possibility," I countered, "that the investment is too high for it to all be changed at once, as well as that the farmers may resist or resent the intrusion into their business." I admitted the biggest fault in my position, that people didn't always want to do what you wanted them to. "That said, the current yields give no surplus, no barrier against disaster or drought to the farms listed here. While the initial investment would be high, it would fix that. One might have to give some incentive, at least in part to change, but with only a bit of time the farmers themselves will see the benefit and adapt accordingly. Within ten years, the estimate on investment would be recouped by the increased taxes anyway. Assuming that it works as laid out."

"You seem a bit hesitant in your position, Alana. May I ask why?" Our instructor seemed to have questions as well.

"Because while this is an exercise, if we were to run it as something in the real world, we would not be playing with numbers and charts, but rather having a deep effect on people's lives. People are not just numbers you can move on a page or pieces on a game board, and you should not treat them as such." I then shrugged. "Anyways, as I said, they are likely to resist anyway if you try to force the issue. You'd do better to find a way to convince them to do it themselves."

"Oh, what a wonderful answer! You're quite correct, my dear, on both accounts." She smiled brightly as she turned to everyone. "What is the duty of the strong?"

"To protect the weak." Everyone answered in unison. It was one of several such answers we were expected to give that was one of the more obvious points of propaganda. Could I really hate that idea though?

Later in the day, I was walking invisibly through the halls. I'd taken to that method to avoid any more attention than I was already getting. I didn't have much to do at this particular hour, and soon enough I'd need to head to dinner. Really, I was just avoiding people while strolling randomly; it was pleasant.

As I passed by one of the empty classrooms, I both saw and heard the discussion going on inside. Pinea and some older boy I didn't know had taken up residence there and were having a bit of an argument.

"You and your whole family disgust me. I can't even believe you'd defend that treachery," the boy hissed angrily.

Pinea seemed on the verge of tears. "There was no point to continuing; all that would have happened is more death. Can't you see that? Father just did what he thought was . . ."

At this point, the guy pulled back, spit in her face, and uttered something I'd never thought anyone would to her. "Never speak to me again, traitorous whore." With that, he turned and walked out.

I was so shocked that I almost didn't move in time for him to miss me as he passed by. He threw open the door and scowled as he left, teeth locked.

Pinea sank into a nearby chair and began to bawl. As I came in, I closed the door, not even thinking about being invisible. As her head popped up, I let that spell fade, revealing myself. She might have once been a noble, but Pinea had always been a friend. It only took a few seconds for me to put a sound barrier on the door, pull out a handkerchief, and move to her side.

After letting her have a good cry while I held her and getting her a little cleaned up, I finally asked, "So what was that all about?"

"There . . . at the end . . . Dad made a deal." *Sniff.* "He had all of his knights turn on the guards in the palace when the signal went off."

"Oh well, it wouldn't have mattered anyway."

"I know. What was he supposed to do, let all his men die? Lose everything himself?" she shrieked. "There was no point to continuing to fight. It was over!"

I patted her back. "The asshole?"

"My betrothed, well, former betrothed, I guess now. I thought he'd understand . . ."

I leaned in. "Then I'm glad he called it off. You can do way better."

She laughed a bit. "Do you think so? I am a disgraced former noble after all."

"Oh yeah. Imagine if you'd ended up *married* to that," I continued. "We can find you someone better. I know some people. I'll introduce you." I tried being as flippant as possible.

"Great, because I think most of my friends hate me now."

"If they do, they weren't real friends anyway. Now, let's go get you cleaned up."

"You're really good at this, you know that, Alana?"

"It comes with being a bard," I said, as if it were the most obvious thing in the world.

"Wish I was one," she said, starting to mope a bit again.

"You should put in for a change then. I hear the forms are a real pain though. Oh, and you have to learn how to sing."

"Oof, guess that's a pass for me."

I didn't know all the details, but I knew enough. I knew that she'd probably hurt from this for a bit longer. She may not have been beaten up or tortured, but she'd obviously lost a lot. Regardless of what happened though, I'd help her through her ugly cry phase. She deserved that at the very least.

"Okay, so I'm going to turn us invisible, because you're a mess, and I don't want to attract attention."

"All right . . ." Pinea seemed a bit hesitant.

"It doesn't hurt or anything, just hold my arm while we walk back to the dorms. Oh, and try not to walk into anybody. That's super embarrassing."

"Sounds like you have experience."

"So much. Once I fell down a flight of stairs, and it was really loud, but nobody could figure out what had happened. At least nobody could see me. I felt like my face was strawberry red as I snuck off." That got her laughing again, and laughing was good. Laughing wasn't crying.

The whole way back, she asked me for more stories. Who was making out with whom and where. What juicy gossip she was sure I'd heard on my wanderings. She wanted the works. Sad thing was I didn't really pay attention to that kind of stuff. When we finally arrived, she rushed off to wash up, and I sighed as I nearly fell into a chair myself.

CHAPTER 11

✦

LOVERS' WORRIES

It took about a week but eventually someone worked up their nerve and came over to approach me while I was working in the practical part of Magical Item Creation. Professor Hern had retained his position after the takeover, as had most of the teachers, but I didn't get much of a chance to talk to him out of class.

"Hello there. You're Alana, right?" the boy said. He was around my age and had pitch-dark hair.

"Yes . . ." I didn't know him, or what he wanted, so caution seemed apt.

"Is it true? Are you General Verren's daughter?"

"I am."

"Mind if I talk to you after class?" He looked over at Professor Hern, who seemed a bit miffed that we'd stopped working and looked distracted. We weren't working with anything too high energy, but whenever we did anything in his class, our full attention was to be on our project.

Afterward, we both stayed behind. Kala had managed to come by, too, and was taking a look. The boy looked a bit awkward, like he wanted to spill out everything he was.

"I'm Tobias. It's really nice to meet you. I wanted you to know. Your dad saved me."

"What?" That was a bomb of a way to start a conversation.

"Yeah, back when Ermath was still a thing. I lived on an estate. The executor there was a monster of a man. He treated all of us like dirt under his feet. I had a minor talent; I could make light. It wasn't much, but it meant that I had a little mana, and every day he made me put as much as I could into an item he had."

"That sounds horrible."

"It was I guess, but I didn't have it too bad. A little mana meant that I had some value to him. Everyone else who wasn't a soldier was pretty much just a slave, to be tossed aside as soon as he tired of them.

"Anyway, when the war came, your father's unit rescued us. It was amazing. I remember seeing him fight the executor. I'd never seen anyone fight like that, and when he'd taken down that bastard, the first thing he did was start freeing everyone. They had a man who was strong enough to rip iron like it was paper, and he went and freed all the slaves. After all the fighting that night . . . when I looked up and cleared my eyes, I could see it then, the auras. The first one I saw was the general, a burning black flame of death to everyone who oppressed us."

He was nearly crying, and I had no clue what to say to this at all. The kid obviously thought my dad was some kind of superhero or something, but I'd never seen any of that. I knew he was strong and fast, but I'd never really seen him go full-on against someone. Even if I had, I didn't have any way to process all this.

"I . . . I didn't really know he was doing that kind of thing."

"Really? What's he like?"

"He's like a dad. Serious most of the time, nice, a bit overprotective if I'm being honest."

"Cool. Hey, me and some of the other new students have a study group going. If you want, you could join us. We'd be really happy to have you around, and from what I've seen today, you are better at making magical items than we are for sure." He smiled as he made his pitch.

"Maybe, but until classes get fully in the swing I don't know that there's too much to do. Can you write down the where and when for me?"

He scribbled a little note on a piece of paper for me before heading off. As he left, Kala came to join me in the now empty classroom.

"How goes your day, oh, daughter of the coolest dad ever?" She giggled a bit as she found a seat beside me.

"Please don't you start too. I get stories, but I haven't talked much to him in years. Well, we've had dinner and stuff, but it feels like I'm getting chewed out every time I go to one of those by someone."

"Fine, fine. He is nice though."

"Baahh! New subject, want to join a study group?" I flashed the piece of paper at her.

"Yeah . . . I wanted to talk to you about that. My order sent me a messenger this morning. I'm to keep everyone at arm's length for the time being. I'm ignoring it for you specifically, but the others . . ."

"What? Why?"

"It's not public yet, but looks like Lord Durin is marrying the former Princess Sophia. As you can imagine we're . . . 'deeply concerned' about it."

As soon as the shock wore off, I took a beat to think. "He's trying to establish himself as legitimate. Even if he doesn't take the title king, if he marries her, he'd have claim. I can't imagine she's happy about it though. He did take her country and like, kill her family."

"The current theory is that he made her an offer to either become his bride, or take a short walk up to the headsman's block. Either that or she's been in on things with him for a while. I don't know what the official statement will be, but it should be clear why the Order of the Lovers as a whole are a bit on edge."

"Forced marriage is . . . not uncommon." I knew that a lot of people were put under heavy pressure.

"Our position is that it should always be willing. In practice, there's a lot of pressure you can exert on family if you want to, but she needs to be able to say no. If she can't . . . I know I'll be pretty mad, and I imagine most of my fellows will as well." Kala was pretty solemn about this.

The Lovers believed very strongly in love, in willing love, and took a violent, brutal stance against things like rape. I wasn't a hundred percent sure what they did, but I didn't want to know either. If he was forcing the former princess to marry him, there would be a lot of rage there. They might keep it quiet, but they'd be pissed he did something so publicly against one of their strongest strictures.

That didn't seem like what I'd heard of him though. I didn't know the man, but my dad did, and the way he told it, Lord Durin was a pretty decent man. I didn't think either he or Mystien would follow someone willing to go down that path, or even my brother. It was a bit jarring to think about.

"What are you going to do?" I wanted to know if this would go bad and how fast.

"Me? Nothing. The Lovers will probably send someone to try and speak with him. There's a bishop to the west who might be asked to go and very politely ask to meet with her. We'll know more from there."

I just threw my head back and groaned. I wanted nothing to do with this, I wanted politics completely out of my life . . . forever. There was a brief moment I considered just running, but then I had a brief mental image of Jackson, and that killed that desire.

"So what do you want me to do? And who knows about all of this right now anyway?"

She looked a bit nervous. "What I want is for this to all blow over, Alana. There's no good end if he's doing something bad, and I do consider that an if. As for what I want you to do? I don't know, and I don't know that you should do anything. I want you safe, but . . ." She took a brief moment. "As far as who knows, I don't know. I'm not high on the list there, and all I got was a letter telling me that he's planning to marry her and to keep everyone a bit distanced until we've figured things out."

"Any other news you have for me today?"

"I don't think so. Were you looking for more?"

"Not really, but I'd personally prefer to get any more bad news out of the way. I find that just throwing it all out and letting the disaster play out is often the best way."

"You do tend to do that. It's one of the things that I love about you." She smiled and poked me in the side, causing me to jump as it sent a jolt up my side.

"Stop that!"

"Oh-oh-oh! I've found a weakness!" For the next several moments, I ended up jumping here and there as she made an attack.

By the time we made our way out of the room, I wasn't in nearly as serious a mood. It was hard to be worried and laugh at the same time.

ROOKE

As I struggled up the side of the mountain, I sincerely considered jumping off. It had been weeks since I'd left civilized lands, and I was keeping myself on the barest drops of my mana through sheer usage. We were far and away from the edge of the kingdom's furthest out city, a place that was still at least nominally loyal, if only because they didn't know that the kingdom had fallen yet.

This far out there were monsters constantly, which was a double-edged sword. It did generally keep most of the chances of enemy soldiers low, but they were hostile, and that was its own bag of fun. I'd run into no less than four mountain lizards in the last three days.

As the next rise came into view, so did my next enemy. The beast looked like a lion, only four times larger and pure white. I wasn't sure if this was going to be one I could win, and the beast didn't look like it was about to leave me be.

As the creature turned and narrowed eyes upon me, I threw forth my first spell. This was obviously something of ice, so I would be focusing on fire. The torrent caused the monster to flee back and give me space, but it was only temporary. The flames roared between us, and I continued to measure my resources.

It charged forward like an avalanche, only to slam into a barrier projected from the little sphere on my waist. I may not have too much in the way of mana at the moment, but items I had in spades. With a quick movement, I threw a small dart.

My enemy dodged the projectile as it sped itself to an incredible velocity, landing with a booming explosion in a tree hanging off the side of the mountain. Between that and the fire we were making a ton of noise, and if I survived, I would have to make my way far from here as quickly as I could.

We had three more passes before there was a flash of silver and a spear appeared. The fact that it was stuck deep into my opponent's neck was helpful. The spurt of blood that shot out shortly thereafter as it struggled and fell signaled the end.

I looked around and finally found my protector. Lord Farren came striding across the snow, cloak blowing in the wind behind him. I supposed that all the noise and smoke had alerted him to my location.

"Hello there, Rooke. It's been quite some time hasn't it?"

I was nearly ready to fall to my knees in relief. "You are a sight for sore eyes. I don't suppose you have any news on His Highness? Or my irksome grandfather?"

"Both alive, m'boy. I'll not tell your wife that you didn't request her first as well."

"She beat me here by about a week!" the old warrior laughed.

"Well, that's a relief. Are we lucky enough to be near?"

He gave a deep laugh as he turned, leading me off once again. There was work to do, and we'd need to get on it.

CHAPTER 12

◆

THE PLANNING

When I came into Combat Spellcasting the first time, I nearly had to pick my jaw up off the floor. Professor Endel had somehow retained his job, albeit with a new assistant (minder) in tow.

"Good, everyone, it's taken a bit of time to polish up all of your slacking from our break, and to bring our new classmates up to speed with where we are, but I can at least tolerate your current progress." He smiled, something a bit rarer these days. "Now, we'll be learning about battlefield tactics next."

We'd already been given some lectures on this in the past, but what he went over now were details on where and when to set up defenses, as well as the logistics. This was apparently something that war-mages ended up doing in the field enough that he felt it an important topic.

What it came down to was that most locations were only so defensible. Anything you put up would only slow down your opponents, so you needed to consider your current mana supply, what you expected to come up against, natural structures like hills, and the cost of the items that you had. It was rare for there to be too much of a budget for magical items used in the field, so knowing what to order was crucial.

The training scheme for this was, to my amusement, a rather complicated board game. It wasn't a square setup like you'd see in the more common ones, but more like something you'd see in movies, with tables and little models. Of course, we just used tokens instead of complex little figurines, but the concept was the same.

The rules were a simple counting system, but you never knew what your opponent would invest in in their defenses until you met them on the field, and there were tons of options for that. It was fun, and we spent several classes playing matches of various groupings. Sometimes we were given more resources than our opponents, sometimes less, sometimes we worked in teams.

After about a week of this, Endel looked out at us. "Good, I'm pleased to see you're thinking tactically about planning your defenses and offenses. Many of you have shown some skill at the logistics, but we'll be putting this into practice now. Games can teach us a bit, but only so much, and there is no teacher like experience." He had a bit of an evil grin. "I have secured one of your off days for just such an exercise. You will be divided into groups of three and have two weeks to prepare." There were about thirty people in this class, so that meant ten groups.

One of our number raised his hand. "Sir, in the game we had resources in the standard warding items, will we have the same?"

"Wonderful question! Each group will receive a 'budget' from which they may 'purchase' items that the school will provide. You may also choose to take the time to build your own, though if you do so, you will need to submit them to inspection by our professors three days before the event. We cannot have you bringing anything dangerous along with us. There will also be a slightly lesser 'cost,' which will reflect the mana and production cost if something similar were used in war."

Our teams were decided that day, and we were permitted to meet in class. The first thing I did was set up a privacy bubble around us.

"Any thoughts?" I asked, looking around.

"I think he's going to assign us to one or more teams with other groups," a boy named Troy offered. He'd been with us in this class for some time.

"Agreed." The other boy in my group was named Leeve. I didn't know much about him, but he was one of our newcomers who'd been part of Ermath before its fall.

"Same, but what should we go for item-wise? Should we take what he has, or build our own? Or both? I'm inclined toward illusion, but everyone knows that so it seems a bit predictable." That got nods.

I had a bit of a reputation for being a pain in any practice round we held in class. My defenses were all rock-solid, and I'd flood the area with illusions. It was a simple trick, but it often worked best for me.

"With you here, we could have good defenses, and I'm not bad in a fight." Troy looked unconvinced that it was a good plan, but it would be a normal one.

"What if . . . what if we went hard in on offense instead?" I asked, looking between them.

"I hate to say it, Alana, but from what I've seen your offensive magic kind of sucks." Leeve shrugged, looking sorry.

"I have some ideas," I offered, and boy did I.

"Okay then, fill us in."

I had one day off before our little battle and I took it. Normally, I might have stayed around the school with Kala for most of the day before heading to our mansion for dinner. Having a mansion was weird, but it was nice in small doses.

A series of letters over the last few days explaining the situation to Mystien and asking him to look over some designs had ended up with me receiving the written equivalent of a "Don't do anything or tell anyone anything important until I look at it!" letter. Sure, it was couched in euphemisms and the like, but the meaning was clear. He'd also been amazingly willing to schedule a meeting on my day off.

As I arrived at the house, he stood there, looking peeved.

"Your father has loaned me a room so that I might advise you." My father indeed was nearby; he also looked peeved.

"Excellent, let's go!" Both of them just narrowed their eyes at my exuberance.

It took a few moments for the items Mystien had brought to be properly set up and for those I simply hummed happily, looking at him.

"Okay, what are you planning?"

"Let's start with the list of supplies and the magical items I want to make." I held out several papers for him, all basic order forms and a sheet with the rune sequences jotted down.

"Standard military supplies . . . non-standard military supplies . . . non-military supplies . . . Okay, I don't see anything too bad here. Let's have a look at your sequences." He poured over the papers for some moments before returning to look at me confused. "Okay, I understand what these do, but why? And how are you going to use them?"

I presented next my master plan, and laid out in steps with diagrams. He studied it; my dad took his time to examine it. Dad just laughed a bit, while Mystien looked at me with half-lidded eyes.

"There is nothing I would be worried about showing here, but I do want you to understand that on a battlefield this would likely get you killed."

"The chances of that are good, yes, or it would win."

"Alana, it is foolish to gamble with your life."

"I'm not here though. These aren't hardened soldiers with a solid command structure, nor are they able to deal with these like a physical magic user would. At least, I don't think they'll be able to."

"This is supposed to be a military exercise, is it not?" Dad seemed to think that not taking it seriously was the wrong move.

"It is, but I know my enemy. They won't know how to deal with this, and they won't know how to work together well enough either. That's a problem with us too. But as long as we have some semblance of order, I'm fairly sure it will work."

"Fine, fine, do what you want," my mentor finally capitulated.

Our dinner that night was lovely. It wasn't anything too odd, but there was more beef in it than I commonly got, even here in Lithere, and beef was tasty.

I ended up in the office of our new Magical Item Creation (theoretical) teacher, Professor Ieala. She was mouse-looking with brown hair pulled back in a loose bun to go with her rather more plain robe choices. I guessed that she was perhaps thirty years old tops, but she seemed to know her stuff pretty well and had approved everything I'd brought to her with little fanfare. That had been a real concern, as was the theoretical idea that our teachers would absolutely be stealing any good ideas we brought them.

In all of my planning for this, I had been sure that I didn't use any new tech, and that I kept all strategy to simple ideas. I'd already introduced more than I had expected to, and putting more thoughts out there that could cause major problems later might come back to bite me.

"Oh, Alana, I'm so glad that we finally got a chance for a little chat," Professor Iaela said. "Your work in my class is quite good, and I'd heard about you speeding through your core development. How are you feeling about your progress?"

"Quite good. My core is advancing steadily, and I feel like I'm getting a better grip on the basics of item creation. As long as I can keep it up, I think I'll be on the right track." I was trying to find a way to stay out of her radar, but it seemed that might be a lost cause.

"Wonderful! Now, I heard the most interesting story. Is it true that you have a sample of sky-metal?" There it was—the thing she really wanted.

"That is what Professor Hern believed it to be, but it's been put somewhere safe regardless of what it is."

"I was hoping to see it sometime, if you don't mind. It isn't often that any amount of that comes around, and it's not a chance I'd want to miss."

I shrugged. "If that is the case, you're welcome to file a request with my parents. If they approve, then it should be fine." This was the nicest way to turn someone down, mostly because everyone was afraid, or at least leery of what might happen if they offended the upper ranks of the military.

"I may do so. On an unrelated note, what do you make of this?" She pulled out a rather standard-looking sequence, which I spent a few moments going over.

"It won't work." I said after considering my conclusion. The item in question was a small light-emitting thing with a broken off/on switch. It looked like someone had tried to fix it and failed miserably.

Moreover, this was clearly a test. The way that it had been attempted would never work. Whoever had done this had gone from a simple "touch here to activate" to a "touch and verbal" but had not set any parameters. We had not covered how to activate a verbal item by touching a spot and speaking. I could probably have done it with what I'd learned from the guide, but there was no reason to let anyone else know that.

"How would you fix it then?" she asked, smiling a bit.

"Like this." I erased fully half of the sequence, taking it back to the simplest on/off parameters I could. "There is no need for complexity for something like this; a simple solution is best."

Judging by her expression, that was not the answer she'd expected or wanted. My guess was that she'd heard I was into some weird methods from Hern, or read some of Rooke's notes, but this was so poor of an attempt to figure those out that it was comical.

"I was hoping you'd make it work as intended. This was supposed to be the basis for a touch and password lock."

"Ah, I see. Well, we haven't covered anything like that yet, Professor; maybe I'll take another look at it later. Did you need anything else?"

"Not presently, Alana, no."

"Well then, thank you for the meeting. Sadly, I have a lot of preparations to make and must be on my way."

CHAPTER 13

✦

PLAN IN ACTION

The day of the event came, and we were all loaded into carriages. Our group was loaded down with items in bags, and we were all prepped. Everything was safe, and all had the ability to give a small flash of blue light and burst of cold when they went off, our signal for an item that would kill/disable the opponent if it landed.

The rules of engagement were similar to the standard ones for any of our training exercises. There were a number of safeguards in place that were supposed to keep anyone from getting hurt, at least seriously. We also knew that Professor Endel and a few others would be around, keeping an eye out for cheaters and those who might try to use more dangerous moves.

Soon enough, we arrived at our training location, another walled-off forested area. There were a number of these, other than the Junkyard Copse, and they were mostly used in the past by very wealthy nobles who wanted a personal hunting preserve. It lacked the warding that particular copse had, instead using a simple wall, but for our purposes that would be more than enough.

"All right, everyone, line up!" Professor Endel looked at the assembled youths with an evil grin, and then began pointing. "You, you, you, and you, you're group one. The rest of you lot are group two. Now for the scenario, group one will be loosed into the woods and have until nightfall to set themselves up, group two will be the pursuing group and will be in charge of taking group one out. If group one has more than half of their players left at the end, they win."

"That seems rather unfair to group two," one of that group's players pointed out.

"It is, but war is often not fair." He left out that this setup would practically force us to fight; without some reason to, we would stalemate. "All right then, group one head out."

I was, of course, in group one and quite happy to be. I felt that our plan would work out better that way. Once we were out of sight of the other students, we stopped for a brief chat.

"So how do we want to do this?" one of my classmates asked. She was a rather skilled wizard and one of the better fighters on our team.

"I'd like you to drive them toward us. Also, we won't be using drums, as they'll be useless once we start."

"What?" another student perked up, in war one normally used a sound like drums, or drums themselves to communicate over distance. Sometimes one would use light and the like, too, but the deep sounds carried well and would easily relay orders. "Light then?"

"Sorry, no. Once everyone is in place, we'll be able to send out a high-pitched sound and a moving light; we'd like everyone to try and drive the enemies to the source." I'd come up with this and would be right there at the center.

"Fair enough, we can set up in a semicircle and ..." The placements for the other groups were decided, made in a way to thin the enemy herd and funnel them into us. Going after them might have been easier in some cases, but for this one we wanted everyone to come to the location of the fight.

SAMANTHA

Professor Endel had designated us as the attackers, and I was ready for it. We'd all been practicing, and going back and forth on what items we wanted. My group was all wizards and we were the best for this. Our shields were good, and we knew our team well.

As soon as the time was called, the three of us moved as a unit. We'd been given time to discuss and come up with the idea of sticking to our own groups. Each group of three would move forward, trying to find the enemy. Once we did, we'd send up one of several designated signals. The only banned color for this exercise was blue. A blue light would indicate that a given person was out of the fight, or that there was a hit in that place if accompanied by cold.

The two girls with me were named Alli and Menae. Menae had put some kind of sound-muffling magic on us while I handled a spell that made the light around us just a bit darker, it wasn't invisibility, but it would make us just that much less easy to spot.

I wanted to laugh. Endel had put all those with the best dueling ability on our teams and had given us numbers. Sure, the enemies had some neat tricks, but in the end, we'd win. Now was not the time though, once we'd taken them down . . .

As I was thinking, a red light flew up from near us, forward and to the right, going high into the sky.

"Enemy found," Allie said, smiling slightly.

As we started, we heard five drumbeats in one of the standard patterns off to our left, one of our signals for "Under attack, need aid." With a look, we turned to their aid. As we did, a green light went up from behind, then more of the standard drum signals started from several different directions.

"What? There's no way all that's happening at once!" I yelled over the booming sounds and flares going up all over the damn place.

"It's something the enemy is doing! They're trying to kill our communication!" It was Menae this time, and she was right. This was all just a ruse to keep us disorganized.

"How pathetic. I can't believe they spent that much effort on this. We still outnumber them and will still win. Forward!" As I pointed toward the opposite end of our entrance, there was a screaming, keening noise.

A brilliantly gold-glowing missile streaked over us, exploding three or four hundred feet behind with a thunderous *BOOM* followed by several sounds of impacts.

"What the fuck! How did they get artillery in the budget?" Alli screamed as the monstrously dangerous projectile passed us by.

"Stop screaming, They can only have gotten one or two. One of the groups must have . . ." At this point, I had to eat my words as four more came flying over, all headed toward different sections of the field.

They had to be some kind of magical item, the range was too far for most spellcasters, and a big burst of energy like that would have been pretty tiring. We were lucky in that they all seemed to be coming from one section of the woods. As one, we turned a final time, heading to where our enemy must be, or at least the most likely area.

We lucked out in that on the way we met up with another of our groups. They'd had the same issue as us and come to the same conclusion. Our new six-person team was a real threat as we stormed our attackers. Even if all of them were there, we could still do some good damage.

It was easy to see where we were heading to as we approached, because of all the light. Not those in the sky, though they probably helped, but the fact that a small meadow had been cleared up and torches were set at close intervals, bathing the whole area in warm brilliance.

That alone would have been odd, but it wasn't the strangest thing. The weirdest part was the bard girl dancing in the middle of the field like it was some kind of stage. In fact, it looked like they'd actually cleared and raised part of the field for her to use as a stage.

"Okay . . . so, we just go take her down?" one of the boys who'd joined us on the way asked as another screaming projectile flew up from near her and arced off.

"Oh no, that's a trap. There is no way that isn't an illusion and she isn't planning some weird nonsense. We go in there and we're done." One of his friends was smarter than he was and nailed it.

"I agree. I don't see the purpose yet, but let's put up our barriers and wait for reinforcements."

Setting up our defenses was easy enough. Alli put down several spheres while we covered her and a small dome popped up. It would keep out anything high energy: no dangerous projectiles, no heat or cold spells, and no lightning. We'd added the last one since we'd heard about this particular bard being known for using it. A person or something small and slow could pass through, but not at great speed, and it would flash to warn us.

We sat there for several minutes, seeing nothing of note. One of the nearby trees shook a bit from a passing wind, and I heard Alli say "stupid pinecones."

"What?" I asked as I turned.

It was at that moment that something small struck me in the kidney. It wasn't hard, or fast, but about the size of a little stick. When it hit, it let off a burst of blue light and a trill of cold that flowed up my spine. The sign that I was dead. Almost simultaneously, the same thing happened five more times to my teammates.

"Ugghhhh." I groaned as I tapped myself to put a blue light over my head, then we made our way toward the point for the dead.

At least, we weren't the first. Five more from my group and three from the opposition were already seated there, playing Endel's strategy game.

ALANA

Back in my previous life, I'd heard about a leader who'd thrown open his doors and beaten drums loudly at an approaching army. The army, convinced that it was some form of trap, had retreated, and the leader had gained the time he needed to gather his forces and push forward.

That was why I was dancing on a stage in the middle of a brightly lit field.

My classmates had fought me time and again, had seen me make copies of myself time and again. Every single one of them would know that this was a ruse, a trap to draw them in, or make them cast at me. Every single one of them would guess wrong, and I could save the mana I'd otherwise need to make myself invisible.

While I bluffed like a poker player with a pair of twos, I instead focused on moving around our light and sound show. They were far out, and I needed a bit of height to get them all where I wanted, hence the stage, but they were doing their job excellently so far.

Troy was sitting on a disc of force quite high up in the air and well cloaked and was in charge of firing our artillery behind and to the side of our enemies. He was doing a marvelous job of herding those that would have been difficult to see from the ground toward us.

As a note, almost no wizards flew. I couldn't really manage that much direct kinetic energy as a bard, but from what I understood trying to manage all the forces while rocketing through the air was both really hard and very disorienting. Some of those who tried ended up flying into large solid objects, like the ground, so few went that route. There were reports of well-protected ones going along a set path, but the mana cost was reportedly obscene.

I could confuse our opponents with all the little items that we had. Most of those were about the size of a ballpoint pen and were either bright flashing lamps or noisemakers that sounded like drums.

Leeve was on the ground, well hidden in the trees, managing the "sedative darts," an idea I'd stolen from the capture team. He waited for someone to come near to the circle of light, snuck them into their midst, and then took them down. I had to admit that from what I could see he was doing a spot-on job, too, he'd dropped like eight or nine people.

Dawn came in its due time, and our game ended. As we all walked toward the meeting area, our victorious team's approach started a line of questions. I was sure Endel could answer all of them, but he'd apparently wanted to wait for us.

"That was funny, but you know in battle that wouldn't work right?" he said as we came over.

"I was told that. I think it would if we refined it, but with the time and what we had, it was good for this opponent."

"What I want to know is how your groups managed to buy artillery items. Those are expensive. And if they were real, the cost would have been unbelievable!" One of the girls from the opposing group demanded.

"They didn't," Endel commented dryly. "Didn't you notice that none of those used blue? That while they made a bunch of noise, they didn't have any wave of cold or even a breeze from their 'explosion'? It was all just sound and light. None of them even came near you lot. It was just something more to throw you off. Oh, and to lead you into their kill zone."

"I will admit that the dancing illusion was a good distraction," one of the boys commented. I could tell he was staring, and not at my face, but I ignored it.

"Anyway, since we're all done now, I think I fancy a bit of a nap." It was late after all, and we had been up for far too long.

◆

CHAPTER 14

EMBERS

Spring passed into summer, and things were fairly uneventful. By the day, my mastery of different kinds of magic was improving, particularly my shields and illusions. It was Professor Etia who helped me with hammering those out even more. The main thing I was working on with them was adding more and more accurate movement magic to them. I wanted them to be able to pick up and carry things, or at least appear to, and that was a real challenge to make look right.

I continued my efforts and by entrance exam, I'd managed footprints. Those were good, but they were very simple and poor compared to having illusions that could fool even experts with how they behaved.

"The cup is sinking into the hand. Put it down and try again. Also, your clothes aren't moving quite correctly. Make sure that the way the fabric flows matches with how dense it is."

I stood in a corner as a mock-up of me put down the cup it was holding and picked it back up. Then I made a slight adjustment to the hang of the fabric on the dress. She was right. It was too flowy for the woolen winter outfit the mock-up was wearing.

"More like this?"

"Better, but remember the thickness of that wool. Imagine yourself wearing the clothes on your illusion and think about how they feel, then adjust for that movement. You don't want it to look like a summer dress or a dancing outfit; it will be too obvious."

I did as she said. Honestly, I doubted anyone would notice, but then again someone like Charles might. He did seem to be able to see through even my invisibility, which still rankled a bit. The flesh texture was worse though, getting the right bounce to a held item, the way it sank into the skin with the skin adjusting around it was no easy task.

"How's the hand look?"

The Elven teacher marched up to my illusion and bent over to look at the hands. "It is closer to an acceptable level than it was before." She turned to look at me where I stood and sighed. "We're done for today, any further practice would be counterproductive."

"I feel fine though."

"I'm sure you do, but you're starting to wear a bit. Go and work on something else for the rest of the day."

"You're right. I didn't know when we started that your standard would be this high."

She snorted at that. "This is the minimum, Alana. My brother is an archer. Did you know that?"

I shook my head. "No, ma'am."

"For him to be considered acceptable, he had to be able to split the shaft of a stationary arrow in ten shots out of ten at fifty paces. Then he had to be able to strike a coin thrown through the air at the same distance ten out of ten times. Once he could do this, he was considered properly trained for his duties."

"That's a bit insane, Professor."

"It is stringent and a high requirement for consideration, but your father could probably do it, as could your brother. If they had been trained since youth as archers at least."

"So I could make it to what you consider acceptable?"

"In a decade or two, you would pass rigor for an Elven illusionist if you study hard."

I just sighed. "That's too much for me, I think."

She laughed a bit. "Don't look so dejected, Alana. You are not as us. While elves will often devote mountains of time to perfecting one art, few would have a grasp of as many disciplines as you. You can summon food, do illusions, heal, and I suspect you're better at creating magical items than you'd like others to know. I myself have never learned beyond the most basic emergency healing spells or summoning of food." Shaking her head, she came over to me. "Even illusions, I know where they should be, but that does not mean that I can do it. I'd wager that mine would be poorer than yours."

"But . . . you know so much . . ."

"Knowing and being able to do something are two very different things. I know the theory behind a number of different types of magic to at least a basic level, but practicing them until I could get them there would stifle my own growth in my chosen areas." She patted my head lightly. "Now off with you. Either relax or find something else to do for a bit."

I acquiesced knowing she was right and scampered off to my room. I did have a project that I'd been working on, and getting in some practice time would be nice.

Settling down at my desk, I pulled out the little basket of inexpensive cloth I'd been using for sewing. Inexpensive was relative I supposed, but it was from older pieces and rags, or else bits that were rather small and would be a pain to work with. All of it was clean, if of a much lower quality than even most commoners wore.

I laid down two pieces and began to hum. Slowly, a thread from one came undone and began to weave its way through the two pieces in a back-and-forth pattern, slipping through fibers like a snake in grass. As my first thread ran out, I carefully pulled on another, continuing my work. I did one side with a back stitch, then another with a running stitch, so on and so on until I'd gone through the five most basic ones for making clothing a half dozen times or so. All of that took around an hour.

"Hi there," Kala said as she wrapped her arms around my neck.

"Yeep! How'd you even get in here?" I yelled as I leaned back, still a bit shaken.

"Your maid let me in. She said you were deep in practice."

"I should never have told her to just bring you in instead of asking every time . . ."

"Probably not, Alana. Anyways, I have good news!" Kala let me go and flopped down on my nearby bed. "Seems that it's unlikely there is anything going on with Princess Sophia. She's going to be staying at our temple for a while."

"That's wonderful! Now you can stop sitting in the corner with all the other priests like some kind of apolitical outcast."

She stuck her tongue out at me. "Also some bad news. We won't be having any visitors at the temple, at least the private areas while she's there, so you won't be able to visit me there on our days off."

"What about those after marks or pregnancy advice?"

"Most will be sent over to the Shield's hospital, though we may keep some of the front areas open. I really don't know yet. Anyway . . . what are you working on?"

"Nothing much for now, just trying to get these right." I held up my piece, and Kala popped up to come and examine it.

"Sewing?"

"With magic."

"Okay . . . but why?" She looked a bit perplexed. I hadn't told her much about my little project, and she hadn't asked about a lot of the things I worked on. I think it was a mix of her wanting to keep everyone a bit back and my paranoia about sharing my work.

"Because my mom won't stop telling me I need to improve my sewing every time I come home. The magic way is easier. I can kind of feel it."

She took a hard eye on each little seam, pulling it this way and that. "They're not bad. Not up to a tailor's work, but not bad at all, and the way you're using the threads from the cloth is nice too."

"Do you sew?"

"Of course, Alana. Our temple doesn't budget much for us beyond necessities, you know that. All the priestesses learn to sew; most of the priests, too, even if they're bad at it."

I groaned. "I feel like I've been left behind on this by everyone! Am I the only person who doesn't always practice?"

"Probably the only girl, yeah. I think noble girls do a bunch of other stuff though, to make their clothes look all fancy. Well, former noble girls, I guess they aren't nobles anymore."

"Do not even get me started on the lectures on embroidery and lace. 'Oh, Alana, you must learn it, it's so important!' Bah!" My mother had gotten more insistent on those as well. I looked forward to the day that I could magic them into existence too.

Kala laughed and reached forward, pulling me to join her on the bed. "You may hate it, but she isn't doing it because she hates you. Your mother is trying to prep you into being a good wife."

"Maybe I don't want to be a good wife. Maybe I want to live in the forest with fruits, sugar, tea, and dancing, lots of dancing!"

"Then you'll have to learn to sew so you can make your own clothes, oh, weaving too," she giggled.

"Aaahhhhhh! My dream is smashed in one argument." I lay back as she snuggled into my side.

"You don't really mean that though, do you?"

"No, not really. Someday perhaps . . . though we can't . . ."

She held my arm tighter. "Alana, we both know that this won't last forever. This is one brief moment for us, before whatever comes next. A beautiful ember floating through the sky that will, too, soon fade away."

I felt my throat tighten. She was right. I knew she was right. "Are you saying . . ."

"I'm saying that I want to blow on that ember and keep it alive for as long as I can. And when it fades, I want it to do so with love, not anger."

I wasn't sure what to say to that. Here I was supposed to be the one good at stories, songs, and poetry, but she'd outdone me handily. Instead, I just stayed there with her, holding her, feeling the warmth and caring as I tried to focus on the now, not what was to come.

I was still a bit sullen a few days later as the little carriage that took me to our house weekly rattled up. I was still struggling to think of it as "home" as I'd only lived there for a few weeks total, a paltry amount compared to The Sky or the academy. My family was here though, and I suppose that's what really counted.

I was surprised to see another, far, far fancier carriage had pulled into my normal spot. It was decked out in gold, with pure black horses to match the pitch-colored sheen of the wood. A few guards stood around here and there, looking menacing.

This had to be another of the higher-ups in the government, and one who wasn't bothered by ostentatious things, unlike my dad. I could tell that the monstrosity of a vehicle was expensive, and I was pretty sure that there were runes on the metal pieces, but they were too far to make out.

The driver helped me down as was usual, and as I came near to my own house, a few of the guards bristled, looking as if they might stop me. It was at that moment my father appeared in the doorway, dressed in one of his few formal outfits.

"Alana, hurry up to your room and get changed. We have guests for dinner." That was all he had to say for them all to stand down.

As I passed through the entry, I saw him return to my mother. There he continued talking to who must be our visitors. The man was handsome, in his late forties or perhaps his fifties. He had dark hair and eyes and a truly regal pose. Off his arm hung a much younger woman, her black hair done up in a lovely silken plait. Both of them wore finery that perfectly matched them, surely custom-made for each.

CHAPTER 15

✦

DINNER GUESTS

As soon as I got to my room, I was tackled by a team of maids. Apparently, my mother had prepped them for just such an occurrence, and they were ready and waiting. I was unceremoniously stripped of my school uniform and forced into a black-and-purple number I was very sure I'd never purchased.

The new dress was gorgeous, with embroidered patterns flowing over it in the same color as the background cloth. They flowed almost like depictions of wind as it passed over me, shining slightly in the light. It even had a small amount of lace on it, but that was thankfully a bit reserved.

"Where in the world did this come from?" I asked as I was sat down so that mother's maid could do my hair.

"The lady of the house had it ordered a few days ago. She suspected that we might end up hosting important guests." She was hurried, but her hands moved with precision that I knew my maid could match.

"Wonderful. Is there anything I need to know?"

"I'm not sure. You did take Etiquette at the academy last year, yes?"

"Yeah, it was required."

"Then act like you're in that class as best you can, it won't hurt. Would that we could have gotten someone to you earlier to get you dressed up."

I frowned, nobody really looked down on the school uniform, at least not as far as I could tell. This was partially because it was for everyone; everyone alike wore it while studying. Therefore, it fulfilled a sort of "evening of the field" function. It was also rather good-looking, so there wasn't much to criticize. While it may not make the same sort of impression as my current attire, it certainly didn't make me look poorly prepared.

I tried to turn as I felt something hard rest against my lower back. "Hey, what are you . . ." I got just a bit of a view of the maid with cords held tight before she cinched the dress. "Wuuhhhh" was my only verbal response to the harsh pulling around my waist and chest.

I frowned harshly at her and she loosened it a bit. Tight corsets weren't really a thing here, at least not as they were generally depicted in fiction. Anything too much and it would interfere with breathing, but there were rough equivalent garments in stays that were worn to act as support. They were mostly cloth and not at all bad. The maid had simply been a bit over-zealous in her haste.

"Apologies, Miss," she said as she withered under my glare. An angry caster was not fun for anyone.

Finally, one of the maids applied a small amount of makeup for me. This, too, was sparing due to my age, but was oddly similar to what was used back on Earth. Powders to smooth the skin and redden the cheeks, darkening of the eyes, and a very faint lipstick that only reddened by a couple of shades. It focused on seeming as natural as possible.

As everything was done, I was hurried out to the hall. There I met John, who wore something that looked almost exactly like one of my classmate's uniforms, only significantly more decorated.

"Are you . . . dressed up?" I was a bit put off as I saw him there.

"Yes, and look at you, no longer in an old outfit in a bar but in a fancy dress ready for important meetings. Must be a change, huh?"

"I wore something similar for a couple of balls back before I was a student, as well as for one of the events there. You, on the other hand, look like you're oddly comfortable."

"Eh, I wear something a lot like this under my armor most of the time, so it's not too bad," he said as he took my arm, leading me down the stairs.

"So who is it anyway?" I whispered as I saw my parents and our guests had moved into the dining room.

"Didn't they tell you?"

"No, obviously not."

"Oh, wow. Well, I won't ruin the surprise then."

I felt my eye twitch as I nearly punched my brother, but at this juncture I couldn't risk making a mess. Whoever we were having over for dinner tonight was undoubtedly important. I did resent slightly that all of this had been dropped on me, but there was nothing to do at this point.

We entered the dining room on schedule just as the drinks were being served and took our seats. Everything was more done up tonight, the table, the clothes, all of it. That wasn't a big deal, but it was a bit off-putting. I was used to my family being mostly informal, and this change was a bit disconcerting.

"You know my son, of course, Lord Durin, but I don't believe you've met my daughter yet." Dad looked proud as he motioned to us.

I tried not to stiffen as I heard the name. It was one thing if a general or some bigwig was coming for dinner, but John had hidden that the leader of the freaking country was here! I'd have to get him back later.

"Greetings, John, my boy, it's good to see you well." Lord Durin nodded to my brother. Apparently, they knew each other enough for that. "And you, young lady, I'm overjoyed that my dear friend has found his missing child. I don't know what I'd do if it had been me."

"Thank you, sir." I was a bit flabbergasted.

Lord Durin had a kind smile, and if that was the Lord of Shadows, then his companion must be . . . our former princess. Knowing it now, I could kind of see they carried themselves in similar ways.

My eyes were drawn back to Lord Durin as he spoke to me once again, his voice kind. "Mystien tells me you are quite the young prodigy. I think he meant to have you join in his new research facility once he's got it going."

"Oh . . . I don't know about being a prodigy, sir, but I've done well in a few things."

"Well, if your brother is any standard of your family's children, I expect prodigy may be the right word. I look forward to seeing what you will do once you've graduated." Then he turned to my parents. "But on to happier news. My dear Sophia and I will be married this winter; the date is to be sent out soon."

Sophia held his arm and was positively beaming as he said it. "We decided to wait until the schools are on break. Most students won't be able to attend, but those who can, may like to." She gave me a bit of a wink as she said it.

I wanted to run from the room screaming, but, of course, that wouldn't be allowed. It was obvious that they'd come back so that she could stay with the Lovers here before the wedding, and that I would be going, regardless of how I felt about it. I generally had a positive view of weddings, but there would just be too much politics in this one for me to want to be within a hundred miles.

"Will you be holding it in Lithere?" Mother asked, chiming into the break.

"Oh no, we'll be holding it at my home." Lord Durin nodded toward her. "Travel arrangements will, of course, be made for those invited."

I wanted to ask some questions on that, but I got the feeling that they wouldn't be answered, at least not here and now.

From there, conversation shifted to rather boring subjects. It was clear that this was a social visit, and there were too many people and not enough security for anything else. I was a bit nervous to try and initiate conversation with such a big player, but I did have to admit that Lord Durin was charming and well-spoken. He didn't seem to mind lulls and was almost . . . casual with us. That was just a bit too weird for me; he was the leader of the country.

After dinner, we retired to the sitting room. The boys went off to one side to drink and discuss their mutual friends while Sophia came to join Mother and me. For her part, she seemed interested, even if she probably had much better things to do.

"So, Alana, you're at the academy, correct?" she asked as we took our normal seats.

"Yes, ma'am."

"And what are you currently working on? I find it so much fun to learn what other casters are studying. You are a bard as well, no?"

"I am, and right now I'm working on some sewing magic. The progression is slow, but I think it'll be useful."

My mother perked up at this admission. I had been keeping it from her until I felt that I had reached a good point, instead focusing on the more common methods while at home. I had a feeling that if I didn't demonstrate what I had accomplished, I'd be getting an earful later.

"Oh, you must show me! Before, we had a lovely woman who worked in the palace who could make clothes with a song. It was a magnificent and rather original use of her abilities."

"I know a tailor in the city who does much the same. He was the one who gave me the idea. Sadly, I find that my skills in that sort of handcraft are below par, and I was hoping to use magic to help make up for it."

That statement had set our guest to giggling. "Oh, I must admit that I always rather hated my lessons on embroidery too." She seemed oddly nice.

I pulled out a small box with some of our practice materials and began humming. Those we used at the house were far nicer than what I used personally, if only because there was more cloth here, and Mother could just use the scraps from her own personal work for practice.

The work was still not quite as good as I would have liked it to be, but it wasn't terrible. The fabric came together in a passable seam within a few moments, and I showed it to the princess. She smiled and checked it a bit, before nodding.

"Oh well, let me show you what I've been working on." There was a bit of a gleam in her eye, and she pulled out a small seed from a pouch.

As she hummed a lilting tune, the little seed began to sprout and grow a stalk, eventually becoming a budding flower on a tall stem. I watched as within a few moments it bloomed, the petals midnight black with small pale white spots all over it, looking almost like the night sky. I'd never seen one like it before.

"Beautiful. What kind of flower is it, if you don't mind my asking?"

She smirked. "That's the trick. This is a spell of my own making that allows me to alter them as I go, growing them into whatever form I like. It's easier if you start with something similar to what you want, but very large changes can be made."

I was floored; that was some seriously impressive work for a bard. Maybe a priest could do it on the fly like that, but I'd done enough healing to know that living things were fragile, and if you weren't careful . . . It took me a few moments to register all of it, and I just blinked. My silly little cloth trick probably seemed like child's play to her.

We chatted lightly about our work for a bit longer before our guests finally had to leave. It was getting rather late, and I was sure that they had more important things to do, but I bid them a happy farewell. Because it was late, I even managed to avoid most of my mom's irritation that I'd been hiding my new sewing work from her, getting only a glare as I headed up to bed.

CHAPTER 16

✦

MYSTIEN'S WORKSHOP

It wasn't until mid-fall that Mystien got his workshop properly set up to his liking. I knew when he did because I received a letter telling me that I was to report as soon as possible. That bristled, I liked him, a lot, and I respected him, also a lot, but he wasn't my current teacher and not family. Well, I had to admit that he was basically family, if only like an old uncle. I might even admit that we were closer than I was with my actual uncle if pressed.

So show up I did. I arrived by carriage to a rather nondescript building in the nobles' section of the city. I thought it might be a storage facility or something based on the outside, but when our carriage stopped, that thought was instantly dispelled.

The doors to the inner workshop were obviously enchanted and made of some variant of steel. The outer door was similar, but looked normal from the outside, a potent security measure. There were runes all over the floor, most of which I couldn't decipher, and all of which I suspected were hidden behind fake sequences. There were even a few guards present, all with auras.

As soon as I entered, I was surrounded by a soft light. It clung to me like a film. I spent a few seconds observing it before one of the guards came over to the carriage and gestured me out.

"Please come this way, Miss. We have a few security checks."

I followed silently as I was led to a panel on the side where I had to put my hand. When I did so, a fair bit of information came up. It was a full health scan that displayed my sex, age, height, weight, and the fact that there was a Lovers' Mark on my outer right thigh. I turned nearly crimson as I pulled away my hand.

"Sorry for the invasion, but it is necessary," the guard said, checking the details against a list. "All right, could you please perform the following spells for me. A liquid based flamethrower, summoning one unit of sugar, and turning yourself invisible. Ah, for the flamethrower, if it's possible to constrain it, could you use this?" He produced a small metal bucket, which he put well away from himself.

It seemed that Mystien was being particularly paranoid here, and after I performed all of those feats, the door was finally opened for me. I entered a small room that, of course, had another door that only opened after the previous one closed. I noticed that it, too, had a number of runes all over the ground, and I suspected that this facility alone was consuming an enormous quantity of mana. Eventually though, I made it through both of Mystien's security doors and into the workshop proper.

"Goodness, Mystien, how much mana are you spending keeping this abomination of a workshop running?" I asked the old man, who was sitting at a workstation engaged in crafting something.

"Surprisingly little, Alana. The main wards are being run through a powered orb, most of what is out there and in here are just used to support what it is doing, or act as foci for its work."

"Um . . . okay, but isn't it still doing some rather heavy magic?" It made sense to run them through a main node, for some uses, but that didn't really answer exactly what was so efficient.

"I used your variable for pi in it. The increased efficiency has done wonders." He didn't stop his work on the item before him as he spoke, even though it looked rather fragile, a spinning group of interwoven rings around some kind of central core.

"What? What increased efficiency?"

He turned and looked at me full-on. "Have you not noticed that you don't need to fill your lamp with mana nearly as often as you should?"

"I . . . I thought my maids were doing it periodically . . ."

He buried his face in his hands before starting to rub his temples again. "Alana, I would wager they were not."

"Oh . . ." There wasn't much to say to that. It was nice to know that I may have made the most efficient lightbulb ever.

"It is your lack of noticing that sort of detail that caused me to make this place. Even Lord Durin raised his eyebrows when I budgeted out what I wanted. I did promise him something that he could hardly resist though."

"Is that what you're working on now?"

"No, no, this is just something personal. I'm making him a crown out of sky-metal that will let him communicate over distance with several of his nearby commanders."

"Good grief, Mystien! You go on and on about me keeping my secrets, then you go and promise something like that. What are you thinking!?"

"I'm thinking that I'm an arch-mage over four times your age, young lady. Nobody in their right mind is going to try and assassinate me, and if they do, I will kill them. It will also explain the origin of certain things you've been leaking out quite cleanly; something I do not wish to have to go through again. So do tell me before you go and repeat those actions." His glare was harsh, extraordinarily so.

I tried to grumble a bit, but when he got irritated, it was almost painfully overwhelming. "Okay . . . So why did you call me here? Did you need help testing the sequences or something?"

"No, I've already taken care of that. I need your help with the sky-metal. I can make it, but it's painfully mana intense and very tiring. I've got a bit more to do before this is ready. Is there anything else you think I should add to the crown as well? You seem to have interesting ideas on that sort of thing."

"Hmm." I thought for a moment before I answered. "Something to stop rust, or patina, or whatever it would be on sky-metal."

"That's . . . not a bad suggestion. I believe that Lord Durin intends this to be the crown for some of his descendants as well. It will certainly be expensive enough."

We worked together, his setup almost exactly the same as the one I'd used when making my little cube of precious metal. It was fairly quiet as we had work right there in front of us and were both concentrating rather hard. I did note that my progress on making more aluminum was leagues above his, much to his visible irritation. Soon enough, we had about a pound and a half of the silvery stuff, and he motioned me to stop.

"You're alarmingly good at that. Do tell me that you haven't been making more without telling me."

"I haven't, honestly this time. I don't want more of this stuff floating around with any possible attachment to me. My teachers searched my room when I made the first little bit, and it was just a small sample."

"You got off easy. Thank you for your assistance. Oh, there was one more thing that I wanted to ask about."

"What's that?"

"Lucien mentioned something about drinks? He's helping with the preparation for Lord Durin's wedding, and they're having an absolute time trying to get enough of your alcohol fluid for what he's calling 'cocktails,' which he's insisting will be a hit."

"Oh, they definitely will be, though you'll need to tell people to be careful. I don't see an issue with making him a few gallons when I get there, or just before, we'll work something out."

"Are they toxic?"

"They're very strong, and don't taste it. If he's bringing in people for things like that, isn't Lord Durin worried about poison?"

"Not as such. There will be a large number of casters, including bards there. Anything that might harm him would have to either be very fast, which would be detected by the testers, or would be easily cured."

That was a bit of change from Earth, but I supposed it did make sense. Magic had a number of similar effects that just fundamentally changed the math on stuff like poison.

"Fair enough, and I know they're restricting access."

He chuckled. "You've no idea, Alana, but I think one day you will. I wonder what you'll make of it."

"Of what?" I asked, actually curious.

"State secret," he said in response, which made him chuckle even more.

I stuck out my tongue, but there was really no reason to press. I suspected that when I did graduate, I would be pressured to work with him here in his workshop. I didn't mind that idea too much, seeing as I liked Mystien, and I was sure some of the work he would be doing would be fun. It had been too long since we'd been able to talk freely without anything pressing to do, and I missed that in a bit of a nostalgic way. So he made up some tea and I made us up some sugar, and we just enjoyed chatting for a bit.

"I'm surprised that nobody is trying to force you into a marriage," I commented when the subject of my own came up. It was something I tried to avoid as much as possible.

"Oh, there have been a few offers, but I'm a crotchety old curmudgeon. I think I may invite Veska to join me here though. You remember her?"

"The bard from Hazelwood?" That was a bit surprising, and I knew my voice showed it.

"Just the one. She and I go back a long way, and I'll admit freely enough that I enjoy her company."

"I'm sure you do." I couldn't hide my smile behind my teacup as much as I tried. I remembered her salacious red outfit.

He fixed me with a bit of an irritated look. "I'm a bit surprised you remember her at all, Alana, you were but a small child when you met."

"Yes, but she made an impression, and I remember how you looked when you came back from your 'meeting' with her, a look I now fully understand." I did giggle openly at this one.

"I'm guessing you never told your father about that one?"

"No, and don't worry, I won't. Good on you, she seems like a wild one."

"Enough about my love life. Who are your current suitors?"

"Oof, can we talk about anything else?"

"Certainly, there are some? Are all of them not to your liking?"

"It's . . . complicated."

He raised an eyebrow but decided that he would drop the subject there. Shortly thereafter, I headed out. I'd nearly forgotten how thick the security on this place was, until I stepped out of the workshop proper and had to go through it all again.

When I finally got back to my dorm the next day, I sat down to work on my current project. It was a simple winter dress. My work with sewing magic had progressed and while I was still far behind Marcus in the art, it was now acceptable. He was on another level, able to meld cloth seamlessly and stretch it like it was pizza dough, but I didn't need that, I just needed enough to get my mother to leave me be.

I'd elected to go with rather dark blues for my outfit, in a princess-line cut, and if it looked as good on me as it did on the dress form now, I'd be quite happy. It didn't seem like something I'd take up often, but it was a good skill to have. Once I'd finished this, I would be devoting more time to other practical things, like finishing the next level of my core, something I was fast approaching even if I was being a bit lazy on it.

As I got the magic going again, I reflected on all the things that I'd need to do soon. Winter would be here before I knew it, and it was sure to bring with it many flurries, both of snow, and of new experiences.

CHAPTER 17

✦

WEDDING PLANS

A few weeks after my meeting with Mystien, Dad called me up to his office after dinner. That was a bit odd, and I knew it was probably something personal, but if it was important it was important. He sat down behind his desk, looking mixed between nervousness and resolve, with perhaps a bit of pity mixed in.

"Alana, we have to talk."

I took a spot in one of his chairs and locked eyes with him. "About what?"

"Lord Durin's wedding. It is a major event, and you do have to attend, even if you don't want to. I know it may be a burden, but I've tried to ask very little of you since you were found. This though I must."

"Like keeping me locked up for weeks?"

He sighed. "That . . . was a mistake. I am not perfect, dear, and I hope that you will forgive me for that and for leaving when I should have taken you with me. I admit that I have made mistakes, but I have done what I thought would keep you all safe."

That rankled. There were a lot of times when people did "what they thought would keep me safe," and it turned out awful to me. On the other hand, after his first major blunder and asking me to keep from stressing Mom, he really hadn't asked much.

"I wanted to go anyway, if I was invited. So there's no issue on that account."

I wasn't sure why he was being so weird about this, if I could go, I defi-nitely would. It seemed likely to be the party of the century, and there was no way I was missing a boatload of fancy people getting absolutely trashed on the cocktails I introduced.

"Yes, I suspected that you would want to go, but . . . you'll need an escort. At your age, you will need someone to dance with, and the like. Understand, Alana, that I rather like Kala, but unfortunately . . . she isn't an appropriate escort for this event." He picked his words carefully, probably expecting me to explode on him.

He was right. As he got to his point, I felt my jaw clench, and I very nearly let loose a scream. I hated people getting involved in my personal life, like this particularly, and he was telling me that she wouldn't work, that I had to find some guy? I could feel tears in the corners of my eyes growing from my sheer outrage.

"Did Mother . . ." This seemed like something she'd push, or at least want to push on me.

"No. Your mother had nothing to do with this, and she doesn't know about this conversation." Me going off on her seemed to be an idea that truly worried him. He might know how mad I was and wanted to avoid a full-fledged family fight. "I'm not telling you that you cannot keep seeing Kala, nor that you must begin courting someone, merely that you must have an escort for this event. You don't have to like them, or have any intention beyond just this wedding. If you don't have anyone in mind or anyone you would prefer, I'll happily arrange something, and I will make it clear to him that this will be only for this occasion."

"I will think on it." I was mad, mad at the world, mad at my father, mad at the fact that I couldn't just do as I wanted.

He didn't stop me as I rose and left his office. I started walking, down the stairs and straight out the front door, the only person who questioned me at all was a maid in the entry.

"Miss, is all well?" she said as I passed by.

"I am going out." It was curt, but honest, and I did just need to get away from here.

I began walking, I'd always loved going out on the city when I was younger, going to the shops and the eateries, seeing what was where. I didn't know too much of the upper parts of the city sure, but I knew enough, and so I walked. I walked along streets that seldom saw pedestrians, most taking carriages or coaches, heading down into the lower parts of the city.

I nearly stopped as I came to the academy. It was just on the edge, hanging just between the wealthy parts and those that were much poorer.

I'd lived here for two full years now. Kala was here; the last part kept me from going in. I needed to talk to her, but I just didn't know what to say, or how she'd react.

I kept on passing the restaurant that Dras had taken me to that one time, down and past the bookstore where we'd purchased the textbook that had helped both of us on our entrance exam, and where the attack on Lief had happened. I kept going, I looked in the direction of the temple district, but decided to give that a miss.

I walked through markets now closing as the sun set, and deep into the city, down to the place that I'd truly called home for a long time. As The Starlit Sky came into view, I felt myself calm. I knew that my parents were a bit apart from me, and that any advice they had would come with ideas of "what has to be" and "propriety" and all that nonsense, but Lucien? He'd tell it how it was. If Jackson had stayed in town, he'd also have a bit of a take, and one that I knew would be honest.

As I came in, I looked around at the people, the decor, the outright noise. It was nice, it was free, the thing I needed to get away from the suffocation around my family and everyone else. There was an open spot at the bar, and as I slid in, a slightly surprised-looking Lucien came over and put a cider in front of me.

"Well, look who it is. Been too long, though I'm not surprised to see you here."

"You're not?"

"No, not after that came in." He pointed over to the corner of the room as I slid him a coin for my drink.

Dras sat there looking absolutely awful. It was clear he'd been crying, and he even seemed a bit disheveled. My head cleared of my own gripes as I saw him, a friend who clearly needed help.

"What happened?" I asked the bartender as he leaned forward a bit.

"Don't know. He doesn't seem to care to share with me, but perhaps with you he will."

"All right, mind if I get a rag?" Without a word, Lucien passed me a clean cloth.

I took the rag and my drink and walked over to where Dras was monitoring his mug. It looked like beer, something that I'd never gotten a taste for at all. He didn't even notice me until I plopped down beside him.

"Hey! What's the . . ." He looked up and saw me. "Oh, hi, Alana . . . Wait, why are you here?"

"I'm having a disagreement with my family, so I'm pissed and wanted a walk, but that can wait. Why do you look like someone burned down your house?"

"I, uh . . ." He finally took a drink and looked up. "Clarissa broke up with me." He looked for a moment like he might start crying.

I didn't really know his girlfriend, well, ex-girlfriend now I suppose, but he had seemed happy with her. It was hard to feel that bad that she was gone, but it wasn't at all hard to understand loss, and that I should be here for him. So I wet the rag with a quick spell and passed it over.

"Here, clean yourself up and then tell me all about what happened."

He wiped himself down with the rag, which was both ice cold and wet, and began his tale. "After the regime change, she just started getting more and more irritated. She was pissed that her family were no longer nobles, that they'd lost a lot of their money and lands, the works."

"Kind of understandable."

"Yeah, I'd feel bad about that, too, but they all made it through, and they were making it work. It just changed her. She got all bitter, and even got mad when I mentioned that I might end up working for the new government after it all settled down. Our graduation is soon, and it's just gotten worse and worse. Then she started blaming other people, the new leaders, the army . . . you . . ."

"Also not uncommon."

"Right. I told her to quit it, that you'd had nothing to do with the war, but she just got pissed at that. In the end, she told me that if I wasn't willing to cut all ties with the new regime that she'd be gone, and when I tried to talk to her . . . She just called me a traitor and left, told me not to contact her again."

"That's terrible."

"Yeah, and then when I went to Mom for help, she just got mad. She'd liked Clarissa a lot, and thought that we'd end up married and blah, blah, blah."

"Moms can be like that sometimes." A fact I was feeling a bit myself.

"Yeah, so that's it. What's your big mess?"

"Short version?" He nodded as I looked at him. "Dad wants me to go to a wedding and to have an escort. He told me that Kala wouldn't do. I've no clue what I'm going to do, or how I'll explain it to her."

He leaned back, just covering his face with the cold rag. "That is . . . rough. I do not envy you at all."

I waited for a few moments to see if he'd say anything else, but he didn't. "You know, a lot of guys would have taken that as an invitation to volunteer."

I heard a snort from under the rag. "You don't want me to. We've never had that kind of a relationship, and it would just piss Kala off if we did go together."

"That is one of my favorite things about you, Dras. That you get that."

He picked up his mug, still leaning back. "Here's to shit love lives and old friends." We clinked glasses, another thing that transferred between worlds, and he drained his without even sitting up, a rather impressive feat.

"Better now?" I asked.

"You know, yeah, a bit." He sat up, and while his face was still a bit off, he did look much improved. He had a sort of off smile on now. "You?"

"Not as bad either. You know what you need?"

"Lots of things."

"To get some."

"Didn't we just have this conversation?" He looked at me with a bit of a frown.

"Not with me, idiot. Come on."

We left our table after I'd checked that he'd paid and headed back into the street. There were dozens of "establishments" around here, and the variety was almost daunting. I led him along to one of the nicer ones, and we went in.

I'd never been in one of these before and the atmosphere was certainly . . . different. There was an older woman at a desk in the entry, and she gave me a raised eyebrow as I pulled Dras along after me.

"All right, I'm just guessing, but I'm pretty good at that, and you are too young." She looked at me harshly as she spoke.

"You're right, but we're not here for me. My nice friend here just had a really bad day." I put several small silver coins on her counter. "Can you find someone to improve his mood?"

"This is not a solution." The objection came from behind me, but I didn't look.

"I can, if that's what he wants." She looked back at him. "But you seem unconvinced. How about a bath and massage, and you see where it goes?"

Dras rubbed his chin as I gave him a questioning look. "Well, a bath doesn't sound horrid, nor does a massage . . . I suppose it won't hurt."

I hoped he felt better by morning, regardless of where it went. Later on, I would muse that I never did find out how far he had gone that night. He never told me, and I never asked.

CHAPTER 18

✦

KALA'S OPINIONS
AND AN ARRANGEMENT

Kala just looked at me. I had explained the situation and she seemed about as pleased with it as I was.

"So you're not just going to tell them to screw off, huh?" she asked.

"I probably could. I could also just leave, but I'm torn. Other than their stupid demand for me to have an escort, I do want to go to this wedding. I met the former princess, and she's something else, and I want to learn more about Lord Durin."

"Okay . . . why?"

"He's different from most leaders I've seen, and I can't really understand it completely. He's a conqueror and by all rights could abuse us, but chooses not to. He seems nice, kind, and weirdly egalitarian. I can't figure out why he's like that, and perhaps getting to know him more will tell me what I want to know there."

"Do you think he had bad intentions?" she asked hesitantly.

"I don't think so. I just can't see his reasoning. Well, at least I hope he doesn't, he doesn't act like he does at least. Bah, I don't know, but my dad and Mystien both think he's a good guy and I trust them."

"Well, I'm not thrilled about the idea of you going to a wedding with someone else, but I, too, am curious about those two. I met Sophia at the temple once or twice."

I perked up, looking over at Kala. "What were your thoughts?"

"She's weird for a bard, very weird."

"I didn't get that. She seemed nice."

"She's quite nice. I just can't put my finger on it." She shrugged. "Anyway, we knew that people were going to be like this. The head priestess has been badgering me more and more recently too. Telling me how I need to find a husband while I'm young and can have as many children as I feel like."

"Okay, I thought my mom was bad. At least she's only trying to make me learn 'womanly arts' rather than asking me about kids."

"Alana, you need to learn those anyway. It's sad that you couldn't even make a dress, just from a practical standpoint."

I plopped down on the bed beside her, crinkling my nose. "How bad is it for you?"

"Not too bad." Kala said, leaning back. "I wouldn't be having any children right now anyway, not until I was out of school, but I'm getting lectures and looks basically every time I go back to the temple."

"Want to come live with me? You could just quit, and I'm pretty sure that I could swing buying my own mansion if I really wanted to."

She snorted laughter. "That's not really possible, Alana. Priests don't leave the orders, not fully."

That made me sit up. "What! Not ever?"

She shook her head. "Do you not pay attention in history?"

This was not a subject I really wanted in on. "Um . . . not really, I have issues with . . . I don't know, it's my worst subject."

At my little admission, she turned and flicked me on the nose. "When priests go bad, when our morals drift into something terrible, we tend to become very dangerous. It doesn't happen often, even with those who do go solo, but there have been a few times . . . when a priest decided that the good and moral thing was for them to exterminate a city, a country, or everyone. One death priest can cause massive destruction, Alana. It normally doesn't go on for long, but it does mean that the orders have groups that are tasked with just making sure that nobody goes rogue. Didn't you know why they take every child that shows priestly magic at such a young age?"

"Okay . . . that's dark."

"No lie there. Battle-mages may think they're hot shit, but when it comes to killing, we priests are the best; it's not even a contest. Then again a bard willing to blow themselves up by focusing several hundred people in one performance can do some absolutely astounding things too."

"Well, I suppose you can't leave and join me in my giant imaginary mansion of awesomeness then. I've had more than enough squads of soldiers sent after me thank you very much."

That got me another snort. "Well, about your wedding plans . . ."

"Not my wedding plans. I think my wedding is still a good ways off."

"About the wedding plans coming up soon then. I think you should go."

"With whom? And if you say Dietrich, I swear I will punch you." She knew I still had a sour taste in my mouth from my interactions with him. He'd sent me a few more invitations to things last year, much to my irritation, but seemed to have given up since the invasion.

"I don't know. You can ask your dad, or go around him and ask Lucien or Mystien what they think. I'm sure the former knows somebody. I'd say see if you could find someone to irritate your dad if you could."

"I could ask Jackson, but sadly he's married now. If I showed up with him, Dad might never try something like this again. I know I don't want Dad to have any say in it. This is a pattern that he needs not to repeat."

At least we agreed that irritating my father would always be a good choice. I got the feeling that neither of us were truly pleased with the whole affair, but Kala was being strangely reasonable. I couldn't ask for more, but it still grated that I had to have this conversation in the first place.

I pretty much ticked everyone in the academy off the list at the beginning. Most of the boys my age were okay enough, but I didn't want too much about this all being spread around. There was also the big divides in our group, and going with one seemed like it would launch me into that political mess.

In the end, I went to go see Mystien. He owed me for bringing me in on his work anyway, and I was fairly sure I could push some names of people I didn't know out of him. As I arrived at his home, a rather less massive edifice than my own, I saw a familiar face coming out.

"Charles?" I looked at the young man in his dark uniform. He'd obviously had some other meeting going on with the old wizard.

"Oh, hey, Alana, how are things?"

"Hmm, not great. Who cares about that though? Why are you here?"

"I work for Mystien. Didn't you know that?"

"I mean, I knew you were in the army or something . . ."

He shook his head. "Anyway, it's good to see you."

I looked over at him. He was a fairly good guy, and while he might not like it, I could ask . . . "Hey, Charles . . ."

"Mmm?"

"So, I'm dating Kala, you know?"

"I know."

"And um . . . I'm having to go to this wedding, but they want me to have an escort." His raised eyebrow prompted me to continue. "And . . . um, I was wondering . . . would you?"

He seemed to consider for a few moments. "I can if that's what you want. Is it?"

"I think so? Er, yes."

He gave me a small smile and just shook his head. "All right, I'll come meet with you soon, and we can go over the details. When is a good time?"

I gave him the next day I had off, planning to meet around noon. He also asked me about clothes and if there would be any major issues he'd need to sort, but I thought it would all be fine.

After a few minutes, Mystien made his appearance from the front door. "Alana, you know that I'm a very busy man, right? Can you come in so we can go over whatever it was you needed?"

"Actually, I think I've gotten it all sorted now. Thanks anyway!"

He looked flabbergasted for only a moment before irritation crept up his features. "Are you telling me you went through all the trouble of setting up a meeting with me, interrupting my work, and now you don't even need anything?"

"Yup!"

"Get out of here! The both of you can just go then!"

Sticking my tongue out at him at this point was, in retrospect, probably a poor decision. I will say that Charles did do the chivalrous thing and try to keep the worst of the cold water the old wizard started hurling at us off of me, but by the time we'd found shelter in the carriage, we were both pretty thoroughly soaked.

"Crotchety old bastard," I said through chattering teeth.

"Good grief, he didn't have to go with cold, that was just mean," Charles agreed.

Soon enough though, we ended up laughing. I had warming and drying spells on the list already, so it wasn't too much of an inconvenience.

MYSTIEN

Sometimes, but not always, my plans went off without any issues. As I closed my door, I threw back my head and laughed. The girl was too smart for her own good and needed a bit of a push sometimes. It was also rare for me to get a good chance to be a bit childish without disastrous conse-quences, and I was in no way giving up this one.

I turned and opened the door into the only real meeting I had today. Veska was sitting by my window, looking superb in her little red . . . outfit was a rather generous word.

"Your angry old man act is something to watch," she chuckled as I sat down beside her.

"Kids these days!" I shook my fist as I tried to make my voice sound even older than it was.

"I was a bit irked when that young man came to deliver those files to you in the middle of our date. Did you plan this? Did he know?"

"Eh, neither of them did, my dear. He's clearly smitten with the girl, and her father will approve of this. Also, I got to have fun, so we all win."

She snorted. "You boys all win, not her."

"Oh? I think she'll win out in the end too. I may be wrong, but we'll see."

"And what about me? Do I get to win?" Veska pouted as she leaned over to me, looking up.

"Well, let us see if you can indeed." I laughed, closing the windows with an errant flick of my hand.

CHAPTER 19

✦

GATEWAY

The day for us to head to Lord Durin's home came sooner than I might have liked. Classes were held off for a week in what seemed to now be a recurring winter break, and my first day was dedicated to the arduous task of getting ready and then traveling there. My mother had been in a flurry of work for weeks, and I was fairly sure that she'd not calm until we arrived. All of my things, save my travel outfit, were already packed in the morning.

We got into a small carriage and headed well out of the city. It was relaxing to just feel it roll along the roads as I leaned back, the slight shaking lulling me into a near sleep. We passed a few fields and several small hamlets on our way. Though I didn't see them, I suspected that well behind us were soldiers who were keeping an eye out for any trouble.

Around noon, we stopped at a waystation. I was glad that these were still around, as they served a valuable purpose for those who weren't super wealthy. These little places, strewn at intervals along most major roads, and some minor ones, served as safe places to rest to the weary traveler. Stopping was a bit odd, being that it was noon and this place was well from any major route, but that was fine.

The first thing that struck me as odd was how empty it was, our group was the only one here. I looked around for a few moments as I disembarked and was a bit surprised at the strange quietness, as well as the fact that we seemed to be stopping for a longer time. Much of our luggage was being unloaded.

As I stretched a bit, Father came up to me. "Come quickly, we're going first."

"Um? Going where?"

"I'm afraid I'm not able to share that with you just yet, soon though. When you are of age, almost certainly."

I didn't really like the cloak-and-dagger nonsense, but I had no reason not to trust him. Our family and a handful of servants were being taken into the waystation first. Charles had come with us, but he was dealing with some other things involving the caravan.

The stone of the waystation entry was clean and well maintained, and the slight heel on my shoes clacked as we entered. It was a plain place, but there would certainly be a small eatery inside where one could get food and drink, before heading to the rooms for visitors.

As the doors opened, I was greeted by a frankly absurd sight. Lord Durin was there, leaning back in a chair and holding a small cup of some drink. In all his finery, he sat here, in an establishment made mostly for peasants, drinking like it was the most normal thing in the world.

"Hello, my friend. I hope you'll forgive my joining you, but I needed a bit of a break from all the hustle and bustle. My dear Sophia is in a flurry of work, and I feel rather unwelcome to be in her way," the man said as we approached.

Dad laughed. "Women can sometimes be like that with weddings, my friend. It is an important day and theirs."

The Lord of Shadows nodded sagely and rose, chatting a bit with Father as we walked deeper into the facility. We arrived at a hallway, and an attendant there pulled out a black strip of cloth.

"My apologies, Miss, but at this point . . ." she said as she approached me.

"There is no need," Lord Durin declared to everyone's surprise.

"No need?" I asked as the man turned to face me.

"None at all. I have been informed by Mystien of some of your work, my dear Alana. He has told me that you have done great service to me and mine, and that you are able to keep secrets when you must. This is one you must keep, one that I hope you will help me unravel in time."

I nodded gravely. When someone of his level tells you that you were to keep a secret, it was important to listen and listen well. I didn't want his direct attention, but that was a lost cause for now, and I was curious. Steeling my resolve, we continued. There were a number of rooms we passed through, the many security measures clear on them. We went down and down until we finally reached a well-protected room.

It was large, even for a cavern, and at the end of it was an artifact that I could tell at a glance was astoundingly impressive. Runes covered the glittering blue opening to a passageway. There was a slight distortion around the stone circle that made the opening. It even felt magical, the way the world seemed to bend around it.

The Lord of Shadows chuckled as he saw my jaw drop. "This is one of the things that aided me in my conquest. Do you know what it is?"

"No, sir, I don't, but I can almost feel the power."

"It is a gate, one of many. Even Mystien is lost as to how it works. He has tried several times to decipher its workings but has yet to inform me of anything of note. I found it and its network some years ago. The Alcubierre Gates, I can tell you that they were owned at one point by the magus Ristolian. Sadly, he left no indication as to who, or what Alcubierre is or was. I personally think it was another magus from his time." Lord Durin waxed on for a bit, loading me down with important information.

That was a name I knew, though I'd only heard it once from our former dean. He was one of those I believed to have been another traveler from my world, and Alcubierre was obviously a reference to warp drives. I didn't know how those worked in detail, but I did know they warped space or something.

"Amazing," I whispered.

"Truly something, instant travel across the world." My father seemed to be watching me, and he agreed.

"Nearly instant. We have been able to figure out that it does take 'some' time to move from place to place," Lord Durin corrected. "At any rate, shall we?" With that, he stepped through the portal.

I followed just after Mom and Dad. The sensation was odd, like being pulled for a brief second as I moved through, to find myself in a huge stone room. There were dozens of similar portals strewn about, turned off, or with a metal grate before them to prevent entry. There were also a number of guards decked out in magical items and with auras that gave me some serious pause.

"Welcome to my home, the Fortress of Ristolian," our guide declared. "Verren, I believe you know your way about. Please excuse me as I have other guests to go and greet." He turned and one or two of his aides joined him as he headed for another of the gates passing through with little fanfare.

This place was strange in a number of ways. Our assigned rooms were right near those of my uncle, who I hadn't seen in years. After he greeted us with gusto, I went out onto one of the balconies. The whole facility was enormous and built in a rather squarish layout. It seemed whoever had made it had used stone and a repeating, simple design. Well, except for the main hall, which was built like a palace and looked like it might have been picked straight out of a children's movie. It was massive and full of towers that didn't seem to serve much purpose.

Our room had a balcony that looked out into the central courtyard, and we were on the upper level, giving us an impressive view. It was a lovely view, a field of white broken up by garden walls and small sections that were kept green by similar heating magic to what I was using to stand in freezing temperatures without issue.

It was cold outside of the buildings, painfully so. Cold on the level of those old videos of people throwing up pots of hot water and watching it freeze in the air. Mother had tried to fuss about me wanting to go stand outside in this until I showed her my warming magic. Then she joined me.

"I didn't know you could do this, dear," she said as we stood at the small railing.

"Of course, I used to really like going out in the snow for walks. It was always so peaceful."

"I've missed too much of your life." She seemed a bit sullen.

"Mom, we both know that we're pretty different."

She sighed and moved to hug me, holding me close. "I know, when you were a little girl, we didn't talk enough. You were always so different, so . . . a bit strange, honestly. I want to be there for you, but I just don't know . . . how." She petted my head as she held me. It was nice, and for the first time in a long time, I just let her, enjoying it as we stood, her hands stroking my hair softly.

"You could stop pressuring me a bit. That would be nice."

She laughed lightly. "A mother worries. I hope you won't begrudge me that too much. I hope one day you'll understand too. I will try though, I'll try."

We enjoyed the moment for a bit longer before she pulled back.

"Something wrong?" I asked.

"Well," she said, sighing. "Sadly, I think we have some engagements this afternoon."

"If we must."

"Don't pout too much, Alana. I'm sure that there will be some you'll enjoy."

We headed back in and checked out the schedule. There were a number of small social events on the buildup to the wedding. There were simply too many movers and shakers here for there not to be. While few of the women here were soldiers themselves, many were married to such and had little to do in military meetings. For that reason, more social things were organized for them and their children to attend while everything else was going on.

The first of which we attended was set up rather like a tea party. There were tables with sweets from all over the country and various drinks. The idea seemed to be to share what products were coming up in your current area, the new trends and foods that could be exported.

Without my knowing, Mom had put together a table for the capital. It had ice cream and one of the more common teas that was popular in Lithere. She knew most of the women who were here with us and seemed to enjoy socializing with them. I recognized one or two of the daughters from school, though they weren't really in my friend group.

There were almost no boys here at all. A few women had what were obviously their young sons, and one or two boys around my age showed up, but this seemed to be more gauged toward girls. I wondered briefly if there were other things going on at the moment and after a simple inquiry got a schedule from my mother. This was the only big thing for today, but she seemed to suspect that I'd want to go to the others soon.

It was impressive. There were dozens of small events like this one focusing on different things. Some were on new kinds of magic that were coming into fashion in given areas, another on food and drink. It looked like mother had brought me along to the one she preferred, but I would decidedly be going to some others before the main event.

It was hard to admit that I wasn't really involved in her social circle at all, but I only saw her once a week at best. It seemed that I may need to learn more, but for now, I was putting together a schedule for my vacation.

CHAPTER 20

✦

DEMOCRACY AND A NEW SPELL

I went to a number of different events, mostly alone. In the time moving up to the wedding, there were gatherings of casters, exhibitions of local foods, there was even a small tournament that I attended to cheer on my brother. It was a party-like atmosphere, rather like a festival from back on Earth.

Today, I found myself sitting in one of the fortress's gardens watching a handful of people try to make art from the ever-present snow and ice. I wasn't sure where these were going, mostly because some of them were really weird. There was one that was a two-story building with lights and ice walls, built in an almost Gothic style. Those mages who liked to use ice and its softer cousin apparently were just having a field day with what they could do.

The judge of this competition was the bride-to-be, who showed up rather late in the afternoon. She moved from exhibit to exhibit and made a few notes. I found it odd that a majority of people still referred to her as Princess, but it did seem right. She gave off the air of a pure and kind princess as she handed the award, a small ribbon, to the winner. That man had made a set of ice rosebushes that achieved an almost rainbow effect in the way the flower petals bent the light.

As she moved to leave, Sophia stopped briefly beside me. "You were Verren's daughter, were you not? I don't believe I saw your presentation."

"Oh." I blushed. "I don't really have much in the way of ice manipulation magic. I just came to watch mostly."

"I see, I see. Well, I'm sure if you want to you'll find something fun that you're good at while here. Sadly, I must return to my preparations, though this little break was nice." With a kind wave, she left me there.

I thought for a few moments and pulled out my schedule. I didn't have anything important going on for the next bit. There were a few different discussions going on shortly though that were of note to me. The most important of which was on the subject of villages and how to handle the integration of them all into our new empire most smoothly. That called to me as a former villager myself, even if it was likely that it would just be impossible for me to do much more than watch. Not that anything would be too important anyway, these were just discussion groups on the subject, not some kind of legal council.

As I sat off to the side, I read through some of the documents on the changes that were happening on the village level. A few things popped right out at me, mostly the changes that were being made toward magic users of all kinds from villages to cities and up.

Based on what I was seeing, they'd kept the idea of leaving casters as a higher class. We were exempt from most taxes with the large exclusion of trade tariffs. There were also provisions for making sure that all casters who wanted to would receive some education. The normal exclusion from forced conscription, though heavy encouragements to join the military were there. The provisions that gave jaw droppingly generous inducements for anyone who had magic using children were interesting too.

The reason for the last bit was obvious, because every nation needed those, and ours was definitively a conquering sort. It would surprise me if Lord Durin didn't have designs of some of the other nearby neighbors, and he'd need lots and lots of soldiers to make them happen.

The inducements themselves were something else. On a child demonstrating an aura or the ability to use any magic, the parents were given a stipend for food, medicine, and housing, as well as a small yearly payment. Of note, female magic users had all of their children included up to age ten, as well as themselves if pregnant. These hadn't gone into effect yet, but I imagined when they did every minor-talented girl in the region would be taking the government up with haste. Full casters might be slower, but I think many would be jumping on this ship too.

"On to the subject of leadership: There are several proposals on how to see to it that local mayors remain of good skill. While they are currently under military command, this isn't feasible in the long term. The Ermathi tried that, and it came out rather brutal. Similarly, there are no more local lords to appoint mayors now, not that we'd want that sort of corrupt official anyway. The leading proposal has the councils of the central towns appointing public servants to the position," an older man stated to the group, which got several people to flip to that section of the provided booklets.

This stirred me from my musings and got me to flip too. I briefly read through the current proposals. They all boiled down to appointing someone to lead the town. Either the local council, or local military commander, there was even one that proposed having local magic users appointed. To me, they all seemed a bit foolish.

"Why not just let the villagers choose?" I asked.

There wasn't a whole lot of speaking going on right now, so it sounded much, much louder than I'd intended. I nearly flinched as dozens of eyes turned to look at me. Some were a bit amused, some condescending, some curious, though all turned to see who'd spoken.

"Care to explain, young lady?" asked the speaker who was the main presenter.

I was glad that he'd managed to at least keep any condescension out of his voice. I think that was mostly because he had an image of impartiality. As I looked at him though, I had no illusions; he decidedly looked like he thought I was stupid.

"Let the villagers choose their local leadership. They will mostly be handling the day-to-day events anyway, and you are unlikely to find anyone who knows those better than the people who live there. They'll also know who in their community isn't stupid, and is trustworthy. Add to that that they'll not resent someone being sent in from outside to control them, and I think it will work better overall." I stood as I spoke, as seemed to be the procedure.

A woman with gray hair and a few lines quirked an eyebrow at me. "What shall be done if they choose someone corrupt or poorly suited?"

"The same thing that would happen if it turned out an appointee was corrupt or unsuitable as well," I pointed out, which got me a nod.

"That sort of option will never work. For a few places perhaps, but the majority will not know what would make a good leader." There was a strong murmur of agreement to that opinion.

"Such democratic institutions are known in some of the eastern city-states," another fellow pointed out. "They have failings, but benefits as well. We may have been remiss in not adding such an option for consideration."

I settled back into my spot to continue my reading and listening. Glad that these people were just the equivalent of a bunch of old codgers having a round table at some conference. Most of what was discussed would seem odd from an Earth perspective, mostly because there weren't even whispers of the idea of equality. Those with magic and those without seemed to be separated completely in their minds, and more as the years went on in mine as well.

I woke up bright and early, tomorrow was the wedding proper, and then everyone would be clearing out. There were a few more talks and the like I'd have liked to go to, but those were later, this morning I had time, and I had privacy. I'd checked and all my family were going to various things they wanted, leaving me well alone.

There was something I wanted to try out, and now was my best chance during this trip. There would be other, better chances later, but I wanted to give it a go before I went back home.

I sat on my bed holding an apple, and I began to concentrate. I breathed deeply as I felt out around me. Magic was a slippery thing sometimes, and often hard to get to do what you wanted, but I knew what I wanted. I tried to visualize space, like it was so often shown in all those sci-fi documentaries and stuff, like a rubbery sheet. Then I reached forward with my mind and tried to bend it, to make a little divot in the sheet like a tunnel, just a small one. I tried to replicate the feel of the gate that I'd come through on my way here. If it worked I'd have my first step to teleportation, if not, well . . .

Nothing happened. I spent the better part of about an hour scrunching up my face in various ways as I tried to pull the sheet, all to no avail. As I lay back, I threw the apple up in the air, catching it, something that I repeated again and again. After a few tried, the apple went off a bit and though I tried to catch it, it landed smack on my face.

"Ow! Stupid apple." I rubbed my nose as I turned to where it'd fallen, rolling along the floor.

It was around that point that I realized I wasn't thinking right again. I didn't need to bend a sheet, sheets were flat. I needed to bend . . . I don't know Jell-O? A rubber ball? Something like that. Regardless, I needed to make three dimensions move, not two.

With this insight in mind, I went back to my focusing. I tried to make a small tunnel, just a couple of inches wide and a few feet long across my room. I focused on the feeling of the portal before and tried to visualize what I wanted. The picture in my mind was a bit weird. I had plenty of practice making weird visualizations real, through illusions, but this was truly strange. Around the areas that I wanted my teleport? Portal? Whatever, I tried to bend space in all dimensions, making it flow and stretch like bread dough.

I strained as my mana flowed out in buckets. Soon though, there was a small distortion in front of me, right in the center of my room, a small spot, maybe a foot wide and four long stretched, pulling against me as it tried to close. Picking up my erstwhile apple, I threw it through.

A second after the fruit hit the front, it disappeared, before reappearing a second later at the other end. It plopped out and continued on its thrown trajectory, eventually hitting a wall and rolling across the floor again. It was seemingly unharmed, that was a victory if I ever saw one.

"Whoooo!" I shouted as loud as I dare. It was followed immediately by "Wooo, OOooooo, OOOoo." I tried to aim at my bed as the mana drain of the new spell hit me and I fainted.

CHAPTER 21

✦

DISTORTIONS AND DANCES

The pounding that awoke me was painfully loud. I discovered soon after that it held no flame to the absolute hate-filled light that now filled my room, slamming into my tired brain like a hammer.

"Alana? Are you there?" I recognized Charles's voice from the other side of my door and sat straight up, an action I instantly regretted.

"Um . . . yeah, one moment." I struggled to keep up as I took a quick look around my room.

The first thing I noticed was that it was dark outside, very dark. I had been working in the morning and must have just knocked myself out for the whole day. There was no way that someone hadn't noticed at some point, but I could probably make it fine by just saying that I'd been feeling off and took a nap. That issue was no big deal.

What was certainly a big deal was the fact that there was still a visible distortion in the middle of the room. I could feel my eyes getting bigger as I looked at it. I had no clue if this was dangerous, safe, or just a weird visual trick, but there was an absolutely zero-percent chance that I could explain that away. It looked like a lens or something, with a slight swirl and color change. My apple still sat on the floor below it, and while it looked fine, I was in no hurry to put any body part into this thing.

"Alana, is everything all right?" Charles asked from the other side of the door, my head was still pounding, and I needed to think.

"What!? Um . . . yeah, everything's fine, I'm . . . I'm good. Um . . . how are you?" Internally, I was cursing, just trying to figure out what in the world to do with this mess.

"Are you sure?"

"Yeah . . . yeah, I'm sure. One second."

I stood up and made my way to the door. My mana had fully recovered as far as I could tell, but I was still coming back from the knockout of using all of it at once. I got to the door and opened it just a crack so I could stick out my head.

"Hi there," he said as I popped my face out into the hall. "There's a party tonight where we'll be going over a lot of tomorrow's activities, and I haven't seen you all day to talk about it. Is there a problem?"

"Um . . . no, no problems, none at all." I thought for a moment before amending my statement. "Actually, just a bit, but like, girl problems." That seemed the surest way to get him to go quickly.

"Oh . . . um . . . like down in the undercity?" I could see he didn't believe me, and his hand was drifting down to the blade at his waist.

It was a bit surprising that they let him carry that, but I supposed that most casters were at least as dangerous on their own. I was also touched that he'd made his face not match his words at all. It was clear that he didn't believe me, and that if I said yes he'd be coming through that door swinging at whatever "problem" he found there. He'd even chosen the perfect words for some assailant to not know how I was answering.

"Not at all like that, actually."

"Do you need me to go fetch one of the maids to help you then?" he said as he began to turn.

"No, nope, I'm good, totally good."

He turned back and sighed. "Alana, if you don't go to the party tonight, it will be noticed. I don't know what's wrong, but you're obviously lying."

"I'm . . ."

"You're really bad at it. Anyway, can you fix whatever the issue is promptly?"

"Um . . . one moment." With that, I closed the door.

"Sincerely?" I heard his muffled voice gripe from the other side of the door.

I could throw an illusion over this thing for the time being, but what if someone walked into it. That would be . . . I didn't actually know, but I was going to go with worst case and move forward from there, so we'd assume bad. That meant that I needed to fix it, preferably without passing out again.

I would have loved to stick around and study this . . . whatever, but that seemed a bit dangerous at the moment. For now, I'd have to do what I could and so I began to focus again. I reached out in my mind and tried to smooth out the area of space that I'd previously pulled, imagining it coming back together.

Luckily for me, it seemed that the world wanted to undo whatever I'd done, and while it was still a strain, it did come back to what it should have been in the first place. As space flowed back how it should be, I got the distinct feeling that I needed to investigate that phenomenon when I got a chance, hopefully somewhere slightly more private and on a smaller scale. For now, I was back to running on the fumes of mana.

I turned and opened my door once I saw that my screw-up was fixed. "Hi there, I don't suppose you would go and get me that maid, would you? I may need just a bit of help getting ready."

Charles narrowed his eyes and gave a quick look around my room. I was fairly certain that he could pick up on things I never would, but after a moment nodded. "Okay, if you're sure you're all right."

"Thanks!"

It was only a few moments before a maid came, and shortly after that I was dressed and ready to go. I was lucky that I'd already been about halfway to presentable and all I'd done all day was sleep after my morning routine. The fact that the maid knew her business also probably helped a lot.

As I walked down the hall with my escort, he looked at me with a quirked brow. "You going to tell me what that was about?"

"Nope." I tried to stay cheerful even though I'd exhausted myself twice today and really could just go back to bed.

"As long as you're all right, I suppose it doesn't matter, but please be careful."

The party was lovely. We were escorted to the main part of the venue, and I was given a small card to indicate where I would be seated tomorrow. After that, we were shown to the hall where the feast would be held afterward. There was one tonight as well. This room had been used for several of the larger discussions and so was familiar to me, but it was still wonderful to see.

The meal was light by feast standards, having only a few courses of lighter foods and a very small amount of wine given out. This wasn't a large party but rather a gathering for most of the wedding guests to get acquainted with the proceedings for tomorrow.

The happy couple sat at the top of the head table, surrounded by high-ranking officials and close friends. From there, the tables were separated by sex with those closer to the high table being of higher standing. Mother and I sat together. We were not the closest but were still nearby enough to hear the louder parts of the conversation there if we cared to. Even from here, I could tell that they both looked rather tired.

Afterward everyone was going off to the dance hall, where those who were so inclined could go through some of the dances that we'd be doing tomorrow. It wasn't nearly as decked out as it would be, and the band was significantly smaller than a true one, but this would serve as a good rehearsal for those who needed it, or who just liked to dance.

"You look tired, dear, will you be joining in the dancing tonight?" Mother asked as she leaned over.

I didn't know if I should take the opportunity or not, but I was surprised she could see how depleted I was. "I'm not sure. Do you know if Charles knows these dances? We'll have to once or twice tomorrow at least."

She blinked at my question. "Oh, I didn't think to ask. He should know some, right? He's a magic user and all and . . . Actually, your father didn't know any until recently. We may need to ask."

It was for that reason that I ended up at another dance rehearsal. They weren't bad after all, and I did know those that were on the docket, months of etiquette classes will do that for you. After a few of the larger group dances, I finally ended up with Charles on the floor. He held my waist with calm confidence and led me through all of the steps at least as well as I could have done.

"I didn't know you knew these," I stated as our second round came to an end.

"I don't."

"What? You're doing better than I am, didn't you practice?"

"No. I'm watching the steps of the other dancers and repeating them," he said as if it were the most natural thing in the world to be able to watch dozens of people and mimic them almost perfectly.

I just sputtered for a second. "That's so unfair, I had to learn all of these by rote."

"Eh, I got used to watching Meg's moves and having to repeat them as she did them."

"You cheater."

He chuckled at my accusation, and we returned to the floor for a few more dances. At the actual party, we'd have to switch partners, but for this it would be fine. He also wasn't bad, I may have personally wanted Kala to be here instead, but it was nice to at least have someone who knew what he was doing, even if he was just faking it.

As we left the dance hall, Mystien approached me, his brow a bit furrowed. We moved off to the side, and he put up a minor privacy ward. It seemed he wanted to speak privately.

"Is everything well?" he asked.

"Yes . . ."

"Your aura looks like you depleted all your mana. Is there anything we should worry about?"

"No, I was just trying out some new spells earlier and didn't realize how mana-intensive they would be. There's so much going on here you know? The ice magic event alone was something else, and while I can make it, I can't sculpt anything like that, yet."

"I see. You know that that will happen though, Alana, please be careful. When you came in late looking like death and strained aura, I was a bit concerned."

"Is this all you wanted? To chastise me on mana regulation?"

"No, though honestly you should be more careful. Didn't we cover that when you were just a child?" He frowned a bit and so did I, but he had other business. "Did you sincerely suggest democratic elections of mayors for villages in the meeting?"

"Good grief, Mystien, they were just a bunch of old farts. It's not like they decide that stuff or anything." I couldn't believe he was asking about that of all things.

He looked like he'd want to bonk me on the head or something, but now was not the time. "Alana, think about where you are. Those 'old farts'—and I do love that turn of phrase—are the movers and shakers of the empire. They are making those decisions. If you were sincere, you could write up details on how you think it might be done. I think your father and I might well support that bid."

I blinked. "You'd put your stamp on it?"

"Both of us lived in a village, Alana, and we know how it can be screwed up. I also don't think it's a terribly bad idea, we might have to try it and work out the kinks, but I'm willing to support that idea."

I thought about how long it would take to do all of that. "Okay then, I'll write down some things and send them over to you. I don't know specifics, but for a general idea, it should be okay."

When I got back to my room, I scrawled out a general layout before bed. Secret ballots, all adults having an equal vote, maybe place a few basic constraints on who could run. It wasn't much of a proposal, but I hoped it would pass. I had it done in under an hour and sent it off to Mystien. Dad was really busy at the moment and he'd not asked for it, but I could answer most of his questions then.

As all that was done I fell back into my bed and laughed at the idea that most of what I'd done today was sleep.

CHAPTER 22

✦

THE WEDDING

The morning of the wedding was . . . hectic. There were few maids overall in this place in comparison to the number of guests. Normally, every important person would have a servant, but since this fortress was secret, that wasn't really feasible. But there were a few who were helping based on a number of criteria. Age was considered quite important: being old was a detriment; similarly young girls hoping to find a husband really wanted the help too. The other was status. It wasn't as all-consuming as it had been back when there had been an actual nobility, but there was no denying that there was still a status divide.

Mom and I broke this mold by not taking the offered help; instead, sending them elsewhere. With a bit of effort and mana, I could do all of my own clothing and hair, and easily enough help her with hers. She, on the other hand, had been living among far fancier people than I normally associated with and had learned more about the cosmetics that were popular right now. I knew how to do most of that, too, but she'd eclipsed me in skill in that area.

I wanted to shake a metaphorical fist at the boys when we finally met to head into the hall proper. With short hair and significantly simpler outfits, they looked like they'd spent a fraction of the time getting ready than we had. That said, I did have to admit that they all looked stellar with pressed semi-uniforms, shined buttons, and polished sword hilts. My male family members had acquired new cloaks as well. Father's had an inner lining that was sort of brindle-looking, whereas John's gray one had some kind of feathers around his shoulders and absolutely looked great with his aura.

Even Charles, though his clothing might have been a few steps below that of my dad or brother, looked good. His clothes were a deep black with subtle purple highlights, which matched my own formal dress perfectly. To go with it, he carried one blade, slightly longer than my brother's and with a shining silver-and-black handle.

"Did you have clothes made to match mine?" I asked after looking him over.

"Um . . . yes, it was suggested that I do so." He looked over toward my dad as he said so.

"And when did that happen?" I asked, narrowing my eyes at the two slightly.

"Lad knew you were inviting him to a major event and came to talk to me, Alana, and be glad he did. It saw to it that there were no misunderstandings anywhere. Anyway, with the two of you matching as you do, most will assume that you're courting and not bother you, or me, with such intentions." I hadn't thought of that, and while it didn't please me that Charles had gone to my father without speaking to me about it, it was decidedly the socially appropriate thing that they speak.

My face must have shown my conflict, which elicited a sigh from my father. Regardless though, I took Charles's offered arm and tried to smile as we walked toward the hall. I really didn't want to deal with suitors, and if this was the best way to keep them away from me, then I could fake it like a champ.

We had good seats, and I had a wonderful view of the ceremony, which was conducted by a priestess of Order of the Lovers. She wore what I could only guess was a formal version of their normal robe, which was far fancier than what I'd seen before. She even had a large medallion with their symbol on it.

After a short speech, she called in the couple, who entered together. There was no tradition of couples not seeing each other, nor any of the many different entry ceremonies that weddings on Earth had. There were a number of traditions, of course, but those had to do with other things like the lighting, which was supposed to be blue for good luck, and decorations, of which flowers in certain arrangements were heavily preferred.

Since this was an event for everyone to put on their best, it was interesting to see that while the Lord of Shadows was in his customary black everything with silver accents, his bride was certainly not. Her gown was a deep blue velvet, reminiscent of the kingdom of Bergond's colors; her waist was surrounded by a thin chain of silver decorated with a frankly absurd quantity of gems.

As they entered, everyone became silent. Thick carpets and smiling onlookers decorated their path to the front. They nodded to the priestess when they got there. She gave a short speech on love, marriage, and all that stuff, standard for any wedding anywhere it seemed, before she invited them to kiss three times, first for the husband, who would bring strength, then for the wife, who would provide stability, thirdly for the family they would make together and a hope for the future. At that point, they were by all rights married, and the cheering began.

After a few moments of whoops and applause, Lord Durin motioned with his hand. "Thank you, my friends, but there are other things to which we must attend now, firstly." With another motion, a man stepped forward.

The newcomer was a bit portly and seemed slightly nervous. "After the death of the previous emperor, the Imperial Senate of Ermath convened one last time. It is our honor to bestow upon Lord Durin, the title of Emperor of Ermath. Long may he rule!"

There was a slight break; a pin could have been heard dropping as Lord Durin nodded and summoned forth another man with a wave. He looked rather like Lord Fallon, if a bit younger and with a more tired face.

"Greetings. After a gathering of the remaining families of old, we have determined that with the disappearance and apparent abdication of Prince Lief and the deaths of the former king and queen, that there was only one potential candidate for ascension to the throne of Bergond. As Crown Princess Sophia has been named such, and married, we do recognize her as Queen Sophia of Bergond. May her rule be fruitful!"

It was clear that he'd been instructed not to mention nobility at all. That didn't mean that others wouldn't think of it as such though, and as Queen Sophia dismissed him with a nod, I tried to recover from my shock.

In the space of a few moments, Lord Durin had made a declaration to all present, and I imagine it would shortly be spread to all corners of his lands. He was not only the ruler, he was the good and legitimate one, and all would need to acknowledge that. The former nobles had undoubtedly been coerced into agreement, as had the senate or whatever, but that didn't matter. He intended to rule without opposition.

"Thank you, both of you, and all of you who came to join us. With our marriage, these two lands shall now be joined forevermore into the Shadow Empire. May it stand forever!" At the new emperor's words, the crowd burst into cheers.

Everyone cheered, most from excitement. I myself did because not only did it seem appropriate to do for someone my dad liked, but I didn't want to attract attention while having a moment of alarm.

With another motion, the crowd quieted again for Emperor Durin to speak. "Thank you, everyone, in celebration of this momentous occasion, I have taken the liberty of having new crowns crafted. They have been made of the purest sky-metal and enchanted such that they shall allow us, and our successors, to rule well and properly." There was a collective gasp at his declaration, something that reminded me that many of my contemporaries considered aluminum to be mythical.

The crowns were brought forth from an inlaid box, and even I had to admit that they were works of art. They were constructed to have bands that waved and flowed around each other, inlaid with jewels and runes that shined brightly even in the full light. First Durin placed his queen's crown upon her head, then she upon his. They each carefully laid the metal bands in place before clasping hands once more.

It did occur to me as I watched this that I was almost literally watching a man put on a tinfoil hat after declaring himself emperor. Had someone told me that when I was on Earth, I'd have likely fallen over laughing. This did not have any humor to it though, and I couldn't even manage a smile.

"Now, everyone, to the feast!" This final declaration drew a great number of cheers. Everyone liked a good meal, even if they were stunned just moments before.

The feasting hall we were led to was the same as the previous night, but the decorations . . . Flowers of every color and shape lined the walls, some glowed, giving gentle light to add to the fixtures. The ceiling was a night sky the likes of which I'd only seen in Lucien's cave, enough to draw the eyes of everyone to it. Even the tables and settings were decked out today, each piece unique but with all sharing the same motifs as the rest of the room. It looked like an evening garden, held in a place devoid of light pollution and adorned with plants only able to be described as fanciful.

It was fortunate that the seats were the same as the previous night because we were all a bit shell-shocked. I found mine, and very shortly the meal began in earnest. Whispers abounded of the declarations, the new empire, the new crowns, all of it exciting and thrilling.

"Where did he find sky-metal? And that much? Amazing. Can you believe we got to see the birth of the new empire too? Excellent!" a nearby girl said in a hushed voice, a series of questions that was being repeated again and again.

I looked about to see how everything was going and found my father sitting and chatting like this was all normal, a roasted rabbit on his plate. John and Charles also dug into their food like there was no big deal, that it wasn't even something to be excited about.

"Are you all right, dear?" Mom asked.

"Fine, just a bit surprised."

"Well, it is surprising, isn't it? That said, you shouldn't let your pheasant get cold."

She was right, and the small bird that I'd chosen as my meal was delicious. After a brief bit of thinking, I came to a simple conclusion. That this was all way above my pay grade and the best thing I could do was enjoy the party to its fullest. So I gossiped a bit, noting who was looking at what and how wonderful the decor was. I ate the food and loved the taste, and I drank the watered-down wine that was served while laughing at the jokes told by those near me.

Once we were all nicely full, it was time to dance. Charles again appeared and led me through several before we traded off and I had a new partner. The new guy was not bad, but he lacked the irritating skill of my escort, who was now leading another girl around the floor. I even saw John and his date taking part. I didn't know her name, but she looked like she was enjoying herself thoroughly.

During one of the short breaks that everyone needed, I made my way over to a small bar where drinks were being served, only to find my former guardian there. We looked at each other as he made me a cocktail, some painfully sweet amalgamation of cherry and orange juices and what was effectively two hundred–proof vodka.

"It occurs to me that I've never seen you dressed up, Alana. It suits you," he said as he put my drink before me. It was very small, and with far less alcohol than any bartender on Earth would have used, but that was for the best.

"Thank you. Is the sky yours?" I pointed up toward the ceiling, which even I would consider an impressive use of illusion.

He chuckled as I finished my drink. "Don't have too much now. The running to the chamber will be soon."

"The what now?"

"The running to the chamber." At my blank look, I saw his jaw drop. "You don't know?"

"Don't know what?"

"It's a tradition in the West, near Lithere and the like. Seriously?"

I heard a laugh from behind me and turned to see Mystien there, with . . . was that Veska on his arm? After I got over the pure outrage that I couldn't bring my girlfriend, but it was fine if he brought a literal prostitute, she began talking.

"Don't tell her. It'll ruin the fun. I'll explain the rules just before we start," she said with a mischievous smile.

"No, seriously, the what?"

CHAPTER 23

✦

THE CHASE

After a few more dances, I met up with my brother to the side of the room. He, too, was taking a bit of a breather. We stood by one of the tables, and he looked on all of the various arrangements before picking up one of the flowers laid around.

"These are great. They tell me the queen herself did a lot of work making original flowers for the event. Look at this one. Have you ever seen one like it?" He twisted the little plant in his hand, looking closely.

"That is a goldenrod, John, it's not one of hers, but they are pretty, yes."

"Oh well, learn something new every day."

"Now, now, John, the young lady there obviously has an escort already. Don't go bothering her about the chase," another guy, ostensibly one of his friends, said as he came to join us. "Pleased to meet you, I'm Alowen. John and I go way back, so try not to mind him," he said, greeting me properly now.

"Oh, we do too. I've known John for so long it seems like my whole life." I tried not to laugh at the guy as he joined us.

"And yet you never introduced us?" He turned toward my brother, looking scandalized. "I can't believe you'd keep such beauties to yourself, my friend."

"You mean my sister?" John asked as he looked at the newcomer. "Why in the world would I want you anywhere around her?"

I laughed and excused myself as they started arguing. I was still quite amused when a few moments later women seemed to be subtly disappearing from the party. As this was going on, Veska pulled me to the side. We made our way, with several other women, mostly young, to a side door.

"Okay, the rules are . . . get back to your room before you get caught," Veska explained, like that covered everything.

"Who's chasing me?"

"Your escort, of course."

"And if I get caught?" Several of those present were already bolting as they made their way out the doors.

"That is the question, isn't it? Now, time to go." She started taking off her shoes as she moved to the door—a good idea, which I followed.

It took only a few seconds to understand. It was a game of catch, undoubtedly, and one invented by horny people. I could imagine now what all the girls and their boyfriends would be doing after their little run. It wasn't hard to think that this was just another one of those kinds of things.

"What if I don't want to run?" I asked, hoping there was an opt-out for this wedding tradition.

"My, my, then you'd just be easy to catch, no?" The way she said it implied that I would both be spoiling the fun for everyone and viewed as wanting to be caught.

There was a loud noise behind me as I bolted from the door. It took only a second to sing myself invisible and silent as I made my way out into the night. I don't know who had thought to head most of the courtyard, but as I began my flight across it, I was grateful for it, trying to do this in the snow would be a disaster.

The courtyard wasn't too big, but it was sizable enough, and as I ran, I could see a number of girls here and there going to hide in the various bushes, walls, slipping into doors along the side. That was an idea. I could probably set up an illusion of a bush or something and just . . .

I nearly fell as it struck me who I'd picked as my escort. I knew of precisely one person who could see my illusions, see through my invisibility, pierce all the many defenses that I normally set up. I could feel myself speed up as I realized the person after me was probably the best person in the whole kingdom to try and catch me.

Wait, if I realized this, then certainly my father had, and Mystien, and . . . Did they think I'd known about this? Did they think that me inviting him was some form of flirting? Did he know? Shit, shit, shit, I needed out of here as fast as I could go.

As I made it to the door to our section of the fortress, I heard a horn from behind me and saw a cascade of guys pouring out of the hall entry.

Each quickly pouncing forward to chase after their target in one giant game of catch. I caught a glimpse of my brother as I threw open the door. He was flying across the courtyard. I had little doubt that he'd end up catching his quarry, but I had my own issues. I didn't see Charles, but then again I wasn't going to stop and look, because if I could see him, he'd definitely see me, and rather made my way along.

It occurred to me that this was supposed to be a fun game. Had I known about it, and just picked someone who had zero chance of catching me, or even better, someone I was into, then I'd be having a grand time right now. As it stood, I had none of those little insights, and so I was fleeing to avoid getting caught up in the amorous contest.

I heard several giggling shrieks and hollering behind and in front of me as I flew up the stairs, not literally, but close enough, and soon found myself at our hallway. I could have cheered, the adrenaline pushing me to my door.

At about that moment, I felt my legs sweep upward into the air. This caused the slightest bit of panic in the half second it took for me to land in the waiting arms of my well-sighted pursuer. As I looked up, I found myself held in a princess carry of all things.

I instinctively grabbed his neck to keep myself steady, breath heaving from the run and panic of my sudden loss of control. As I dispelled my magic, I saw him chuckling.

"Didn't you know I'd beat you here?" he asked as I tried to compose myself.

"I didn't know the game existed before a few minutes ago when Lucien told me."

That got me an outright laugh. "I forget sometimes that you seem to be oblivious to everything that you're not dealing with directly."

I stuck my tongue out at him as he carried me into my room, toward the bed. "Nothing is happening tonight, so don't get any ideas," I nearly growled at him as he sat down, leaving me in his lap.

"Your father beat you to that declaration by several weeks," he snickered as I untangled myself.

"As long as we understand each other," I huffed.

"Understand each other? No, no, I don't think I understand you at all." He reached forward slowly, giving me plenty of time to move as he brushed a lock of hair from in front of my face. "But I hope one day perhaps I will." My heart fluttered a bit as he turned and left, making one last declaration at the door. "Now, if you'll excuse me, I've some other mischief to go get into." With a small waggle of his eyebrows, he was gone.

I sat there feeling really rather divided. I cared for Kala, a lot, she was close, warm, and happy. Being together with her and all curled up somewhere or other made me happy like nothing else. At the same time, there wasn't really any physical attraction, and while it made me happy, it wasn't the same. That little flutter was like nothing I had ever had with her.

All of that made me feel terrible. Did I want to continue as things were? Did I want them to change? Were my mind and body in two different opinions on the matter or was it all me? The guilt that I was feeling attracted to someone else was crushing, and it didn't change anything at all for the time being.

Many of the guests had left, as they were going through some massive cloak-and-dagger scheme to keep the fact that they'd been taken through quiet portals. That left me a few days to both dive into my core for expansion and study of the guide and to work on my new teleportation.

The latter of which I did very, very carefully. The mana cost was on another level even compared to the other spells I'd worked on. My power personally had been growing hand over fist as I attended school, and this year was no exception, and it still almost flattened me to move that apple. So I started even smaller, pebbles and the like.

This led to a few discoveries. A couple of them were about the distortion I'd created on my first attempt. It was mostly the product of sloppy casting and a lack of preparation. I'd not had anywhere near enough mana or practice with the spell in the first casting to do it very well, but as I worked on my visualization, it reduced dramatically. After a few rounds of practice, I managed to get some teleports without any distortion at all, or at least none I could detect.

Which was fortunate, because of some of my other early experiments indicated that the distortion, while harmless, did allow things to pass through it. Stuff coming in from the side seemed to just sort of . . . mold around the teleport tube, and while I wasn't sticking my hand into it, the stick I used seemed fine after several passes. If it went through the proper end though, it would certainly stick out the other side, which seemed a bit more dangerous.

It was more dangerous because the distortion broke down over time on its own. That itself was another important discovery and one I was very happy to make. It meant that I was not going to have to fix them all manually if I needed to move something in a hurry. My stick though, if left inside did not fare well, and as the wrecked bit of space righted itself it caused more and more pulling, until the piece of wood shattered and left its area in bits, some of which were very small. I considered the danger of someone being in there when one failed, and that gave me pause.

The guide was, as always, rather unhelpful. In fact, all the menus in the core were kind of like that. I'd tried every iteration of "find" I could think of, but find, locate, look up, and even control + find had all been duds. There was no information on warping space, either, or at least nothing obvious from what little I could locate in the documents. I wasn't sure what that meant, if the gates had used some trick of the core, or if there was something altogether left out, or if maybe the mage who'd made them had found another hack to put in magic.

Before we left, I did put in a request to get a look at "Alcubierre's Artifacts," but that was soundly denied. I did receive an answer though, and from Emperor Durin himself no less. It was flowery, and longer than it needed to be, but boiled down to: "You're still in training, go finish up, and I'm quite pleased that you want to work for me, I look forward to you taking that position." It was a sensible response, even if I didn't like it.

That done, I had nothing to do but wait. With no other distractions, I bemoaned what I would and could say to Kala. How would I tell her all that had happened, and that I even felt sort of attracted to others, or anything about that whole mess? I was so unsure and worried that I was in a dreadful state of mind by the time I made it back to my room at the academy.

It was shortly after I arrived back that she came to see me, joining me in my room with her normal smile. I guess my face showed something though, because as she looked at me, her face fell a bit into a much sadder smile.

Kala sighed and sat down, looking at me with an almost regret. "Well, it looks like we need to talk."

CHAPTER 24

✦

BREAKUPS

ell, why don't you tell me what happened."

"I went to the wedding. I don't know if the news is out yet, but we now have an emperor and a queen, so there's that."

"He declared himself emperor? Okay, let's go over that first."

"All right," I told her. "Some big fancy-looking guys from the senate of Ermath came forward and declared that they'd voted him emperor, and then a bunch of nobles from Bergond came and declared Sophia to be the proper queen of the land now that her brother is gone and parents are dead."

"That is . . . going to have some implications, yes. Anything else you can tell me?"

"The whole event was basically a festival. So I'm not sure that there's much to say there. Did you know about 'the running of the chamber' or whatever?"

"Huh? Yeah, of course, it's a standard wedding tradition . . . nobody did anything to you, did they?" She sounded genuinely concerned, like she'd found why I was a bit off.

"Uh, no, you've met my dad, and I bet you can guess how he'd respond after I got done setting them alight."

"I always forget that you can do that."

"Because I never feel the need to start fires, but that's not really the point."

"Then what is?" she asked as I flopped down on my bed. I looked at her and got that sad smile again. "Oh, I see."

"I'm sorry, I didn't mean to . . ." I wanted to cry as she came to join me.

"It's all right, Alana. I knew you weren't interested in me in a number of ways. We both also knew this was coming. We'll still see each other, too, so it's not goodbye. Things are just changing."

"But it hurts."

"Yes, that is one of the worst parts about love. It's so magnificent, so beautiful, that when it changes, you always miss what it was. That's how you know it was real. My order has teachings on that too. Would you like to hear them?" I nodded, not really wanting to speak. "Love never dies. Things change, people change, but love, real, actual love, it never really dies. It may change, fade, or become something new, but it's still there, and it will always be. What we had was not as most love is, but it was something, and it was worthy of enjoying."

"That's . . . I like that."

"It's peaceful isn't it? I do hope we can remain at least friends, in some way. Though . . . it may take some time before that truly works. At any rate, you missed a good bit while you were away."

"What?" I looked up to see her smiling there.

"Yeah, sorry I didn't go first, but I thought this was going to be a bad one and wanted you to have something to distract you when it was done."

I lidded my eyes a bit. She knew that I hated people trying to make decisions for me, but I guess she wasn't hiding anything in the end. "Okay, what happened?"

"Your friend Dras. His ex tried to murder him."

I sat up straight, looking at her in shock. "WHAT? Is he okay!?"

"He will be. It's a bit rough right now, but he's stable. You should go see him as soon as you can, he's at the Shield's hospital."

"I . . . um, okay, we should talk, a lot, and . . ."

"It's fine," she said with one more smile, and we left my room. Immediately, I began making my way back toward the gate while she moved off.

Getting a ride to the hospital was easy, in that my dad's carriage was still at the school. They'd had a few things to unload of mine, and the driver didn't have anything pressing, so he took a small break to socialize while I was . . . breaking up with Kala. I cringed as I thought it, but there was nothing to do for the moment, and I needed to go see Dras.

The driver was less than enthusiastic about me giving him another couple of jobs this late in the afternoon, but he would get over it. I took the time to scrawl a quick note to my father as I rode. My family would certainly know I'd left the school, and telling them was not a bother. Dad might even be able to help somehow.

As I rushed into the hospital, I was in a state. It was fortunate that someone had come by and told them that I would be visiting, as well as the fact that I knew several of the members of the order who could vouch for the fact that I was, in fact, who I said I was. Normally, those who'd had someone try to kill them had tighter security, but that had managed to get me through without too much hassle.

As I entered his room, I nearly fell over in tears. While I'd been told he was stable, he looked anything but as he lay there on the bed. As I came closer, one of his eyes opened and he cracked a slight smile at me.

"Hey there, Alana. How's it going?"

"How's . . . Dras, what happened to you?"

"Yeah . . . about that."

Three Days Earlier

Dras

I had about a week, or so I'd been told, until I found out if my application had been accepted. As I was set to graduate from the academy next year, there were a number of places that I could go to work, but there were some things that just couldn't be ignored.

One of those was that the girl who I considered one of my best childhood friends was the daughter of one of the most powerful men in the city. It might have been a bit wrong to use that connection, and her connection to her former mentor, but what were connections for, if not to help you when you needed it, and I didn't plan on doing anything wrong.

For now, I was back at the old house, in my old room. I wouldn't be here much longer regardless of what happened, but I thought that perhaps one last stay with Mom and Dad was something I owed them. I didn't get to see Dad nearly enough, not since I was really little, and Mom . . . well, she loved me, and that's what counted.

I stood and headed downstairs; there wasn't much to do until everyone came back from the wedding, but I could take care of things here at least. I walked over to the large brass item in the living room and began pouring mana into it. This simple little thing would keep the house warm for the winter even after I left. It was nothing too complex, or too expensive, but I'd managed to put an absolutely obscene mana supply into it so that even if I didn't get by to visit too much, Mom and Dad could stay warm. To go with it were several small lamps here and there in the house of similar make.

"You don't have to do that you know," came the high-pitched voice from behind. The same thing she always said when she found me charging these up.

"I know, Mom. I just want you and Dad to have something in case I'm gone for a bit."

"I'd rather have you around more, Son. Have you heard any word?"

"No, I told you though, lots of people are out of town. I'll know a bit after they all get back, but I'm sure I'll get it. Crap, they basically invited me to apply."

"That's not what I was talking about and you know it!" she snapped.

"Mom, she's not coming back." I could feel my mood darken as I spoke; we'd had this argument before.

"Maybe if you . . ." she stopped as I turned, the look in my eyes must have been a giveaway.

"I know you don't mean ill, but it's enough. You weren't there, you didn't hear her or see her. It. Is. Over." I breathed for a few moments. "I'm sorry. I need to go clear my head."

She reached out and touched me as I moved to the door, halting me there. "I'm sorry, Son . . ."

"It's okay. Love you, Mom."

"You too. Will you be back for dinner?"

"Yeah, I'll see you then." I kissed her cheek and headed for the streets.

There wasn't anywhere particular on my route today, but getting out a bit would be nice, and I could even earn some coins if I wanted. At this point, I knew enough bars and brothels that I could make a round charging items, tattoos, whatever all day. With that, food, drink, and . . . other services would be easy to come by.

It was astounding how many of the working girls preferred to pay that way to cash. Lots of the seniors at the academy spent far more time than needed on their days off engaging in such things, but for me, I wanted the money. It would have been a betrayal back when I was dating Clarissa, one that I wouldn't like, and now, eh, girls were easy enough for a wizard; we had money, power, status enough for most.

Today though, I just walked, at first unsure of where I wanted to go. It was ice cold outside, with snow falling all around, not like that was a real issue, but it meant that I stood out a bit. First I headed up toward the market, to see what was open; after I was done, I thought I'd stop by The Sky for a nice warm drink.

The market was well enough dead. Sadly, as the winter went on, nobody really stayed open. The stalls and shops didn't do enough business to keep things running, and it was too cold for much besides. There was one small shop that I frequented for more general things, but they didn't have anything I needed or wanted, so I just kept going. On the way, I bumped into a man. As I looked up, I saw his frown and quickly stepped aside. There was no need to be impolite.

Freshly fallen snow crunched under my boots. It was still only midafternoon and there was plenty of time to spare, but wasting it all wandering about that city wasn't nearly as fun as it had been when I was a child. I thought back on those days as I approached The Sky; my old haunt was still one of my favorite places in this city.

As I stopped to look upon its edifice, I heard the sound of boots behind me. I turned to get out of the middle of the road, and as I did, pain bloomed in my side. With a scream, I instinctively cast a spell, a powerful mix of heat and kinetic magic that blew my attacker away from me. Unfortunately, that also took his knife, which ripped its way through my flesh as it was violently pulled back.

I finally got a look, and it was the man from the market. He'd stabbed me with some kind of large knife, but why? I certainly didn't carry much on me and didn't look like I did. Between that and the aura of heat I always let off, he should have known that I wasn't someone to fight. Now he was crumpled into the side of a house like a rag doll, his spine as shattered as the plaster behind him had been.

With a gasp, I tried to hurry to The Sky, I was bleeding badly. Around that time, I heard the voice.

"Well, I suppose if I want something done, I'll have to do it myself." Clarissa moved from the corner of my vision to the road in front of me. With a move of her hand, a whip-like spell sprung forth, hissing on the ground where it touched.

"What? Why?" I gasped as she struck, only to find that I'd put my own spell in her way. "Clarissa, stop this, it's madness!"

Once I'd cared for her, and I thought she for me, but now she sprang forward, casting as she came. Neither of us were trained in battle magic, neither knew the ways to strengthen ourselves against magic, with proper shields or proper attack spells, but that didn't make us any less deadly to each other.

I pulled out my old fire ribbons; they weren't really suited to fighting other people, but they were almost instinctive, and with a bit of kinetic power fused into them should prove useful against her whip. She struck, and I blocked again and again, both of us hampered by the fact that we were basically flailing like children.

"Do you know how many I lost, Dras? Do you know how many of my friends and my family died when they took the city? Cousins I'd known since I was a girl, friends I'd grown up with! I could have dealt with it if you'd just wanted to keep out of it, but no, you had to keep being friends with those traitors, and now, now you want to go join them?" she screamed as she attacked, moving to and fro with her whip snapping in wide arcs.

"Stop! There's no point to this, no point to any of it. The war is over! There's nothing more to do, just stop, you have to stop!" I begged, I didn't want this fight, didn't want to hurt her, or anyone else really. I just wanted to live a good life.

As she moved forward, once again her weapon turned in an odd way, screaming toward my face. I jumped back as it came down, slashing across my visage in a burning arc. That wasn't the end though; when I fell backward, it kept going, to my right forearm and straight through it. As I landed on my back, my ribbons failing, I could see it there, my own hand laying a couple of feet away in the snow.

I tried to push myself up with my other hand, she slammed her knee down on it, straddling me. I looked up to see her with my good eye, her enraged face now tinted with pain, fear, and shame.

"I'm sorry, Dras, I really am, but I have to do this. I have to show them that I'm still loyal to the crown, that I won't turn against them." Tears bloomed in her eyes as she turned her whip into a blade and slowly moved it toward my neck. "I'm so sor—"

The only real rule to fighting a caster was to never give them time. The lance of white-hot flame that slammed into the back of her skull was why. My good hand was still there, still able to throw spells. I'd just needed time, and while that spell wasn't meant for combat, it would certainly serve. Her face didn't survive, but I thought I saw just a moment of surprise as the beam of heat that could melt iron, was designed for melting iron, hit her, vaporizing her head.

As the body of the girl I'd once loved fell to the snow beside me, I tried to reach out, only to find the stump couldn't. I wept where I lay, broken and bleeding onto the cold stones of the street. Soon enough, I heard cries of alarm and the calling of names. As I started to drift off into a sleep that might well have been my end, I heard a deep singing and the warm light of healing pulsed over me. A final look up showed Lucien's assistant barkeep there, his hands held over my wounds as he sang for me.

CHAPTER 25

✦

THE HAMMER FALLS

Dras was in an absolutely brutal condition. He had a missing arm and eye, and his face was split in a heinous way. Through all of that, he still had a smile on his face. It was sad and pained, but a smile nonetheless.

"I'm sorry, Dras, I know what you did . . . must have been hard."

His eyes darkened a bit, the pain clear on his face. "Not like I had much of a choice, or either of us did from the sound of it. The way she was talking, it was like someone was forcing her hand. I've told the guards who came to investigate, but . . . Alana, there's no way to know if there's some of this still in the academy, if there are others trying to kill people there as well. I want you to promise me you'll be careful."

I nearly laughed. "Dras, I have no plans on getting involved in any kind of fight like that if I get a choice in the matter. Just rest up and get healed, and let those who know what they're doing deal with the mess."

"Fine, fine, one more thing . . . My mom really doesn't like you, and she's probably going to find some way to blame this on you, even if that's stupid. You mind avoiding her until I can get her to see some reason?"

"You want me to avoid your mother for the rest of her life?"

"Ha-ha, no, but when you come by, can you hide yourself until you're sure she's not around, at least for a bit? The priests will be pissed if you two start going at each other in the hall or something."

"Fine, but only because it's you." I gave him a wry smile as I left.

In the hall, I asked to speak to whoever was in charge of his healing and was quickly introduced to a slightly tired-looking priestess.

"Hello, I'm a friend of Dras," I said as I looked at the woman. I knew many of the priests around here, but she was unknown to me.

"Hello, dear, was there something he needed?"

"Not as such no. I was just wondering how long it will take for him to be healed, and if there's any way I can help."

"Ah, I see. Well, the only real issues are the hand and the eye. The other things are mostly superficial and can be done with relative ease. Losing a limb, on the other hand, is a lot of mass, and eyes . . . eyes are a nasty piece of work to fix, they're complex and fragile, and just generally take a lot of time. At his current rate, I'd say he'll be back to full functioning in about a month."

I was quite glad that there was nothing like HIPAA in this world, back on Earth, the doctor might well have told me nothing. "Is there anything I can do? I know a bit of healing myself and if it's an issue of mana . . ."

The woman shook her head. "No, no, dear, the lad has plenty of mana to pay for the treatment to go as fast as possible. The simple fact is that fixing things like this just takes a bit of time. He'll need to eat to replenish his body so we can keep on building more onto the hand, and as I said, eyes are just messy."

She patted me on the shoulder before sending me on my way. There was nothing for me to do here and tonight.

I could summon matter out of thin air, somehow, and so could wizards to some extent, but I got the feeling that that little trick was beyond priests. Our training seemed to indicate that they couldn't just make things like that. They could manipulate to an insane extent sure, and even speed the growth of plants and the like to astounding levels, but the matter they used always seemed to come from somewhere. A bard powerful enough and well skilled enough in healing might well just be able to conjure him a new hand. Sadly, I was neither of those things, so I would just have to wait.

After my greatly irritated carriage driver returned me to the school, I found my way back to my room and collapsed. The whole night had been a bit much, and I knew that there would be more to come.

It didn't even wait until breakfast the next day to arrive. When I woke up, my maid came in, holding a small letter for me. it was easy to notice my father's handwriting, something that I'd gotten more used to since he often sent me small letters like this at home.

Alana,

We are still investigating what happened to you friend. Surely, you've heard by now, but it seems his former girlfriend tried and failed to kill him. I'm not sure what exactly happened, but the reports that I received when I got home were concerning, and I'd like you to stay at the academy rather than go and see him. If you could, try to stay in public areas and remain close to others as well. Kala, in particular, may be a good choice, as while she won't interfere in politics she might well protect or heal you if something goes amiss. I want you to avoid being alone if at all possible, at least until we can find out more about things.

With love,

Dad

Wow, he didn't even know he was twisting the knife. I finally get my family's blessing to spend as much time as I want with Kala now? I just leaned over into my pillow and screamed for a moment. At any rate, it looked like he'd written this last night, before he knew that I'd already been to the Shield's temple, and there was a nearly 100 percent chance that someone would take offense at my going there too.

I skulked down to breakfast shortly thereafter, in no mood to really talk to anyone. When I arrived, I found Pinea off in a corner, looking rather stressed. I could have sought out someone else, but she needed a friend, and so did I, at least one or two more would certainly help. For a small mercy, Kala wasn't here right now, and I was still on the fence about how to deal with her at the moment.

"Hi there, how are things?" I asked, moving over beside her.

"Honestly? Not great." She looked like she'd been through a lot in the past few days.

"Something happen?"

"Yeah, a few things."

"Still having problems with . . . well, lots of people?"

"You have no clue. It used to be that I was always on top of things, front of the line, always had to be first and now . . . Heck, about a quarter of the people here won't even talk to me. Most who will are not really people I was friends with before. For what too? I didn't even do anything, it's like they hate me because of who I am." She leaned back rubbing her temples. "I don't even know who that is anymore either. Used to be I was the daughter of one of the highest noble families, and now, now who am I?"

"Well, that last part is easy. You're Pinea, the sincerely devoted to causing scandal. Honestly, you should be a bard with how you act sometimes." I pointed at her with my fork. "You're the girl who went and got a dancing outfit behind everyone's backs and threatened to wear it out into the street, the one who's made more dirty jokes than half of our dormitory combined."

She blinked and sat up a bit straighter. "Alana, everyone thinks . . ."

I cut her off. "Who cares what everyone thinks? Okay, I care a bit, but I need to work on that in a bad way, particularly with those close to me. Any advice?"

"I know you're just trying to cheer me up," she said.

"Is it working?"

"Um . . . kind of. As for advice . . . mostly, I think I was just being rebellious to you know . . . rebel. Now what is there to buck against?"

"Society's expectations in general, people you don't like, the fact that Atali dancing isn't a common hobby." I was making a list, both for herself and me.

"Oh, but it should be." She looked off into the distance, gripping her hand as if declaring a deep truth to the universe.

"Agreed."

We had to go to class now, but our dance class was later, so I agreed to meet up with her then. I knew I was kind of a bad friend, and I didn't even have that many friends, but it always seemed that I was running off when they needed me, and dragging them into a whole mess when I was around. Perhaps that would never change, but one could try at least.

I tried to do as my father commanded and keep to the main hallways, never too far from anyone. I even tried to keep close to those students who I knew were connected more to the new government than the old. At one point, I even walked between classes with Dad's fanboy Tobias. He was nice, if a bit short and scrawny, and his penchant for light magic meant he could do some neat things. The downside was that he would really prattle a lot about all kinds of stuff, too, which I didn't really know how to deal with all that well.

While he talked, I looked around the halls. Today had been a weird day for a number of reasons. First there were certainly a few extra adults in the halls. Here and there, a knight or an older mage walked around on some business or the other. I suspected that this was to keep an eye out for any trouble after what had happened. The other big thing . . .

"Okay, so there have been like, I don't know, seven or eight people missing from my classes today," Pinea said as we prepped for Atali Dance. Tobias had split with me just before I got here. "Have you heard the gossip?"

"I haven't. I was hoping you might have. You were always better at that sort of thing than me." I had no shame in admitting it; she had been far more plugged into the school.

"Right, so did you notice who was gone?" She seemed a bit giddy as we waited.

I counted in my head, thinking about who was missing. "Former nobles, particularly those who'd been more loud or outspoken about how unhappy they were."

"See! You can pick it up. That asshole got grabbed this morning I hear; someone came in and pulled him right out of the breakfast hall. Oh, I wish I could have seen his face." She looked vindicated and had a rather nasty smile on her face as she pictured it, not that I could have blamed her.

Her ex was a piece of work. After their breakup, he'd gone around being so rude about her even I had heard a few things. He'd managed to keep it from being spread around why he was mad, but it was clear that he was. There were even some nasty rumors about her behavior in private, which if I were honest, might really be true. I wasn't personally bothered by them, but the general population was full of prudes.

"You're not worried about yourself?" I asked, her family really had been high up in the kingdom's hierarchy before they fell.

She snorted. "Hardly, that whole crowd reviles me, and my only friends now are outside of it. That and I've done my absolute best to keep my nose clean. After what Dad sacrificed, I have no plans on causing trouble."

We were still warming up when Professor Etia arrived. She led us through our paces one after another and then began a lecture on stomach movements. They were hard to look at when we were all still in uniform, to her immense chagrin, but she tried.

About halfway through the lesson, there was a knock on the door. When our teacher opened it, there was a grim-faced pair in the hall, sweeping their eyes over the assembled girls. They settled on Pinea with finality.

"Well, fuck," she said as she walked over to them, not making a bit of a scene.

CHAPTER 26

✦

INTERROGATION

PINEA

This was a part of the school I'd never been to. We were deep in the ground, under the more normal item-creation labs and workstations. From a glance, I could tell that this place was far more secure, and even then it looked like it had a few additional protections as well as a handful of guards. It was clearly an impromptu prison or the like. Based on what I was seeing, it had been here forever, though based on the size, it probably only ever saw one or two people.

I was walked past what were clearly cells to a slightly nicer, if plain, room. There was a table and two chairs, and I was invited to sit, which I did, of course, since that "invitation" was clearly a command.

I waited in silence, able to almost feel the presence of guards outside the door. It wracked my nerves something awful. I had nothing to do, nobody to speak to, just the silence and the small pair of candles that was set here for light. It at the very least wasn't cold, as one might expect a dungeon to be.

After a few moments, a young man walked in. His full military attire stretched and moved with him as he sat down across from me.

"My apologies for the delay. I had another guest to attend to." He sounded as not sorry as was possible to be, like my waiting was some just punishment for some failing on my part.

Not so long ago, I could have spit acid at him and raged, demanding he be punished for making the daughter of so high a house wait like a servant. Now though, that would be a fool's move. My house had fallen, and while we still had some power, it was no secret that we were being watched and that any attempt on our part to rebel or resist would be met with finality on the new government's part.

I looked up. This man could kill me if he so chose, and there was little I could do. He knew, and I knew that with a word all manner of terrible things could befall me, or my family. So I spoke carefully and respectfully. "No need to apologize. May I ask for what reason I am here?"

"Of course, of course. You're aware of the incident between two of our esteemed academy's recent graduates?" he asked with a light smile.

"Yes, my understanding is that there was an attempted murder."

"Quite so. That on its own would be cause for alarm, but based on the perpetrator's words and actions, we came to believe that there might have been some group involved. Would you know anything about that?"

"No, sir, I have no desire to be involved with anyone like that." No matter how hard I tried, I knew that I wasn't succeeding in keeping a slight tremble from my voice.

His smile widened a bit. "I will be clear with you, Miss Pinea, I do not personally believe that you are part of any rebel groups." After my exhalation of relief, he continued. "Nor do I think you want to be. That said, I do believe you know who might want to."

"Th-th-there are a few who have expressed displeasure at Lord Durin's . . ."

"Emperor Durin's," he corrected, still smiling.

"A-a-apologies . . . at Emperor Durin's new rule." I didn't have to feign even a bit of fear. That little misstep was still a minor faux pas, but soon enough it might well be considered an insult.

"When things had first changed, when the kingdom had fallen, I had been taken to my father. He had told me many things, what he had done, why, and importantly, where we stood now. He had known our new emperor before, and so his advice was thus. I was not to bring his wrath upon me. If someone who I knew had done so to themselves, I was to act as if I knelt before the chopping block, fearful, begging for mercy, but without even the slightest bit of resistance. Our new ruler was a hard man, he had said, but not one prone to harming those who were no threat, and not one who would seek to harm me without reason. If I gave up, surrendering wholly, it was likely that his blade would never fall. However, if it seemed that I might fight . . . there would be no mercy upon me."

"Ah, I have heard as much. Their names, if you would be so kind." He produced a pen, paper, and ink, sliding them across the desk to me.

I looked at him. This was a test, a test of loyalty. While my father and my family had officially declared our allegiance to the new regime, I needed to do so personally. With a shaking hand, I took the pen and began writing. I knew who was most unhappy and began there. Name after name did I write, people who used to be friends, distant relatives, those I'd known since I was a small child. It was painful, painful to know that I might be the end of them, but if they had turned against the new leadership . . . there was little I could do.

After a moment of thought, I drew a line between the bottom part of the page. "The, um, the ones below the line seem unhappy, but they're not being particularly loud about it." That done, I slid it back over to him.

"Why, thank you," he said as he looked over the paper. "Nothing truly surprising here. Ah, we did have your quarters searched, I hope you understand. They found nothing of note, but you should be informed." He quickly rose and opened the door, motioning for me.

I did not have to be offered twice. Trying to keep everything together, I rose and moved toward the door, eventually walking down the hall with the man whose name I didn't even know. About halfway down the hall, I saw another person brought in. At first, I couldn't tell who it was, until he came far enough down the stairs. There I almost froze looking at the eyes of the young man who might have once been my husband.

In an instant, I watched those eyes harden to sharpened steel. "You bitch!" he shouted as he lunged.

The world seemed to slow for an instant. Almost everything moved at a crawl as I saw the glow of some spell form around his hand, drawing up to release it at me. The only thing that seemed to move were the guards, while all others looked caught in the moment they freely turned, and with a quick movement and the flash of steel, the instant of us all being trapped in ice was over.

A line of blood splashed across my face, and I screamed in terror, trying to flee backward. I heard the thud of a head falling to the hard stone floor and the soft wet noise of fluids pouring out. As I turned, a strong arm held me aloft so that I wouldn't fall and couldn't run. The face of the man who'd interviewed me moved before my own, blocking my view.

"Look at me, look at me not at him. You don't need to see that." His voice turned hard for an instant. "Cover him, you lot who made that mess."

"No, no, please!" I begged.

"Calm, calm, you're perfectly safe. No one is going to hurt you, Miss Pinea. Look at me, you're safe." As soon as I stopped trying to run, I was released, and the interviewer, whose name I didn't even know, handed me his handkerchief. "Don't look." He said as he firmly led me up the stairs.

"You killed him." I barely managed to speak as we left the lower area. I wiped my face, trying to get off the blood, wincing as the cloth came back with crimson marks all over it.

"Yes, but that spell seems unlikely to have been something to tickle us."

"You killed him," I repeated.

"I did not want him to die. Sadly, he did force our hand. I did not think he would have that type of reaction when I arranged for you two to meet."

"You arranged . . . why?" When I looked at him again, he had a different smile, kinder, apologetic.

"I was hoping that he would admit something, say something we might use. I did not anticipate that level of hatred. Please forgive me."

"What?" I was so confused, the stress, the fear, the disorientation.

The agent pulled out a small sheaf of papers from his jacket pocket and handed them to me. As I read over each, I got more and more alarmed. My habits were here, my favorite foods and places to eat. There was a section on the route my carriage took to return me home on my days off and the times I liked to leave. Another had descriptions of my favorite outfits and several drawings to accompany them. All of my daily schedules and routes were listed.

"We found those when we searched the young man's room, among other things. The reason we thought it unlikely that you were with their little conspiracy."

"He was . . ." I could hardly finish, but the evidence was all here.

"Probably planning to kill you, yes. Another reason we wanted you pulled from your classes, just in case he tried anything. Though I will admit the investigation was our main motivation."

"But . . . but why?" I asked.

"Why did he wish your death? Surely, that is obvious." Sadly, it was.

"Why did you even consider protecting me?" I clarified. The old kingdom might have done so, but I held no real status now. A commoner before would probably only have been followed, to see what happened.

"It is the duty of the strong . . ." he began.

"To protect the weak." I'd attended enough Civics classes that the answer was almost automatic now.

He walked me all the way back to the entrance to the girls' dorm, stopping with me at the ward. "Well, Miss Pinea, this is where I leave you. You should take the rest of the day off from classes to rest."

"Yes, I think I will." I paused and handed him back his soiled handkerchief. "Forgive me, but I don't seem to have caught your name."

"I didn't say it. Though there is no harm in telling you. I am Alowen. I would say it was a pleasure to meet you, but it seems in bad taste."

"Thank you, Alowen, please be well." I tried to be polite, but in the end, I just couldn't concentrate.

It only took a few moments to make my way to my dorm. This section of the school was, for the moment, blissfully empty, and so nobody saw me wandering blankly to my room. The banisters slid under my fingers as I slowly took the stairs, each step plodding, almost numb.

My maid was, in a small blessing, still not here. I closed the door and quietly made my way over to the waste bin, where I fell to my knees and emptied my stomach. I retched and retched as all of the stress of the day hit me at once. My fingers gripped the receptacle until they hurt and tears flowed freely down my cheeks.

Once it was all over, I rose on shaky legs like a baby deer and moved to clean my face at the washbasin. Several times I did this, washing away the streaks, then gulping and spitting out water to remove the bad taste. As I looked in the mirror, I thought about how I'd nearly died, nearly been murdered by a former lover. That, of course, sent me right back to kneeling before the waste bin, the smell overpowering as I retched heavily once more.

Finally, truly sure that I was done, I gathered my things and headed to the baths. I needed to soak in the hot water and scrub away everything about this day.

✦

CHAPTER 27

IF YOU DESIRE PEACE . . .

I wasn't sure what to do that evening when I found my friend in the bathroom, crying as she washed herself over and over. I tried to talk to her, tried to comfort her, but in the end, it was a bit beyond my capabilities. To that end, I went and found someone far more suited to the task.

"Hey . . ." I said as I approached Kala.

"Hi, everything okay?" She still seemed in a good mood, a tiny bit down perhaps, but not too bad.

"Um . . . I need some help with Pinea."

"What kind of help?" Kala looked at me with a tiny bit of suspicion, and I scratched my head.

"She's . . . in the baths, and I think something happened, but I'm not sure, and something is clearly wrong, but this is far beyond me."

It took only a beat for her to process that and silently she rose, walking toward the bathing area. She was in there for a long time, and I decided it was best to ask some of the other girls to go and wait for a bit. Eventually though, they came out, and Pinea made her way back to her room.

"What happened?" one of the girls nearby asked after Pinea had left.

Kala sighed. "She saw someone die today, and I think that was a first for her. That kind of thing, particularly if it's violent, will take a little bit to process."

That got a series of nods, and the rest of the dorm went back to basically normal. There were a few whispers here and there discussing who could have died, or how, rumors and the like. Most of those shut up with a bit of a glare from me, or at least they went somewhere that I couldn't hear them. Pinea was a friend, and I didn't want people spreading things about her with ill intent.

"You told them the truth," I said as I moved on the couch opposite Kala. It was a weird feeling, but it felt like where I should be.

"Yes, there would be other rumors otherwise. She's been through enough and doesn't need that kind of thing floating around about her."

"Yeah, you're probably right. So . . . how do we proceed?" I spent about a second putting up a basic privacy barrier as we began to talk.

She looked at me for a moment, and in that time I could see it, pain, exhaustion, a slight feeling of betrayal, but also care, love, and hope. "I still like you, and I still . . . want to be around you. Not as much perhaps, but sometimes. That said, I think it's best if we spend a bit of time apart." Then she sighed. "I'm still a bit raw, Alana. I hope you understand."

I could feel my throat tighten. I still liked her, in my own way, but she was probably right. "Okay," I said, "I'll try to stay away for a little bit. I really am sorry."

As I rose to leave, she reached out and gave my hand a light squeeze. "Thank you for trying to help Pinea. I think she needs a friend right now who'll look out for her."

"You know my past, Kala. I wasn't sure where she was, but I'll do what I can to help her." I tried not to think about it too much, but in my short second life I'd seen far too much violence.

"I know. If you need any more advice, or help . . ."

"I'll ask, thank you." With that, I left.

There was no easy way to deal with breakups, but for everything this might be the least stressful I'd ever had. There was no screaming, no anger, no refusal to deal with each other again. Perhaps it was because we both had known that it wouldn't be forever. Perhaps it was because Kala was an absolute saint. I wasn't really sure.

Over the next few days, I spent a good amount of time with Pinea. We'd been going to classes sometimes before, but now I made a point to walk with her when I could. I also invited her to come and join me for studying. We talked about all kinds of things, but not what had happened. That was fine; she'd tell me if and when she was ready.

We were in Civics today and talking about how it was important to let the various priest orders handle their own. There was a strong sentiment that while the government needed to be independent of them; they also needed to work together wherever possible. In particular when it came to finding and training young priests.

This all seemed a bit odd to me, and from beside me I heard Pinea inquire. "Professor, will L . . . Emperor Durin not try to recruit any not involved with the orders?"

"No, absolutely not. Have you not covered Arnim in your History course?"

There were a few nods, though hesitant, and I noticed several of the priest students wincing and looking rather uncomfortable. One other student volunteered, "We heard that he caused a massacre, but not much more, Professor."

"Well, you should have. Arnim was a priest who lived a few centuries ago, while the orders were still forming and solidifying their rules. He was, by all accounts, a kind and gentle man for most of his life, protecting the weak and healing the sick. There were even reports that he helped with the local crops in his area. He wasn't much of a standout, but was a valued member of the community, and well liked . . ."

She took a gulp of water as she led us through the rest of his story. Arnim, after years of service, had a family, a wife and two daughters who were the loves of his life. He doted upon them, as only a father would until one day . . . one day a group of bandits came to town while Arnim was away helping the local lord. When he returned, he saw what they'd done to his house and to his family.

In a rage, the priest had tracked down these men and slaughtered them, killing them to a man. They begged for mercy but found none in the spells of the distraught priest. That normally would have been the end of it, but Arnim found documents when he searched their hideout. The papers showed that both the local lord and several of his near neighbors had known about the group and allowed it to prosper, in exchange for them primarily targeting his neighbors, or those the local lord didn't care about.

Arnim's fury was inconsolable, and he marched on the local lord's city. There were few priests then, as there are now, and as he passed through the gates, men died in a wave. He didn't seem to care, didn't seem to be bothered as more and more guards came to fight him, only to die in the street. They tried arrows and the like to kill him, only to find that he healed himself as he walked.

He strode to the lord's keep, slowly like death itself and within killed scores, each falling like grass before a scythe. Soon enough, even the lord of the city fell, his betrayal leading to a gruesome death. Arnim stood there, above the city staring at the carnage he'd wrought, declaring that all those men had deserved to die.

He then proceeded to go room to room through the keep, killing servants and those who hid. That was until he stumbled upon the room of the lord's daughter. The small girl was naught but an innocent child, fair in skin and hair, who looked almost like Arnim's own beloved girl. As he hesitated, weeping, a soldier managed to strike an instantly fatal blow to Arnim's head, ending the rampage.

In the end, he'd killed nearly three thousand citizens, soldiers, and others who'd either gotten in his way or just been in the wrong place at the wrong time. The people of the time had been stunned, shocked that this man could go and do such a thing. There were inquiries, investigations, and questions about what he'd done, as well as how he'd done it.

These things were not a first. It seemed that every few hundred years that a priest would go on a rampage, killing indiscriminately. There was even a term for it, a death priest, for the destruction they caused. The Order of the Shield had been the first to act, putting forth new rules after Arnim's slaughter to help find and train new priests, to identify them and make sure they were safe, or to retrain them if they were not. All of the other orders had agreed almost instantly.

"And that is why it is important that young priests, for a time, be removed from their families and trained, so that they can be assured safe for everyone. No civilized country has tried to stop this in quite a long time, and Emperor Durin agrees."

"But, Professor, don't priests need to believe what they're doing is right?" a boy asked.

"Naturally, that is important, but tell me, can a priest not become confused and perhaps think that many people deserve to die?"

There was silence in the room as we all processed it. I had a rather large concern, because to me it sounded like the priests were just brainwashing all of their successors, each generation making sure that the sort of hatred and rage that one man had shown was cleaned out regardless of what the child wanted, or the parents wanted. Would that damage them? I wasn't sure, several of the priests I knew were pretty awful sometimes, but at the same time I knew a few who were downright wonderful.

*　*　*

At dinner that night, Pinea sat with me. The two of us ate as we chatted about the day and the classes that we didn't have in common. Around the time that we finished, she looked over at me.

"Alana, if I were looking to learn some defensive magic, where would I start?"

I gave her a hard look. I'd practiced for that class for going on a year now, and it was still hard. There was a lot to consider, what she could do, what she should do, where she might practice . . . There was also not much to consider as the answer was easy enough.

"Pinea, that's a hard road, but you could talk to Professor Endel. He's tough, but fair, and he might teach you a few things. Honestly though, why do you want to learn it?"

She looked a bit afraid. "I want to be safe."

"Well, from common threats you can use items, that is a more immediate solution, if not a very good one. You can also learn to harden your aura, which is good generally against magic."

"Will you show me that? Personally, I think Endel is a bit too hard on students and I know you won't be too mean. You do owe me a favor anyway . . ."

I sighed. "Save the favor for something I don't want to do. This, on the other hand, is fun, and I can show you the basic exercise in under an hour. After that, you just have to work on it, like using a muscle to make it stronger."

She nodded, and after we were done with everything else for the evening, we moved off to a side room. There I led her through the process of pushing out her aura, making it stronger so that it would resist any magic trying to enter it. She sat and sat, concentrating as slowly it materialized.

Pinea's aura was a vibrant pink that wavered around her, not like an inferno like my father or my brother, but like a dancing candle flame. It was pretty, and her pushing on it harder and harder only made it stand out stronger.

After a bit, I pulled out one of the small balls of cold we used to practice in our combat class and threw it. It wasn't strong by any means, but the aura burned part of it away, only letting a bit of it smack into her.

"Oh! That's cold!" Pinea yelped as it struck.

"Yup, but it doesn't hurt. It's what we use in class to practice."

"So what, if I get good enough, I won't feel it at all?" she asked.

"It will get weaker and weaker until it fades completely, at least at that level. The thing is that the stronger the caster, the more you'll have to resist. It's one of those things that's more like wearing a pillow on your stomach, if someone kicks you there, you'll still hurt, but you won't hurt as bad. Does that make sense?"

"That doesn't seem particularly useful." She frowned a bit. "Can't I stop it completely?"

"Maybe with shields, but those take a lot more time. Also, it's crazy useful, you remember when I got attacked back in my first year? The whole terror incident on our combat class?"

She shivered. "How could I forget? A bunch of people died."

"Yeah, and I probably would have, too, if not for that technique. Don't get me wrong. It still hurt like nothing I had experienced before, but I lived, and getting passed it is the first big hurdle."

Pinea nodded, chewing on what I'd said. "Okay, this is great, thanks!"

"I'm thinking about some protective items too. I've got a few ideas, but most of my ideas tend to be wonky, so see what you can come up with as well. Who knows what we could need?"

After a few more rounds of practice, we agreed to call it for the night. She looked as tired as I felt, but I had a few more things to do. Mostly, this was to work on my core, it had been too neglected, and I was determined to finish it as soon as possible now. I wanted some personal things to protect myself and my friends, and if I had to take care of that on my own, so be it.

The next day, I waited after class to talk with Professor Ieala. Her approach to the theoretical portion of Magical Item Creation was solid. I got the feeling that she knew less about it than Professor Rooke had, but she was far, far better at explaining a lot of the workings of what we were doing currently. She was also less abrasive, which made her slightly more popular.

"Professor, I had a question if you don't mind." I asked as she was packing up.

She smiled. I'd avoided her for the most part since our first meeting, keeping distant, but not rudely so. "Certainly, Alana, though if one of my best pupils is asking, that must be some question."

"I'm looking on information about shielding items. In particular I'd like to know about those that are made to shield from kinetic attacks."

"I've seen your grades in Combat Spellcasting. Are you telling me you don't know how to shield against kinetic attacks? Because I'd have a hard time believing that."

"No, Professor, I certainly know that, but those shields are slow to put up. I'm looking for something in case someone surprises me."

"Oh, I see. Well making those is possible, something small that you can turn on if you're assaulted can be useful."

"What about having it turn on automatically? We've covered some different signals. Can you have it put up a shield if an attack is detected?" I already knew from the guide in the core that this should be doable, but what was doable and what most people considered to be possible were two very different things.

She stopped to think for a few moments. "Hmm. I've not heard of anyone ever doing that, and I can think of three problems you will decidedly find if you try." At my questioning look, she continued. "The first is that the mana usage will be higher than normal, much higher as it has to constantly be looking for an attack. If this item is functioning constantly, that means it will constantly be draining its mana. And even if that drain isn't too bad, it will need to be recharged fairly often. That will be expensive. The other is defining what an attack is. If you set the bar too low, you're likely to set off your shield all the time, not very helpful in day-to-day activities and potentially dangerous. On the other hand, if it's too high, it runs the risk of becoming useless. Even setting those parameters is not well understood, so that may be a challenge." She got to her last point finally, tapping her chin with a finger. "You'll also need to get the timing right. I'm not sure if the item will be able to respond quickly enough to be useful in an actual combat situation."

"That doesn't sound very encouraging."

"On the other hand, Alana, I think you should absolutely do it. Work like this is how magic progresses, and even if you fail to make something, you can use how you want, you may discover something useful somewhere else. Please make sure to take good notes. If you bring me results, we can go over them." She perked up giving me a bright smile. "Oh, and I'll send you one of the more common sequences for a standard shield item, you might find it useful as a place to start."

I knew she was just using this to try and build a relationship with me. She clearly wanted some of my research, particularly if it was something novel. I can't say that I was too bothered. She'd be getting nothing that Mystien didn't approve of me giving her, and she was helping me. If she planned to milk me for all I could tell her, there was no reason for me not to reciprocate. I'd even expected something like this when I came to her.

Mystien,

I'm writing to ask for any advice you might have on shielding items. Particularly, I'm looking for something like a kinetic shield. I'm fairly certain I could manage one of the standard ones, but those are static and need to be activated. Is there any way to make an item that just slows things over a certain threshold instead? Or activates if it senses something like that?

I'm not sure where to go on this and while Professor Ieala gave me a few places that will probably be issues, she didn't have any solutions.

Thanks,

Alana

MYSTIEN

That girl was on the other side of the city, in a school full of magic texts, and still sending me letters about theoretical and insanely useful things. I did not have anything like she was asking. There were those who'd made similar things, to be sure, but normally for royals, and even then, only for short period use. I could probably cobble together something like that if I truly needed to, but it wasn't something that was either needed or my area of study. I sent her a letter telling her as much in response, since she'd at least come to me for advice.

While I wouldn't tell her, I was also pleased that she was making connections with Ieala. Her new professor was a smart girl, quite so, and I couldn't help but be glad that they might end up working together. Ieala had one major flaw, in that she lacked the art needed to make truly stellar magical items. She knew the concepts that governed them, certainly better than most, but she just didn't have the . . . flare, the little bit of umph that made for a good sequence writer.

She was also the most conniving, research-burrowing little woman I'd ever met. She'd ingratiate herself with people and learn all she could, not out of hostility, but out of a desire to grow. It meant that she was very, very good at gleaning things. It also meant that she wasn't allowed within five hundred paces of any lab I worked in, and all of my assistants were forbidden from so much as holding a conversation with her on the weather. I'd have to warn Alana again not to go discussing too many things with her that she shouldn't, particularly with the gates, but she was a smart girl and, for the most part, was doing a . . . passable job keeping her secrets hidden from anyone other than her father and myself.

I sighed and turned back to my real work. The gates were proving to be quite good at hiding their secrets, and no matter what I did, I got very little back in usable information. That was frustrating, but there would come a time when I figured out something. For the time being, I was pouring over the remaining notes of Ristolian, not the originals, but some copies. They were in some kind of code, and it was taking me a bit of time to parse some of the meanings. What I was sure of was that they were pointing to him doing some work on the Elven continent. Perhaps that avenue would render some use.

✦

CHAPTER 28

PREPARE FOR WAR

ROOKE

I walked along the halls, not that there were all that terribly many. This facility had never been designed for a lot of people, and as such was quite small. It traded comfort and size for the fact that it was also quite secret. Its general was known to the higher-ranking members of the kingdom as one of several places they could evacuate, but the exact location was known only to a few, which meant, in theory, that we would have the chance to see people searching for it before they got here.

In practice, it was clear that if our enemies wanted, they could send enough men to flush us out and would likely kill us if they did so quickly enough. It seemed unlikely they would, given the casualties they would take, but they would win. We were leaning on those odds for now, because we had nothing else.

As I went by several other rooms for families and the few who had come, I reached my current project. There was much work to be done on the warding of this location, which could turn it into an actual fortress and not a small facility afraid of being crushed. Getting the wards up to snuff was point one. It might not matter much if the full might of our enemies came down upon us, but it would at least keep a small force from wiping out the lot of us.

After several hours of slaving over sequence after sequence and beginning the process of forging numerous magical items, I was interrupted. "How go things, lad?" Lorrae asked from behind me.

"Slowly, old man, very slowly, is there even a point to this?"

"To a point . . . in the end, we'll have to take the fight to them. We've already seen that a defensive war is not in our favor." He seemed more sullen than he used to be, not joking or jibing at me.

"That's got to be some kind of joke. You saw their offensive power, if their defenses are anything near it, then . . ."

"Then we will lose. I'm not saying it's a good gambit, but the only one we have. If we can cut the head off of the beast, then perhaps its body will begin fighting itself. That's our only play right now. Without an army, without far more people than we have, it's the best we can go for."

"Too many variables." I said, frowning at him.

"I know, but it's the only path any of us can see."

"I'll get back to my work then," I grumbled as I turned away.

"When you're done, we need to start on some offenses too."

"Yes, Grandfather."

VERREN

I sat in the meeting room, side by side with my fellows, all the generals and most of the advisers of our fledgling empire gathered for this.

"Greetings, gentlemen," Emperor Durin said as he sat down. "Let us begin with the obvious. After our work in both the empire of Ermath and the kingdom of Bergond, we've garnered a name for ourselves. We've also made more than a few enemies. General Lenore, if you will."

The woman indicated stood, she was skilled at her art, a monster of a battlefield tactician and supply chain organization, and one of our best. "Of course, my emperor. To our east and south, we have the nations of Oronir and Litea. Both are now eyeing us nervously, and we expect that they will be waiting for our attack. Ermath had a form of truce with them for the past several years, and they're not particularly strong, but it would be a foolish move to underestimate them. If they think we're likely to overtake them, they may act. On our north, there are a number of small city-states, no real threat, but they may serve as an aiding force for any remnants of our defeated enemies. We believe several are already hiding there."

"We will have to deal with our neighbors eventually, but if possible we should rest to shore up our reserves first. Keep an eye on them for now," Durin declared as he looked out at the rest of us. "And for the remnants we were speaking of General Verren, what are the goings on in your district?"

I stood, addressing the head of this group. "A few minor attacks, my emperor. Current evidence suggests that they are most likely just individual groups, a few nobles here and there who are displeased about the change in governance. While we aren't discounting the possibility that there may be others behind their actions, we have not found evidence of it yet. The incidents we have had have been . . . unorganized, messy. I've got men working on it, but the patterns are varied and not particularly effective."

"And, General Klendle?" he asked as he turned to my counterpart.

"Much the same as General Verren, Sire. There has been some success in capturing some of the wayward princes, but the Ermathi leadership apparently spent all their time trying to make as many as possible. I'm having difficulty figuring out how many legitimate and illegitimate heirs there *were,* and some are bound to slip through. If only by dint of them not being well enough known." He seemed irritated about that, and I truly understood.

"No matter, so long as none tries to make a claim on anything, we can capture them as they come. And what of those you have taken?" he asked, quirking a brow.

"If they are compliant and willingly acknowledge the situation, they are being reeducated, as you commanded. Those who try to fight are being disposed of, of course. I will say that there have thankfully been few of the latter." I got the feeling that he didn't really mind killing the youths, but he knew that most of us found doing so distasteful.

"I am glad that there aren't many. Now, on to less unfortunate business. We've seen several proposals on turning over day-to-day operations, of these I think three have merit, one of which comes to us from General Verren's daughter. Let us discuss these. The sooner we can free our soldiers from their holding positions, the better." As Emperor Durin spoke, servants passed around the proposals.

After a long discussion, Emperor Durin finally declared the victor. Surprisingly, it was Alana who had come up with the winning bid. There were some changes made to her original proposal, of course, on who could stand, what powers they would have, and all of that, but most of it remained the same. We'd run into several points at which the more military-minded of our council had disagreed vehemently, but when it was pointed out that none of them had lived in a village, they had to concede that they might not fully comprehend the situation.

That decision was only for the smallest of communities, of course. For the larger ones, the winning bid had come from a panel of advisers in the civilian section. Basically, the larger cities would be ruled over by a council; each member would be chosen to represent a different section of the city, with a military governor to act as the head and to overrule in case of conflict or tie. I, of course, would be retaining the position I had in Lithere.

I had to take a gate to return home, followed by an hour-long run. I wasn't as fast as I had been in my prime, but I could still easily outpace some of the fastest horses. I'd never get tired of using my strength to push myself like this, the wind rushing through my hair and fresh air almost forced into my lungs by the speed.

My wife met me after I'd cleaned myself and readied for bed. She brought me a cup of the cheap herbal tea that I preferred and sat with me for a few minutes. This might well be the highlight of my day, something I'd missed too often because of war.

"You look tired, dear, is all well?" she asked.

"Nothing particularly wrong, just . . . I never wanted to rule anything, it's taxing. It's a shame we couldn't just live in peace like we used to."

"I know you hate it, but that's why you're right for the job. My heart tells me that you'll never fall to corruption like those damn nobles did, because you never wanted to rule in the first place." With that declaration, she kissed me lightly and pulled me toward our bed. It was late after all.

ALANA

After spending weeks working through the mass of information Mystien had sent me, along with my own work, I finally had an outline of a ward I liked. Between the normal class schedule, which was still absolutely brutal, and trying to get my core up to the next milestone, I had less time than I would have wanted.

I did manage to get to the second level of the core, and it was a massive improvement. The notes in the guide seemed to believe this was truly the basic level of what I should be working with for any real magic. It wasn't a small step up, but almost a skyward shot in complexity. My old work could only have held a few lines of sequence here and there, but now, each could hold several functions, even if they were significantly more complex. That was a huge escalation.

This particular item consisted of five total functions. Three were detectors and two active uses. There was a detection for an on/off switch, turning on either the full function, or the other detectors, depending on what was needed. The other two detectors looked for changes in velocity or in temperature. I'd wanted something better, but the velocity mechanic seemed to be the best way to go about it. Finally, the active functions smoothed out either the change in velocity between the user and whatever was approaching, or the change in temperature.

I'd decided to add heat/cold protection because there was no good way to take the cost in mana of running an item constantly down too much. Adding the second function was not a large addition to cost in comparison to just having the damn thing on all the time, and if I was going to have to pay for it, I at least wanted my mana's worth. It *should* take the worst of any fire- or cold-based attack trying to enter the protected area. I was sure it wouldn't stop things going out, but it had limits on what it could handle.

The velocity warding was not exactly what I'd envisioned, but it would stop arrows, crossbow bolts, or massive pillars of water from killing me by slowing them down to a fraction of their initial speed. It was imperfect perhaps, but I'd rather be wet than a small red stain on a wall. It also never escaped me that an arrow could end my life as sure as any other human.

I'd shoved them into various pieces of jewelry for myself, Dras, Pinea, Kala, and Charles. I still cared deeply for Kala, even though we now spoke far less. Pinea and Dras had already been targets, so I had no qualms about giving them an extra bit of protection. As for Charles . . . I'd been a really shitty friend to Charles over the years, and this was something I reasonably could share. There was nothing secret here, just commonly known sequences arranged well.

Once I'd gotten it all ready, I made a test mock-up. I didn't want these out in the wild until I knew it worked, and I knew one professor who would certainly help me run some quick numbers in exchange for the item. After that, it would all be a matter of getting the time to make all of them.

CHAPTER 29

✦

PLANNING FOR FUN

On our next break day, I ended up managing to get all my friends together. This wasn't an easy task, due to conflicting schedules, timetables, and the fact that some of them weren't in school. But after a lot of planning, and no small amount of personal irritation, I managed it.

We had secured a room at my home, both because it was spacious and Dras was having some issues with public places as of recently. I didn't blame him for that at all, but it meant that he was far less likely to go and get a drink or whatever he did when he wasn't in class. As we sat around playing the local analog of chess, which had room for up to twelve players and a whole slew of irritating rules, I pulled out my boxes.

"What's all this?" Kala asked as I passed them around.

"Well, after recent events, I decided to do what I could for my friends' protection. These are some items."

Dras narrowed his eyes at me. "And what do they do exactly?"

I gave a brief explanation as each tried theirs on. I'd gone for anklets for myself and Pinea, while making Kala a bracelet. Bracelets were common for women, and anklets for those dancing, but the latter could easily be hidden if desired, so it didn't matter much. The boys both got rings, as men in our society didn't wear other jewelry very much. I wouldn't say it never happened to see a man with bracelets or whatever, but it wasn't common. Getting all of the enchantments to fit on such a small item had been an absolute pain in the ass, but after a bit of work, I'd managed it, though they both looked kind of like school rings.

While Charles was trying on his, Dras put both hands on the table.

"Look, Alana, if these do what you said, do you know how much they'd cost? Even just to run them is going to be costly."

I looked at his arms. He was whole now, with little other than the clearly regrown skin on his limb and the faintest trace of a scar on his face, but I couldn't forget how he'd looked in the hospital. I still saw it in my mind when I thought about him too much, lying there, covered in bandages with only the one hand able to do anything.

"I don't suspect that you'll be using them all the time, but if things look dicey, it's something you can use without training or the like." I sighed, looking up to meet his eyes. "Look, I know you don't like taking expensive things, but keep it, hopefully you never need it, but . . ."

"Thank you, this could really help," Charles said, still looking at his ring. He was still a bit short on words, but he looked up to give me a brief smile.

"Same. After what they showed me during that interview . . ." Pinea shivered.

Kala just gave me a light smile and nodded.

"I suppose I am being a bit of a jerk. These don't contain any weird stuff though, right?" Dras gave me a bit of a look. I sort of deserved that, since the last piece of magical equipment I'd given him had been taken away for containing a trace amount of military technology.

"No, perfectly normal stuff. I had Professor Ieala help me with the testing. Anyone could do it, but most don't bother. Either you don't need it, or there are cheaper methods of defense for most people." I nodded. She'd been rather disappointed when she saw my sequences, because they were fairly straightforward.

"Thank you then. Hopefully, we won't need them."

After that, we went back to playing "not chess." I hated it with a passion, and barely understood the rules, but it was popular among the wealthy. It was a bit embarrassing how I was the only one who struggled here, my friends having learned the various rules over their lives for the purpose of interacting with nobles and rich folk. Even Charles and Dras, who were both decidedly from the lower classes of the city were quite good, though none of us could hold a flame to Pinea.

There were two groupings of pieces, one could move north and south primarily, while the others could move north/southeast and north/southwest primarily. They all did this on a hexagonal game board, and there were several distances they could move in each direction, much like pawns and queens.

"So," Pinea began, after having destroyed us all collectively again, "do any of you know of any good balls happening? I've tried to get word on some even though it isn't the right season, but it seems nothing is going on."

"I don't, and frankly don't mind all that much." The rest of the table looked at me, but I hated some of those I'd been to.

"Come on, Alana, everyone loves a good party," Pinea objected. "Heck, you could organize one yourself if you wanted to. I bet your parents would be thrilled. I'd even be willing to help. It would look really good . . ."

"I do love a good party, but what I consider a good party, and what most of noble society thinks is a good party are two significantly different things. If I threw one, it would likely be the talk of the town and might be the cause of no small quantity of scandal."

"I'm in." Pinea didn't even blink as she answered.

Shortly thereafter were these responses: "Sounds fun." "Worrying, but what do you have?" "Why exactly? You're always fun."

"Is this really the best time for this?" I asked, looking at my friends tiredly.

That got me a series of nods. This began an argument that lasted no less than three full games back and forth. Personally, I would love to throw a massive party, but there was no occasion. And frankly, I wasn't sure I wanted to deal with all of the blowback that would certainly come. While I was holding the line, my father decided to make his appearance, throwing a wrench into the works.

"Are you lot still going? I didn't know you enjoyed games this much." He regarded us with a slight smile.

"We're trying to convince Alana to throw a party," Pinea said, beating me to the punch. "She's being very contrarian about it. Which is weird for a bard and putting a damper on things."

"Come now, Alana, I may not be much for social events, but a small party might do some good." That statement seemed to go against everything I knew about him.

I looked at him with hard eyes. "Who are you, and what have you done with my father?"

"Alana, your mother has been pestering me for far too long about how we should be acting more in accordance with how people think their rulers should. She thinks we should throw a ball or two, or something. More social events for the young of our lands would be right on what she would like." That made more sense. Mom could be relentless when she got on a subject, and a month or two of badgering might well make him jump on any opportunity.

"We were discussing how what I think a party should be like would undoubtedly create mass scandal." I answered, and it seemed to cause him some amount of worry.

"Does it include public sex or nudity? Or any other illegal activity?" he asked. "Or anything dangerous, or potentially dangerous to either the participants or the country?"

"No, most of the people I know are a little too pent up for that. Depending on your definition of nudity, I imagine someone will wear something like the professor's dancing outfit." I tapped my chin as I thought.

"Emperor Durin wants to establish new traditions, and I hate the old ball format. If this succeeds, and your mother is mollified by having more social events, then I'm fine with it. I'll see if your brother will help. If you can fold in some of the things from the Ermathi part of the population's traditions, too, that would be excellent."

"I . . . can't believe you're giving permission for this." I was stunned.

"Your mother and I will be out of town for a few days. I'll see to it that it overlaps with one of your off days if I can. Who knows, if you pull it off, everyone wins. We get new traditions, your mother gets off my back, you have fun, and everyone is happy. Use the ballroom and edit your guest list carefully."

With that, I was grabbed by Pinea, clearly attempting to silence me. "Don't worry, we'll make sure to help!"

He left shortly thereafter, and several of my "friends" started laughing at me. After a brief moment of introspection, I decided that if Dad wanted me to throw a party, a party would be thrown. There were a number of things I'd need, but I knew that those were hurdles we could make with ease.

"Fine then, if my father okayed it, then I won't have to deal with anyone's whining when it's done. Pinea, Kala, can you two come up with guests? We'll also need everyone possible who we can reasonably trust from our dance class. Invitations, too, make sure people don't wear clothes they will mind getting a bit mussed."

"Got it," Pinea said. She was practically bouncing.

"Charles and Dras, we are going to need a band. We'll talk later on specifics, but if you can secure a handful of bards that work together, that would be great."

"Where are we getting money for that?" Charles asked, a valid question.

"We shouldn't need too much for this, but I can make you a bit of sugar to sell or something. The band can be one from the lower part of town. Talk to Lucien. He probably knows someone who can put on a wild show."

"What will you be doing?" Kala asked.

"Refreshments and party games. I'll grab my brother to help and see if we can fold in some of the old Ermathi traditions too. He might know those, or know someone who does."

As it turned out, my brother didn't know any of the traditions I was seeking. He did know a few people from the old empire there though, and they were both trustworthy and very willing to help. We spent an afternoon going through all of the different things they could think of, trying to find something that fit with the atmosphere. When I brought up the idea of festivals is when we really started to hit on to things I liked.

One of their summer celebrations had involved a sort of fighting. Well, all of their celebrations involved fighting; it had been a rather militaristic society. In their case, it had been done on poles over a pit of coals that was hot enough to burn, but not kill anyone who fell into it.

I threw in a bit of old game-show ideas to change it over to water, and since they were already using staffs, the idea of padding them a bit for safety didn't go down too badly. This hadn't been one of those somber serious traditions, but rather something idiotic teenagers did to impress girls with how strong and daring they were. When I suggested doing it about fifteen feet up, they'd stopped whining and jumped on board. The only issue would be the setup, but my brother assured me he knew someone who could probably pull it off without any issue.

That settled, I began my work on food and drink. It was the job of a good hostess to provide refreshments, and I had just magic to help make sure that it was a wild party.

CHAPTER 30

✦

PARTY TIME

I had had less than a full month to prepare, but when the night came I was ready. The guests would be here shortly, but for the moment I needed all of my skill. For while the decorations were up and the games were in place, now we needed to mix the drinks.

I had no less than five distinct cocktails in place, all sweet, along with three separate beers. It had taken a full afternoon of getting drunk and un-poisoning myself to get through all of this, but it was well worth it. The mixtures of fruit, liquor, sugar, and spices were all right, and I had even managed a passable mojito.

"Wow, I dig the mushroom aesthetic," Dras said as he arrived.

Our whole ballroom was illusioned to look rather like a cave, the light primarily coming from fake glowing mushrooms on the walls. Jackson was kind enough to provide it for me, but I was paying hand over fist for that, mostly in alcohol and cocktail recipes. Both were easy for me to get, so I was not a bit bothered by that.

My other friends were coming in shortly, too, those who'd helped me with setting up this mess. Pinea had a whole group in the background getting dressed for their various performances and making sure to apply cosmetics or illusions over their Lovers' Marks. Charles was doing his last sweep to make sure everything was in place, and Dras had just arrived with the last shipment of food for the party. It was small dried dates, stuffed with nuts and tossed in honey, a personal favorite from back on Earth, as well as some bacon flowers.

The guests arrived in waves, and soon enough everything was in motion. It was going rather slowly, because most of those here had no idea how to truly get down and have fun, but it was my job as hostess to remedy that issue.

"So, how does this work?" said one boy over by a giant wheel that we had one of our bartenders manning.

"I'll demonstrate," I said as I bounced up.

It took only a few seconds to spin the wheel, during which I hummed a happy tune. The little arrow ticked past section after section before finally landing on one of the slices. From there, I was passed the drink that I'd won. Had I cheated so I didn't get one of the bad ones? Maybe. Did I regret that? No.

"You spin the wheel, and when it stops, you get the drink indicated," I said as I downed the significantly weaker than normal shot, which was almost entirely fruit juice. This world might not have a drinking age, but too much alcohol was bad.

With a nod, the guy spun the wheel, and our now smiling assistant handed him his drink. Within a few seconds, he'd followed my lead, but unlike me was sputtering and coughing. His face was red, and he looked rather irritated.

"That's terrible!" he declared. He'd received one of my personal amalgamations that involved rather a lot of star anise. I'd called it a "falling star" as a joke.

"Yup, there are one or two that are bad. Most of them are good, but if you land on one of the unlucky ones, it's pretty nasty."

Several of the guy's friends had started laughing, and now the game was off. Each wanted to try their luck, and based on the number of spellcasters present, they either wanted to cheat to hurt their friends or to help themselves. That was fine by me; cheating at party games was a good and time-honored tradition.

There were several other similar party games, including one where someone tried to get a prize from a pool with only their teeth. I'd had to adapt that one a bit, since normally I'd want a girl dressed as a mermaid in there with the prize. Sadly, there didn't seem to be a lot of info about mermaids. Perhaps they existed in this world, but if they did, they weren't a popular story where I lived. Regardless, a rather soaked Dras was demonstrating wildly with several of his friends, and it was garnering attention.

The sound of drums led to the main attraction of Atali dancers, who rotated in and out from a large circle. Several would go at once, having their turn before moving to the side to take a short break, and soon enough one of the girls in the audience went to join them. This led to several more, myself included. Planting the first couple had been easy enough as I knew most of the girls from the Atali Dance class.

That attraction went on for quite a while and earned no small amount of whispers. It was clear to my guests that this was no normal ball, and that their expectations could be left at the door. That was aided by the fact that after a few rounds, one or two of the dancing girls just joined the rest of us while in full costume.

"I need a slight break," Pinea declared as she joined me in observing things. She had been going for the better part of half an hour now and was dripping sweat.

We got her a berry-filled ice water, and I turned to her. "Want to go see what they're up to outside?"

I could barely hear the cheers from where I was currently standing, but that I heard them at all from inside indicated that it was going well. At her agreement, we went to go and watch. Two boys, Tobias and another whose name I didn't know, stood high up in the air. Each had his pole to stand on and several more he could reach, and a staff in his hand.

They were ducking and weaving, jumping, thrusting, and parrying, and as I looked on, the young fanboy sent his opponent careening to the water below. Another boy soon joined in on the fun to the cheers and encouragement of all those watching. I had a feeling like they might be at this for a while.

"Oh, hi there, Alana . . ." One of the guys I knew from my Combat Spellcasting class froze as he saw Pinea in her outfit, clearly ogling her, something she seemed to rather enjoy. He stood there soaking wet and slack-jawed for just a moment.

"She's taking a break from the dancing inside. How are things?" I asked, trying to pull him out of his brain-lock.

"Um . . . great, tons of fun. Seems like I might have missed a few things though . . ."

"Then go and enjoy them. Dry yourself off before going inside," I said, motioning him away.

The two of us shared a giggling fit as he turned and tried not to run inside before going back to watching the matches up in the air. At some point or other, I think most of the boys tried it, if only to prove they weren't afraid. Even the lads sent falling into the water were greeted with well-meant jibes and pats on soaking backs as they left.

Things went on well into the night before people eventually started to head out. Kala had managed to convince several of her priest friends to help in giving all of the leaving guests a quick sobering up, not that we had anything that was all that strong being given out. It still mattered as I didn't want to cause too much trouble for people.

The morning after every good party involved cleanup. Magic, of course, made this significantly easier, and since I'd years ago come up with a simple cleaning spell, most of it was kind of trivial. As I was telekinetically tossing cups and plates onto trays for the kitchen to wash, I discovered something.

"Oh my," I said.

One of our dancers had at some point lost her top, leaving it sitting on a chair not far from the area. I blinked and laughed. It clearly wasn't Pinea's. It was less than ten minutes later that I found the girl in question, one of last year's graduates, curled up with another of my guests under a nearby table, quite asleep, and thankfully otherwise clothed.

"Hey, wake up!" I yelled, sending them both popping up and into the bottom of their hiding spot.

"What!?" *Thunk.* "Ow! Wait, where . . ." The girl quickly covered herself as she registered things.

"Lost this?" I asked, offering out the missing article.

"Um . . . yes, sorry . . ." She blushed brilliant red, putting it back on, and the young man with her failed to look away.

"It's fine, grab something from the leftovers if you need it before heading out though." I waved them over to a small table that still had some of the extra food on it. Neither of them seemed to need my help, and I did have work to do.

John wandered in to join me at some point, looking still a bit tired. He was blinking the sleep from his eyes as he walked over, grabbing a few things on his way. As he passed, the happy couple was leaving in a hurry.

"Were they . . . ?" he asked as he watched them depart.

"I don't know and don't really care," I said with a shrug.

"Whatever. Last night was great, we need to do that again some time."

I just snickered and went back to my cleaning. It may have been minimal effort, but it all needed to be done.

I got a letter at school, an actual letter from my father when he'd returned. I knew that our little gathering had been a hit based solely on what I was hearing at the academy, but apparently word had gotten out. Not in a good way, I'd succeeded in causing a decent scandal.

He'd received several complaints and questions about what exactly had gone on. This had not been aided by my brother who was rather wild in his descriptions of everything. The fact that we'd gone in a completely different direction from a normal ball was simply unacceptable to a number of people, including my mother once she'd understood what kind of dancing had been performed.

That said, I didn't get the feeling that he was at all irritated. He sent me the letter to "reprimand me" as was his job, but I'd gotten his express permission and even orders to go a bit wild. Whatever . . . I'd know soon enough.

Regardless of what he did though, it wouldn't much matter. I'd introduced enough new ideas to the students of the academy that I was fairly sure that we'd have a good rotation of celebrations going in the next year or two. Setting trends was good fun like that.

CHAPTER 31

✦

BREAKING AND ENTERING

My third year seemed to fly past me. Between all of the many things going on and the work I was doing, it was summer again before I knew it.

My work on portals was progressing, but I'd run into a hitch. The cost was just too high. I'd managed to practice it until I could now reliably move an apple or something around a room a few times without passing out, but it was slow-going. There had to be an answer beyond "use more mana" because that was obviously not what the gates were doing, but I couldn't work it out.

I suspected part of it was that they were fixed points. If they were somehow connected, that might end up meaning that their connection was far more stable. While that was probably true, I wasn't sure how that was being done. Did they need to be in specific places? Was it something to do with the gate architecture, some form of spell that it was running when they were on? Without more time to study them, I couldn't figure it out, and I wouldn't be getting any of that for another year or so at least.

While I chewed on that little issue. I continued to work my way through the guide. I looked to be getting near the midway point now. This should have been something I finished in a year or two, but the lack of good organization was still a big mess. There were references to other parts that weren't labeled, and no explanation of how to find them, meaning that I had to spend far too much time wandering around looking for simple answers that I should just be able to search. It was really less of a guide and more the ramblings of an expert jotted down about things he thought about when he thought about them.

You'd think the "help" function would be useful, but here it honestly wasn't. The problem with it was you had to know what you wanted for it to help you, and if I already knew what I was missing, I wouldn't be missing it. Frankly, that seemed to be an almost completely useless thing from where I stood. I suspected that whoever had made it had some better use, but without them telling me what it was, or something in the guide, how was I to know?

Regardless of my gripes, I was still learning loads. Between my classes and my own research, I was now easily one of the best, if not the best at writing sequences in my year. I'd learned to pump in multiple functions and adjustments, and now that I had a higher-level core, I could start to get into some really interesting bits. These were mostly layering things one atop the other and in complex trees of behavior with if/then statements, that took otherwise simple actions into much more useful methods.

It was one night as I was sitting, bemoaning my current state of progress that I received a letter. This one wasn't much, a simple notice from Professor Endel that we'd be having another military exercise on our next day off. It oddly didn't say what we'd be doing, just where to show up and when for the event.

Our next Combat Spellcasting class came soon enough, and our teacher wasted no time in getting down to business.

"Good morning, everyone, I'm sure you've all gotten my notice by now." There was a murmur of agreement. "Excellent, now, I won't be telling you what you're doing, but I will tell you that you will all need whatever basic rations you think are important for at least a day. This exercise will test how you respond to situations that are unexpected, as you won't always know what you're going into."

Several hands went up, only for him to shake his head. "No questions on this one. Now, let us proceed on today's topic, common monster weak points."

This was something we'd go over every now and then for this class. There were a number of monsters that could differ considerably from place to place, but most of them shared locations to attack, joints, eyes, brains, and the like. Since these creatures were what we'd be fighting when we weren't going after other humans, those were important to know.

After class, I joined with a few others in discussion of what we'd be encountering.

"Well, definitely monsters of some kind." Troy looked around at the others.

"Sure, but any thoughts on what kinds?" a girl asked.

"Who knows, heck, we might even be going into somewhere that has a lot of variety." A few of the others looked at me as I jumped in, nodding as they thought on it.

"The Copse Junkyard again?" One asked.

"Hmm, I don't think so. We've been there a few times now, so it wouldn't be a surprise. That's what he was talking about, right?" Troy was right, even after the attack there we'd gone back once or twice for other, less strenuous exercises. Even if we only had a few of these days a year, they still added up here and there.

I sighed as I looked about the room. "Well, if it's a surprise, we have only two options I suppose. We can try to figure it out, or we can let it come as it does."

"Isn't one of those cheating?" asked the girl from before, whose name I thought was Samantha.

"Is it? It might not be what Professor Endel wants us to do, but war isn't fair, and going in blind is stupid."

Troy looked at me. "All right, I'm game, you lot?"

The girl looked a bit worried but nodded, as did everyone else in the little gathering.

"Okay, so here's what I'm thinking . . ."

The thing about breaking into Professor Endel's office to steal the info was . . . we didn't need to. Well, some of us would be trying, but I didn't honestly expect that to work. There were multiple parts of this plan that were easier to decipher, and many, many avenues that would have decidedly less security.

First of all was the fact that the vast, overwhelming majority of any plan involved having more than one person. Knowing that, and that we only needed to know where we were going opened some routes. We could go after his new assistant (minder) and see what we could learn there, but that seemed about as likely as trying to get the info from Endel himself, not very.

So we broke into three pairs to look into different areas; this fit our group of six well. One was after the professor's information, one would try breaking into the office, and one would be looking into the transports. I was in the last, because I thought it had the best chance of success. All of us were, of course, under strict instructions to bounce if it looked at all hairy, better to fail than to get caught.

We always took carriages wherever we were going for these events. It stood to reason then that we'd be taking them on our next outing. With this information in hand, and a guess that the carriage operators would both have a schedule and some notes, we aimed for them.

Few people who were raised among nobility thought much about all of the many workers below them, and that was a huge flaw. For each student, there were a number of staff, be they our maids and manservants, the cleaners who took care of the main part of the school building, or the staff who dealt with any of the other general service, like moving us around. That was a flaw in my view, one that we needed to exploit.

Troy had joined me as we sat on a ledge overlooking the small stable. It was off of the main building, nearer to the gates. We were here just after our classes ended and while we could see a few lights still on, things were definitely winding down over there.

"Being invisible is weird," Troy observed.

"You get used to it. Heads up, looks like the last light just went out."

"All right then, we wait about a quarter of a bell then move. How do I know where you are while we do that by the way?"

"You'll take my hand . . . obviously. Be ready to deal with any wards on the building or anything like that." I could, of course, sense him to some degree, being that my spell was covering him, but the opposite was very untrue.

As I counted the last of the time down, I nodded, sighed a bit at the useless gesture, then took Troy's hand. "Time to go."

We moved across the drive silently, I'd worked the spells out for that years ago. His addition to this started here as well, as he'd cleared the normally dirty area while we waited, removing any dirt and dust that might have given away our footprints. By doing it slowly enough and over the whole drive, it didn't look very obvious, but might prove important if anyone was watching.

As we reached the building, we needed to make a few quick decisions. Neither of us knew how it was warded, if at all, or where. We also didn't know what the locks on the doors or windows looked like, and what might come of those. Troy moved forward and took a quick look at the main door, checking the seams for runes, or the signs of obvious warding. That done, he tapped my hand twice, a signal that there were wards, but they were minimal.

Next we needed to check windows. It was likely those were protected, too, but if they were there was only one solution. A quick look over revealed that the first floor ones decidedly were, and floating a mirror up to the second floor let us know that those were protected as well. That was unfortunate, but not unexpected; we'd just been in a war for several years, and our school would have been a primary target.

We students were somehow given a pass by the school's normal warding, but we couldn't bet that these would be the same. That said, everything had a weakness, including wards. If we didn't care, we could just break some of the connections and be done with it, destroying them. That wasn't an option since we were both trying to be sneaky and not disrupt the school's functioning. That left us with draining the magic from them.

Something like this wouldn't work for the main building, but this wasn't nearly as well protected. See, sometimes magical items that have a charge need to be drained, for whatever reason. If the item is damaged, this can be dangerous, but for a well-functioning, well-built thing, this is no big deal. There were tools for it, and Troy set quick to work on pulling out all of the mana in one of the windows.

As he finished, I carefully undid the latch on the other side with a small spell and slid up the glass pane. One of us would need to stay there to make sure that the magic didn't refill from any connected area while the other got inside and looked around. Since I was both the more sneaky and smaller of the two, I got job number two.

This place was quite literally a barn, and it took me only a few moments of looking around to find the small office-like area attached to it. Here, the workers could drink tea and go over their assignments, and like most break rooms, it had a nice, friendly board with papers on it. From there, I only needed to find the order for the day and time of our departure, easy since I knew roughly how many of us there were, when we were leaving, and from where. I quickly marked down our destination on a map of the city I'd brought for just such a situation and slipped back out.

Our little conspiracy met again right after breakfast the next morning. The other groups had failed, but that was due to them not finding a good way into where they were going. I'd thought that the office group might get something, being that one of their people was supposedly practiced at ward bypass, but he'd taken one look at it and called a retreat. Endel had also apparently stayed in his office until almost curfew, so no luck there either.

I laid out the map we'd managed to secure and frowned down at it. "Just a location, but I've got no clue what's there."

"Not much," our other female conspirator answered. "That's the back end of one of the parks in the old nobles' district. The only thing there is an entry for one of the little creeks. My brothers used to get in all kinds of trouble for using it to get down into the . . . undercity shit." The last word was drawn out as she realized our destination.

For my part, I just buried my face in the nearest padded chair and screamed.

My little crew showed up to our event decked out. All of us had lamps, a couple of bottles for water, rope, and basic climbing gear to go along with our normal overnight equipment. Some of my companions had brought food and water, but I honestly would rather save the weight. I'd taken to wearing a variant of our armor that had legs instead of a skirt, rather frowned on normally, but if I was going to be climbing ladders, quite important.

Upon seeing us all gathered, our professor looked at us, then at the rest of the group of students. "Good work, but to whomever did it, it is of note that one should take pains to hide their footprints in places with loose ground, like stables. Particularly if your feet are smaller than those of the men who tend to work there and you leave a ward obviously drained of mana."

I felt myself blush a bit and tried to hide my face. We might have gotten out without being caught, but leaving clues like that behind had been a bit sloppy.

Regardless, we were shortly split off into groups of three. I was joined by Troy, along with Alli, a girl from my class I seldom worked with, who I knew to be of the "commoners" grouping. I suspected that I'd been placed specifically with those not too related to the nobility for this, and all of my other groupings after the incidents earlier this year.

We were all piled into one of the carriages, along with our gear. Each of the three of us had our standard-issue armor, along with what we considered a basic provisions pack. Those had been part of our instructions, but everyone had chosen their own flare to put on it. It was strange, but the former kingdom's military had been only barely organized from the top down, and we still had a bit of that.

"So, do we have a plan?" Alli asked as our carriage pounded down the road.

"We don't know what the mission is, only where we're going," Troy answered.

That got a raised eyebrow. "Where?"

"The undercity," I groaned.

"I've never been down there. Don't suppose either of you have?" Troy shook his head, but I sighed and took over.

"It's going to be dark and difficult to navigate. The undercity itself is not too dangerous in most places, but the latter part of that statement is vital. I don't know how deep we're going, but as you go lower and lower, the danger level rises quickly. We're likely to see rodents of unusual size, along with any number of other minor monsters that have set up shop."

"Okay, so you've been down there before. What's our maximum danger look like?" Alli seemed the kind to get all the info she could, which was good as far as I was concerned.

"There are some rather large and extremely dangerous monsters down there if we go deep enough. We might also become trapped, but I'm guessing Professor Endel has taken some precautions with that. The worst things I've seen were not something we could fight head on, but everything has a weakness. If we run into anything too big, we'll just need to leave its territory." I breathed in, thinking on my experiences.

"The bigger issue will be navigation. It is a literal maze down there." I leaned back thumping my head against the wood. I still didn't have a good answer to that problem.

During the rest of the ride, Alli and Troy asked me a few more basic questions, some of which I could answer, some of which I couldn't. I'd only been to the undercity once or twice before, so I wasn't really an expert on the matter.

When we arrived at our destination, everyone got out and followed our professor to a hidden opening from which flowed a creek. The tunnel itself was perhaps fifteen feet wide, with a ledge along one side. He put up a light and refused to answer any questions as he led us into the darkness.

We didn't walk far before he turned to a sealed door and opened it with some form of key. From there, we went down, probably walking for a good hour with Professor Endel leading as his assistant followed behind to make sure none of us got lost. When we finally stopped, it was in a large, fairly empty room, easily big enough for us all to stand in comfortably. All along the walls were doors, far enough spaced that they probably led to very different paths.

"Good day, everyone, and welcome to the undercity." Endel looked out at us as he produced a bag. "Everyone, take one of these, and then we'll begin."

Each of us got a small item, decidedly magical in nature with a number on it. It glowed faintly as the assistant professor took down the numbers. While waiting, all of us checked our gear, by this point experienced enough to know not to bring much, but still nervous that we had everything.

"All right, now that you have those, don't lose them, each releases a trail that can be tracked in case of emergency or failure to return to the surface on time. They also have a time-keeping function and will change color at halfway through our exercise. When that happens, you are to immediately head upward. Your goal for this exercise is to go out into the undercity and hunt; you will gain points based on what you succeed in taking on, along with making your way back to the school. Questions?"

"How far down are we?" I asked, since nobody else seemed to know what to say.

"Roughly seven levels, as commoners measure them. This is as far down as they would go, because any lower and magic will be needed to combat what you find. I know for a fact that this section of the city goes down at least twice as deep, but I would not advise you to delve too much lower."

"Anything else we need to know?" one of the boys in the class asked.

"Do not split your group. If you come back to the surface without all members, or confirmation that the missing ones are dead, you will be considered to have failed this exercise."

Since everyone seemed ready, he began by taking the groups one at a time to the doors. Each was quite locked, and the group was let out after a word of encouragement from Professor Endel. When I was smaller, I would have viewed seven levels as something near legendary, the best ratcatchers I had heard of barely touching that. I supposed that the city might well have some more professional non-magical soldiers who could easily go that deep though.

Soon enough it was our turn; we'd been left for last. As our teacher led us over to the last of the doors, he opened it with a loud grinding.

"Now, I've got expectations for you lot, since you prepared for the undercity and all," he laughed.

"Professor, we . . . actually, yeah, that was us. Well, not Alli." He corrected himself as he got a glare from the girl in question, I couldn't do anything but laugh.

"Intel gathering is important, lad, but so is secrecy. We'll talk about that when you get back. For now, good luck." As I left the portal, he slammed the metal door home with a final *thunk*, letting the silence overtake us.

The undercity hadn't changed much, well, at least as far as I could tell. It was cool, dark, and quiet, and we set out forward, no point in trying to keep back. As we trudged along, we ran into other groups once or twice, but fairly little else.

While we found a few monsters, most of those were painfully minor to us. Any of our group could kill a giant rat or the like with pretty minimal effort, even me. We took on about a dozen of those as we passed along. It was hard to gauge, but I was pretty sure that these were bigger than those higher up, perhaps there was more ambient magic down here or something.

"Ugh, more rats, can we get something else please?" Alli complained as we made our way into what looked like an old sewer, having just taken out a couple more of the beasts.

We opted to follow this for a bit, it was easy to walk and didn't look like it had any other students going down it. It went on for perhaps half a mile, curving slightly this way and that, but strangely empty. After a time, we came to a drop-off, opening into a cylinder of some kind.

"Neat, some kind of drainage?" Troy asked. As he did, Alli got close to the edge, looking down.

I nearly missed it as she was grabbed. The reason this tunnel had been so empty feeling but not covered in webs. It was huge; the furry legs snatched her like a fly before a frog, pulling her off to the side of the tunnel opening.

"Alli!" both of us yelled as she was pulled away.

Troy didn't miss a beat, preparing a spell as he rushed to the side, a flaming bolt swirling around his hand. I tried to stop him but was just a beat behind as he leveled it and let loose, the spear of flame screaming toward the monster and taking one of its legs.

"You idiot, you can't use fire, it's . . ." I watched in horror as the worst began.

The spider was as big as a horse and holding our teammate in two of its legs, its face over her body as Troy's bolt slammed into it, taking one of its appendages. The fire then hit the light coating of webs behind and began spreading like lit spiderwebs always seemed to do. The monster dropped Alli, who was shaking and gurgling, looking like she was having a seizure from where she landed on a much lower web.

"Shit," Troy said as he watched the monster turn toward us, the fire spreading all along the walls in a wave.

"Really! Deal with that thing. I'll get her!" I started singing as I swan dove toward Alli. Behind me, the spider jumped toward the tunnel entrance, only to be met by a hail of ice shards from Troy.

As I approached her in my dive, my speed seemed to drop rapidly, nearly jolting me as I slammed into my companion. I'd have to think about it later, because now I had work to do. On her side, clearly visible through her armor were two largish holes, leaking an angry yellow-green fluid. The wound could wait. I immediately decided as I worked my song into an anti-poison spell.

When I'd come to the academy, I wouldn't have been able to fix this; it would have been a death sentence. As it stood, the sheer amount of venom in her was giving me trouble, but I was making progress. Bit by bit, I was pulling away the killer fluid, yanking it forcefully from her trembling body.

Behind me and Alli, the sounds of battle continued, eventually ending with both combatants flying from the tunnel. Troy was no slouch and was giving the beast a good showing, a blade of ice shoved into it as ichor sprayed. Invertebrates were tough customers though, and the spider flailed in rage, trying to bite its enemy.

As they fought, the fire spread, and before I was done, it started hitting the strands holding our web in the air. One after another, they began to burn, each lost letting us droop lower and lower until we swung toward the wall. As we impacted, I lost my spell.

"Ice water!" I yelled up at Troy. It would cool the monster worse than it would any mammal, and the water might help with the quickly spreading inferno.

A small mercy was that the fire didn't have too much to burn, while it was going quickly, air was sucked from below to feed it, so from my point the smoke wasn't bad. I could see it approaching us though, and that was no good.

I would have liked to keep working on Alli, but there was no time. Soon the web would burn and we *would* fall, and I had little I could do about that. Instead of healing, I wrapped her in my arms and legs and began to sing up my best kinetic shield, trying to make the outside a bit bouncy to act as a cushion when we inevitably tumbled into the darkness below.

I didn't have to wait long, and as we fell, I embraced her, singing with all my might as we fell down into the abyss.

CHAPTER 33

✦

RETURN TO THE DEPTHS

The air screamed in my ears as our plummet continued for what seemed like hours. In reality, it could only have been a handful of seconds, but the fear of the darkness below made my heart pound like a hammer.

I didn't see it so much as feel it when the ground rose up to meet us, hitting first the same bubble that had shielded me when I'd jumped toward Alli, and then my own shield in quick succession. The sensation was jarring, but more like falling onto a trampoline than concrete as we slowed, the lack of a bounce was odd. Instead, we just settled onto the uneven ground.

From somewhere nearby, I could feel a powerful wind entering. My guess was that as the fire made the hot air go up, that from below rushed in to replace it. Above me, I could see the blaze continue, a few pieces of smoldering web and the like falling much like I had. Of note was one bit that I heard more than saw, a large mass that crunched as it landed nearby.

Soon, that was followed by my other teammate. Troy descended in a controlled fall, a light in his hand to let him see where he was going as gravity did most of the work. He landed near the other item, his cast-down opponent. As I looked at him, I could tell he was struggling. His breath was hard and sweat shone on his forehead.

"Alli?" he asked before coughing roughly.

"Alive, but badly hurt, and we need to move."

"What? Why?"

"That smoke is going up for now, but that will change as it cools when the fire runs out of fuel, assuming it doesn't continue on down here. I do not want to suffocate or burn to death." I was a bit sharper with him than I should be, but as he'd been the one to start the inferno I wasn't too worried.

"All right, I can feel wind coming from somewhere, so let's look around . . ." He turned his light to the ground, and I almost retched.

The "ground" so to speak was a massive pile of corpses, rats, unidentifiable remains, a few that even looked human. All of the bodies were covered in webs and desiccated, what would have been the fate of our comrade had we not gotten to her. The bones crunched as Troy looked about for the source of the air, eventually shoving aside several dead things to reveal a pipe, perhaps four feet wide.

There wasn't time to waste and we headed in. Taking only a moment to cut out the spider's fangs. I sung as Troy led the way, trying to remove the venom in Alli's system. It was hard going, but I suspected that stuff was far nastier than I wanted to know.

We had few options on where to turn as we went. This was obviously drainage into . . . somewhere, and clearly ancient, but that didn't help us much. After about twenty minutes, I felt we were far enough from the mess behind us to be safe and asked for a break at the nearest room.

We found one shortly, a small rounded junction of sorts that was devoid of anything hostile. Here we stopped to regroup and get our friend back on her feet. While I hovered over her, singing quietly Troy set up some lights around us and even some basic barriers around the openings. It wouldn't do to be surprised again.

I had to get out almost all of the venom before my patient stirred, groaning pitifully.

As the last few drops left and my spell ended, I spoke. "Alli, can you hear me? Are you okay?"

"It hurts, it hurts," she wept from her spot on the floor. "I want to go home." Her voice was weak, far too weak for comfort.

I started up my healing spell and was shocked at what I felt. Even though I'd done what I could to remove it, the venom had still ravaged her body. The muscles particularly felt like they had been almost . . . cooked or something, broken and shredded. Her heart seemed unaffected, which was a small mercy, but the rest of her was in pretty bad shape.

I cast until I couldn't anymore, falling to the ground beside the now passed-out Alli. Sleep took me, too, the mana loss having been too much for me. I suffered nightmares of large monsters and dying friends before I awoke, jarred by the image of a beast closing its jaws around my neck.

I found Troy there when I awakened, looking slightly worse for the wear. When he saw me rise, he smiled.

"Good, can you keep watch for a bit while I rest? An hour or two would really help." At my nod, he found a corner to curl up in and drifted off in seconds.

It was lonely for that time, the tunnels mostly dark, save for the few lamps we'd brought. I considered continuing to work on Alli, but she was alive and I didn't want to exhaust myself while on watch. A quick check of my anklet showed that my suspicion was right. It seemed to have read me falling at something as an attack and tried to shield it, draining it almost completely from the two falls. I wasn't sure exactly how long my own vigil lasted, but when I noticed that the little tools given to us by Professor Endel had changed in color, I woke my companions.

"Hate to say it, but we need to move."

Alli groaned as she tried to rise, slowly making her way to her feet with a grimace.

Troy looked over at her. "How bad?"

"Feels like someone is shoving needles into me, but I can walk." I saw her set her jaw as she stood to her full height.

"We'll work on that as we go," I assured her, and she gave me a small smile.

With no obvious paths up, we moved forward instead. There had been a brief conversation about going back and trying to get up that tube, but it seemed neither of the wizards thought they could levitate themselves up with their current knowledge, much less our whole group.

Soon enough, we came to a small pipe that we could get through; it was also our only path unless we wanted to backtrack. Since this seemed out best option, we made our way into it, pushing for foot after foot, hating the whole process.

When we popped out, I felt my own eyes widen. I knew this place, this huge room with its columns and thousand-year-old stonework, and the water below. The same cistern I'd found myself in years ago, I now found myself in again. As an added bonus, I could sense the beast that lived here, flowing around in that water.

"Oh, shit, I know this place," I said.

"Really?" Troy looked a bit relieved, but that ended as the water in the room began to churn.

It seemed likely that the monster down here had lacked in food for long enough that it had ended its patient waiting, and as it rose I wanted to panic. The cephalopod didn't quite match anything I'd seen back on my world, its body too long for an octopus and too rounded for any kind of squid, not to mention that it seemed to be the size of a cottage and living in a tiny amount of liquid. It rose from what must have been a slightly deeper part of the old cistern and turned its eyes in our direction. They would have looked dead if not for the predatory intelligence in them.

The two wizards aimed as it gripped columns, pulling itself toward us at speed. As tentacles grasped this way and that, they shot bolts of fire and ice at it, one slamming after another. For my part, I sent illusions circling it, running this way and that, which it tried to smack with a few errant swipes.

The battle, such as it was, didn't take too long. Troy was cautious, making quick and exact spears of ice to damage its limbs. Alli, on the other hand, seemed to have some anger she needed to work out, and absolutely pounded the monster with a torrent of flame. Both approaches worked for this fight, and before long, it was little more than fried calamari, even smelled kind of good. Alli tore out its beak as proof of death.

"So," Alli turned to me as she breathed out, "you said you know this place. Is there a way out?"

"Yeah . . . two potentially, though one might be collapsed, and the other is a path up one of these pipes. It's really steep. Let's see if we can clear the collapse first."

Within a few minutes, we'd made it back to the region that had Charles trapped for years. Cracks now littered the walls, making me quite nervous. The stairs had all but fallen as well. A quick look around showed that not too much had changed on the center level.

A look down revealed one of my old opponents, still stuck there without stairs to allow it up, it dragged itself around in a small circle on the ground.

"Shit, is that a golem?" Troy asked, leaning over the balcony to look at it with me.

"Yes, and there are two; we need to get up a level. Can you manage that?"

"Yeah, let's go." Between the two wizards, we shortly reached the exit.

It was a collapsed mess, but behind those rocks was our way out. Golem number two had managed to remove itself and now stood roughly where it had before, right where the collapse started. To my great irritation, it seemed none the worse for wear.

"Let's take it down," Alli voiced, grimacing slightly as she spoke.

"No, since this one turned my leg into mincemeat, it's mine." They both looked a bit taken aback, but no matter.

I'd grown since last I met this iron asshole. I sang, and like before, he didn't move. I motioned and my team joined in, a simple song, one to the morning sun. I felt the power build, higher and higher until I carefully chose my target.

It would have been unsafe to let too many things loose in this messed-up tomb, but lighting didn't cause all that much damage to rock, and the thunderous strike that I sent forth rocketed into the contraption. It glowed as I led the strike along its surface, melting the runes that kept it powered and moving one by one until it fell forward, several of its joints now slag.

I fell forward, too, having put a bit too much into that. From my place on the ground, I laughed and laughed. Years ago, these automatons had been an issue for a team of four, but now I could take one mostly on my own. It helped that it didn't move or fight back, but I'd take my win and smile.

My wizard friends carefully cleared away the rubble, using magic to levitate the rocks out one by one. It was nice to watch, and I had a few minutes to recover from my mana usage before we continued on our way.

It was kind of hard to pick our way back up, as I'd only been this way once and then in a bit of a state. We did manage though, even finding the body that Charles had taken the club from so many years ago. I looked back on his words of respect that day, and how he'd treated the dead.

"I'm sorry my friend took your club. Please take this instead." With a light movement, I pulled out my knife and laid it down beside the corpse. It seemed right, and losing that wouldn't be any real burden to me.

When we reached the surface again, I could tell from the look in the sky that it was late. If I had to guess, we had only barely enough time to make it back to the school before we set off a search party. That in mind, we all headed at speed toward the academy. If we lost grades for being late after that mess, we were all going to be pissed.

We huffed as we made it back to the gate just in time.

Professor Endel

My "assistant" Moran may have thought me a fool going out before the time was up, but as we stared at the carcass she ate her words.

"Those are . . ." The spider before us was not well known, but this particular mutant's venom was a nasty piece of work.

"Not something students should be messing with. Come quickly. We need to find them."

Nothing like that should have been on the seventh level. There wouldn't have been enough ambient magic there, but the shaft . . . it went deeper, and some might have come upward. It must have been something that was recently broken through as well, as these tunnels were checked every few years for big monsters, and that was a new addition.

Seven levels down should be easy for a student to handle, but now we were much further. The path showed that all three of my charges had made it lower. I'd known something was wrong when they were so late coming back. It had been decades since we'd lost a student on this exercise, and I wouldn't be starting now.

Alana had a knack for finding trouble, and this was certainly something that had her scent on it. She also had a knack for escaping, which was good, because if his daughter died under my watch or came back injured, General Verren might well gut me.

Both Moran and myself were using magic to speed our way along the path, and each shock took us less time to process. The dead cave giant cuttlefish was no joke, but the last . . . the remains of one iron golem were still hot, it having been partially melted by my erstwhile bard.

We marked the other golem for retrieval before continuing. We sped along after them, and I didn't breathe any easier until we reached the surface. I was only truly happy when the guards at the academy gates had told me that all of my students returned whole. One had made her way to the infirmary, but they were alive, and even back on time. I'd only missed seeing them by an hour or two.

CHAPTER 34

✦

GRADUATION AND GARDEN TALKS

Alli spent several days recovering fully from her spider experience. That said, we still got excellent marks on our underground activity. Our group had gone deeper and killed far more impressive monsters than any other, so there was no contest. The fact that we'd made it back just in the nick of time didn't look good, but nobody could fault us since we were technically within the time we needed to be.

After that little foray though, our class got a stern lecture on dangerous elements to use together. My guess was that Professor Endel had the same issue with Troy's battle tactic on the spider as I had. So he gave us all a number of different situations and made us drill a bit on where and when to use certain things.

As with all things, time marched forward. Soon enough came the end of the year and the graduation ceremony. I'd never been to one, not that I couldn't, I'd just never wanted to. This year though, I did need to attend, as it was time for one of my best friends to make his exit from our institution.

Dras had already secured a job working for one of the research facilities under Mystien. His skills would have managed it on their own, but I personally prodded the man more than once to make sure that it would happen. Nepotism was alive and well even after the fall of the nobility.

I mused on these as I stood in the audience at his graduation. It was a bit like one from any high school or college on my previous world. There were stands packed with well-wishers as our dean placed a belt on each of the new graduates. It was a wide silk thing, clearly meant to signify status. A number of those in the audience worse similar ones; the colors had changed slightly over the years. You could tell that almost all of the alumni wore blue ones from the former kingdom, while the newer graduates were getting those of a deep black.

There were only separations for those who were family and those who were friends. Though in the past, the nobles had been given the seats closest to the graduating students, no such tradition held anymore. Now, whose parents got to be closest was determined by a set of exit exams. I was proud to say that I could easily see Dras's mother right at the very front.

The clothing on display was kind of . . . weird. The parents and guests tended to wear whatever formal attire they chose, lending an almost party-like atmosphere to the event. The only rules seemed to be that academy graduates wore their sash or a replacement, and some of the more physical-type mages wore shining breastplates. The current students who attended wore their uniforms, with what I assumed to be a slightly different uniform for those in the knight program.

The graduates wore their uniform as well, with a handful of variations. Those who were healers or had taken that class designation wore a variant that had golden threading around the edges. There were a number of other edgings for other specializations too: blue for water, red for fire, green for those who'd gotten high marks in Magical Item Creation classes. Those who'd passed their Combat Spellcasting classes were wearing a set of leather armor. Dras, of course, had a red edging to his uniform, which suited him quite well.

As far as ceremonies went, this one wasn't too bad. Sure it dragged on a bit, but nothing like those on Earth did. Perhaps it had been worse in the past, with nobles and the like, I didn't know, but now it was pretty quick and clean.

Immediately after, everyone split off into groups to go to their various parties. Most of the restaurants in the city were completely packed, and so we had to settle for one that was a slightly lower-class establishment than we might have liked. It was still only a short walk from the academy, but down toward the lower part of the city rather than further into the wealthier parts.

Dras and his father were a riot. I had never really known his dad, but the two of them seemed to be having a grand time. He hadn't ever talked much about it, but from what I understood, his father worked almost nonstop. Tonight though, they were telling jokes and drinking.

About halfway through the festivities, the two of them left his mother and me alone for a bit, having gone to find either more drinks or whatever bard was performing tonight to request songs, there seemed to be an argument on which should be done. Moments after they left, she turned to me.

"Thank you for helping him get into that school," she uttered. It looked like she was eating a lemon as she said it, but the words alone caught me off guard.

"He worked hard for it. I didn't do anything but help him a bit on the path." I tried to look away.

"Don't be modest. It's rude. I don't like you, but without your help, my son would never have achieved his dream," she said, sighing. "So, when can I expect you two to marry then?"

"Never."

"What?"

"Never, it's not like that and hasn't ever been. If you asked him, he'd tell you the same."

She just stared at me for a while, seemingly lost for words. It seemed that even after everything, she still thought I was trying to steal away her son. It was patently ridiculous to me, but in some odd corner of her mind, it probably made sense.

Eventually, the boys returned to us, and Dras came near. His dad looked a bit spent from the night, even if he was having a good time.

"Hey, so one of my classmates is having a party and I just got invited. Do you want to go?" he whispered to me too loudly as he leaned over.

"Sure," I said, grabbing my coat as I looked at his parents.

"Go on, you two have fun." His dad waved us off. As we were leaving, I could swear the man turned to his wife and said "So . . . when are . . ."

After we left, we ended up at the house of one of Dras's friends. One of those who, like him, hadn't been a noble before everything happened, but rather a commoner, well, a merchant's son. This party was impressively similar to the one I'd put on, with the addition of a few new games and a rather well-stocked wine bar instead of cocktails. People were still having a hard time getting ahold of pure enough alcohol, though it seemed that Lucien had spread the spell to a few of his bard friends, as had I.

The evening was fun. The music was good, as was the dancing, and I made it back home before anything troublesome happened.

QUEEN SOPHIA

Today found me in my personal garden. I hummed idly as the vines twisted and re-formed. Botanical magic had always been my personal favorite, the flowers bent to my will and never tried in response to bend me.

"Hello, my love." The calm words caused me to turn.

The voice didn't surprise me, as only one other person was allowed in this room. Not because it was his home, and he could go where he pleased, nor because of some insistence. My dear husband had offered me this private space to do as I pleased, and only after my repeated invitations had joined me.

He was of the opinion that everyone needed somewhere that was theirs alone, someplace that they could go when they wished no disturbance. It was a bit of an odd idea, but a nice one. When I'd been younger, I'd been followed all hours of the day and night by servants, guards, and ministers who'd seen to my every desire. I was told that many who heard that longed for such things, but it was stifling. I never had the chance to just be myself, to do as I wanted without any reports to my parents, or judgment from whatever hangers on I'd been assigned.

It was why I had hated them so, a hatred that had only grown when I'd met Durin. For all of their expectations and desires, he met them with a simple response. He wanted me, not some image of a perfect princess, or a brood mare for royal children. No, he just asked what I wanted, and when he understood, all he wanted from me was myself. I was happy to give it all to him, and in return I gained him, a trade I felt I'd quite won.

"Husband, come and join me." I pulled him over to a pair of chairs as he looked at my current work.

"New project?" His eyes flowed over my work with a light curiosity.

"Not as such, no. Just making a new piece to fill out a spot I don't like."

"Ah I see, it is lovely." He smiled as he looked over at the section I'd been working on.

"I doubt you came here to discuss flowers with me. Is something wrong?"

"Not wrong, my dear. I've simply come to speak with you on the disposition of a few of the more rebellious nobles from your home."

I felt my jaw clench. We'd had a few incidents where some of those who'd made it through the war ended up turning on us after surrendering, or trying to establish contact with my brother and his little band. Frankly, I had little patience for such individuals.

"Do with them what you will. We gave them the option to fall in line, did we not? I see no reason to extend any further kindness if after everything they still won't obey."

"In an ideal world, we could capture your brother and get him to call off his resistance. Force him to abdicate all his claims and live out his life somewhere . . . controlled. As it stands though, that isn't possible, and while I know it irks you, I ask that you temper your anger." He gave me a rather knowing look.

"Those nobles conspired against us; their punishment was just." I stood and faced away. It seems he'd gotten word of how I'd dealt with some nobles from the former lands of Bergond who'd tried to find and join up with my brother. I was completely within my rights as the queen of those lands to hand out whatever punishment I wanted. Not to say that he couldn't overrule me if he really chose to, but in theory I could.

"I am not questioning your displeasure at them, my dear. You've every right to that, but when you confiscated all of their goods you left their families paupers. Now there are children with nowhere to turn, who likely feel resentment to our government. You know, for a fact, what those who are cast out are capable of. I'm merely asking you to see such children are provided for. Allow it to be a show of your kindness." As he spoke, he wrapped his arms about me and I blushed, perhaps I had been a bit hasty in how I'd responded.

"Very well, in the future I'll leave them with enough to live on, and a house or something. They still need to be watched though."

As I turned to face him, he gave me a quick kiss. "Of course, watch them. It may lead us to other rebel cells, and thank you."

"You owe me," I said, pouting upward.

"Oh, and what do I owe you?" In response, I waved my hand and a literal bed made of flowers appeared on a blank patch of soil nearby. Giggling, I escorted him into it.

✦

CHAPTER 35

YEAR FOUR BEGINS

Before I could start my fourth year, there was something I had to do. I didn't want to, well, okay, I kind of did, but at this point, there was no arguments to be had. It was a requirement for my continued participation in classes.

That was why I now found myself in Marcus's shop. No matter how much he complained, he was still the best tailor in the city and I couldn't really go to anyone else. The man himself knew, or at least suspected why I was here and gave me a scathing look as I came up to his counter.

"Marcus."

"No, I already told you no." He didn't even seem to consider what I planned on asking him.

"You are the best in the city, and I trust you more than anyone else with this."

"There are a number of other tailors and dressmakers who will be happy to help you. I had my fill with that little monster Pinea, and . . ."

"And what? If I thought any of the others would do as good a job, then I'd go to them."

He harrumphed, "I've already turned down others. Why shouldn't I turn down you?"

"Because if you do, I'll get one elsewhere and then tell everyone I got it here. I'll upsell it as hard as I can to as many of my companions as possible, and even if it's not as good, I'll make sure they know where to come. Or you could help me out and I can have conveniently forgotten where I purchased it."

"You would actually blackmail me with that? Would you really do such a horrid thing?" He gave me a hard look.

"Eh, probably not, but I'd still be pissy about you turning me down."

"I'll make a deal with you," the grumpy old tailor said as he looked at me.

"Hmm?"

"The rumor is that you came up with a spell to make drinks. Teach me how to do that, and keep that I'm doing this again to yourself, and I'll do it."

I nearly laughed. I would happily have shown him that spell anyway. With a smile, I held out my hand for him, "Deal."

"Come in the back then and let's get this over with."

"Oh come on, it's just a dancing outfit. It's not that bad."

He didn't say anything, instead getting straight to work. It was a marvel to watch the man in his craft. I'd learned enough about this kind of magic to know that what he was doing was the work of a master, honed over years into making what he considered to be works of art.

The whole process took less than an hour. He'd rushed it I was sure, but that didn't mean that it wasn't better than anything else in the city. It had certainly helped that I knew exactly what I wanted, added to the fact that there wasn't much involved in this particular operation. Of note was the fact that while he was working, Marcus had the most peaceful of smiles.

The finished product was perfect. A pair of long panels covered me below the waist, if only barely, hooking onto a bottom that much like Pinea's looked like it didn't really exist. The top was a more complex affair than hers had been, with off-the-shoulder bits and several cords peppered with decoration.

After trying it on and the last few adjustments I changed back into my normal clothing. I wasn't my friend, and wouldn't try to cause problems in the city. As I returned to the front with the outfit in a small box to pay the tailor scowled at me.

"You always seem so grumpy, but you also seem to enjoy the work." I quirked a brow at him.

"Just because I like making clothes does not mean I like dealing with people, particularly when those people can be a thorn in my side."

"I'll admit to being a pain in the neck, but at least I gave you something different to work on."

He rubbed his temples. "I'm married, you knew that, right? I think the outfits are lovely, and making them is a challenge, but . . . Well, I don't really like seeing women other than my wife half-naked, makes me feel disloyal. Also, it's weird with some of you girls. I've known some of you since you were children."

I grimaced a bit as I finally understood his objections. Perhaps I had been more pushy than I should have. As I looked back up at Marcus and put away my new clothing, I sighed.

"I won't tell anyone where I got it. To be true I had to for school, the professor insists that fourth years have one, and I wanted the best I could get."

He huffed, but on my way out he called after me. "Oh, girl, your measurements have changed a bit since you were last in. Come by when you need to get your skirts lengthened again, and I'll handle it for you." That was about the best that I was getting as confirmation that he'd forgiven me. Either that or he was telling me I was gaining weight, which I certainly wasn't.

School settled in much as it was before. As more new students came in, I couldn't help but notice that not only were the classes bigger, but they also contained almost no members of what I would refer to as members of the "former noble" faction. Sure, some of them were former nobles from one place or another, but of those, they didn't fall in with the remnants of the malcontents, not that there were many of those left now anyway.

We now had to dress out before Atali Dance. Professor Etia would unceremoniously oust any girl who didn't show up in a proper outfit, something I suspected she wanted to do from year one, but had been forbidden to enact. Now though, we were at the mercy of her demand.

I looked better than most of my peers did on this account, matching well with Pinea and even getting a nod of approval as our teacher went over our outfits on the second class of the year. That was good, as I would have hated to be in the group of two or three who she outright told needed to get replacements.

Other changes happened in Combat Spellcasting. For one, we had far larger groups for our exercises now, and we were all drilled hard on monsters like we never had been before. We also got a new spell to learn that would help us retrace our steps in certain encounters. Everyone was expected to learn it and it was fairly similar to what the item we'd had did. Professor Endel seemed to think this was needed so that we could go backward, should we ever enter something like the undercity again.

The biggest changes by far though happened in Magical Item Creation. Both sides of that class had spent years drilling us with the basics and now we were getting to some really juicy things. We all knew the sequences well enough that we had a good understanding of how to make them work, but this year focused on making them work together in ever complex ways.

Our first major project was an item that moved through a series of different steps based on a few input runes. These could be touched to turn them off or on and allowed for a much wider array of function. That, in itself, was very cool, but I now finally realized why the core had been putting so much more emphasis on the movement of physical items than our normal class did. It allowed for things like dials and items that would run through ever-increasing complex designs.

With the mixture of what I was learning in both, I even managed to create an item that would change the active sequence based on some inputs. The changes weren't too big, mostly moving one section for another, but because the runes were tied as they were, it was just possible to do. I got the feeling that the designer of the guide knew how to do this, too, based on what I was seeing. I also felt that he'd forgotten to write down specifics on it. This form of change went in my "do-not-tell-anyone-about-this-for-now" bucket while I looked into its current existence in society.

With those changes going on, I fell hard into my own personal research. The sewing spell was going quite well, and I was now confident that I could meet my mother's expectations with ease, which was good enough for me to let it to the side for now. Portals were still a beast, but as I practiced and worked out the kinks I could almost feel the mana cost reducing. High-cost magic worked like that, and before too long, I could portal myself across my room. It was hard, but possible.

Most of my nights I spend working on either my core or the guide though. I was getting close in the latter to completion, and from there it would only be a matter of finding a way to securely make something akin to an appendix, or at least a physical copy with page numbers, and chapter headings, and a freaking table of contents.

It was on one of these nights in the spring as I worked through my current chapter that I found it. Clear, concise directions, written as a note down below a major section. I wanted to scream and rage, and beat whomever wrote this with a stick as I read through it. It was all so simple. Why did they have to be such a damn bastard about it!

CHAPTER 36

✦

"HELP"

The "help" menu flashed up before me as I brought it up. I was more than a bit pissed that this was how he had decided to do it, but whatever. I casually wrote out a small code in it, a simpler version of my lamp code, that only used a small rune as an off/on switch. The whole thing took maybe a minute to do.

When I hit "go," I was bombarded with the amount of messages the thing gave. First and foremost was the initial one, saying that it *should* work in the real world, followed by a number of notes and comments on other ideas and improvements.

The first was one of the problems that led to issues with larger sequences in this world, namely that they had to be manually tried out. There was a long history of people writing sequences that pushed the limits of what could be done, only for there to be some critical error somewhere in the coding. Since each and every one had to be basically handwritten, this could cause immense delays in trying to figure out what, where, and how to fix it. The initial function of "help" was to test it out, to see if there were any such critical errors.

Just below this was the copy/paste button for putting my now checked code into something. A function that had I been paying attention to my physical body would have caused a small twitch on one of my eyes. It truly would be a great help in making new items going forward.

Below this was a mass of information. First came the list of basic functions and definitions of exactly what they did. This had a drop-down menu attached so it could be hidden easily. There were even implications that it could form more drop-downs for various sections. Below that there was a list of similar and suggested functions, along with their definitions, more like a "Hey! I see you're using a touch switch, have you considered a verbal switch? Or a thermal one? Or a physical on/off clicker? Try one of these!"

After the functions were listed, with their annoying suggestions, came the properties we were using. It recognized that I was making light, and so included was a few important notes on it. It had various wavelengths and what they could be used for, definitions on how that was all decided, and finally a color picker for visible light. The last bit looked like it had been stolen straight from some Earth drawing program, and would let you choose an image before it output the wavelength.

The worst part was the little blue coloration to some of the words in all of it. With an internal scream of rage, I mentally poked one, only to see the relevant section of the guide pop up before me. That bastard had gone through all of this effort, and he hadn't even put in basic bits so that people reading the guide could navigate it. It was just fucking irresponsible!

I was also confused a bit. How had nobody ever found this, even by accident. Well, obviously someone had, but had found the whole mess so incomprehensible that they'd never shared that. Worse, someone might have understood and gone to great lengths to translate the English, and then really start learning. It would still be really, almost impossibly hard, but with a few codes to use as a Rosetta Stone, then it might just be possible.

Since nobody had told me it meant one of two things. In thousands of years, nobody had written a sequence in the "help" menu, unlikely but possible, or, they had, and had kept it either secret, or considered it unimportant. The final option was honestly pretty likely too. If someone didn't realize what they'd wandered into, then they might well just ignore it, or only tell a few people as a novelty. Many secrets had been lost that way.

I closed everything down and sat up in my bed, where I rubbed my temples. I had quite a bit to think about. Had someone else found this? Had they understood the English? Why wasn't it well known?

The answer to the first question was that yes, some probably had found it. That much was easy to guess.

Had they understood the English? Well, I did, and I was guessing that at least one or two others had been born from my world into this one, so they may have. So again, there had probably been a few at least who understood parts of it.

Finally, I had to consider why it wasn't well known. It was possible that there was some cabal somewhere that read English almost as good as a native speaker and was working hard at being monstrously powerful. It was far more likely that if anyone knew what it did, or how to read parts of it they kept it to themselves, and perhaps their children.

Magic users were a bit secretive about their advancements. These things could change large swaths of society and any little shred of power was one to be hoarded in the mind of the average wizard. There was nothing like Wikipedia, or even the idea that knowledge should be free. I knew from my education here that this place itself only bestowed what we needed, and my guess was that the professors were learning and hoarding secrets of their own.

If there was someone else out there using these menus like I was, then I wouldn't be surprised. I also couldn't blame them for hoarding it, as I wouldn't be sharing my own knowledge, at least for now. Perhaps one day, I'd be able to teach others, but that day was not today. I could just use it and add it to my list of "don't tell anyone, not even those close to me" with my portal spell.

With a sigh, I lay down on my bed. If nothing else this was going to make my grades in Magical Item Creation go straight to the top of my class. Thinking on that I finally fell asleep for the night.

As my year continued, I realized that being a fourth year here was a bit different, mostly in that as it wore on more and more of my classmates came of age. Since birthdays weren't really celebrated here we knew based on season, I was in the first batch of us to turn eighteen, of course, alone with only one or two others.

It came with a number of extra responsibilities and freedoms as far as the law was concerned, but so far as my day-to-day life, not much changed. My family had a small, brief celebration of my coming to age, but it wasn't seen as that big of a deal.

The onset of puberty was a much bigger deal for girls, but my family had missed that. I hadn't talked with anyone about that kind of thing so nobody had known, but normally that was given some celebration. Traditions like that still weirded me out sometimes, but what could I say? It was normal for everyone else around me, so there was nothing to do about it.

I didn't even have to worry about finding a job, something that most in the end of their third year, and certainly in their fourth were concerned about. Those of us who would have to work, or who wanted to take an apprenticeship somewhere to learn more about our chosen subjects were scrambling. On the other hand, I was pretty much told where I'd be working when the time came, not that I really wanted to work anywhere else. Mystien's labs would certainly be one of the most interesting places in the city, and while it may not be as lighthearted or fun as working in a tavern, I knew that I'd get a peek behind the curtain. Seeing the secrets was all the inducement I really needed.

I mused on this as I stepped through one of my portals. It didn't really go anywhere, just the other side of my room. The sensation was not quite the same as those that the emperor was using, but these were set up on the fly instead of items, some discrepancy was to be expected.

I had to take a moment when I stepped out. I still had enough mana to keep on at it for a while, but I had real worries about what would happen to me if I were to run out of mana midtrip and had therefore set up my own safety rules while practicing. The first among these was that I should have what I estimated to be three times as much mana as I needed for any trip I took personally.

While the mana drain these things put out was a monster, practice with any spell made it that much easier. I knew this from personal experience as time and time again I'd had to develop my own magic, and this was no different. Now, what I needed was to work on this spell until it was almost innate, shaving down the drain bit by bit until it was more manageable.

A knock on my door pulled me from my thoughts. "Come in," I said, looking up to see who it was.

"Good evening, dear." My mother opened the door slowly and joined me, finding a seat. "Alana, I know that you hate it when I get involved, but . . ."

"But?"

"Well, every time you come home, all you do is sit in here and work on your core or magic. You need to go out, make friends, attend balls, perhaps look into potential . . ." She didn't need to finish, as we were both aware.

"Mother, I spend my time at home relaxing. You know as well as I that my schedule at school doesn't allow me much of that." It did happen that I found practicing magic to be one of my favorite hobbies and almost never got tired of it.

"I know, dear, but, there are several events you could go to. Or at least pretend you want to go to. Most of the girls around here are at least looking into their future prospects, and you seem to be . . . well, ignoring them. I worry that one day you'll find yourself an old maid."

"Is this really a conversation we need to have right now?"

"If not now, then when? As it turns out though, now is a good time. I just got a list of parties that are being held, and we have invitations to several. I was hoping that you might choose a few to attend with your father and me."

"Mother, my history with formal events is . . . rather mixed."

"I know, but you need to go to at least a few. If it helps, your brother is being pulled along too." That gave me an idea.

"Shouldn't you be having this conversation with him too? He's a good bit older than I and still has nobody." If bothered by your parents, deflect onto a sibling, this was a hard rule in every universe.

"His issue is different. He's had a few . . . dalliances, but nothing that stays. Men are different, too, dear, as you well know. If he gets married when he's forty, there will still be no problem. The emperor himself is a good example."

I pouted at the unfairness of it all. "Fine, I'll go to a few, but no promises on finding anyone."

"That's all I ask, dear." With that, my mother left, leaving in her wake a list.

I knew a few children of some of the families listed. Boys and girls who were in my classes, or at least attended the academy. Mother had gone through the hassle of even listing out who had children at my school and their names, along with the names of several other figures from each of those on her list and brief descriptions. I couldn't help but notice that she'd focused on single men. It annoyed me, but if she'd gone through all the trouble to compile or have this made for me the least I could do was be bored at a few balls for her.

✦

CHAPTER 37

TRIALS AND EXAMINATIONS

I found myself bored as expected at one of the parties mother had suggested. It wasn't the worst thing in the world, just not really my scene. We were around half a dozen dances in and while I was participating, my heart just wasn't in it.

"I think I like your parties better," Dras said as he moved over to my side.

He was attending for similar reasons to myself, ostensibly to find a spouse. The main difference being that he seemed to be taking the whole matter more to heart then I was and was clearly enjoying himself at least a little.

"Thanks, how are things?"

"Well, care to dance?"

"Certainly."

We caught up a bit as we danced. He told me how he liked his current job. The research was fun apparently, and he was getting to learn a lot of specialist things. I was left out on specifics of course, since he worked for the military, but I was glad he was happy. Near the end of it all, he pulled me to the side to speak more though.

"Hey, Alana, be careful, okay?"

"About what?" I asked, my brow quirked.

"Rumblings from up north. Nobody is really talking about it, but many nobles who were unhappy with the regime change are disappearing, while the others are staying oddly quiet. Nobody knows for sure if something's up, but . . ."

"I'll make sure not to take too many wild adventures for now then."

"Thanks."

It was nice to have someone plugged into the current regime who would actually tell me anything. Dad and Mystien both thought that I needed to be protected for my own good but also kept well away from anything important. They may have kind of had a point as being near important things tended to end with me coming up with new and over-powered magic, but it was annoying, nonetheless.

From there, we separated, and some guy who looked like his baby teeth hadn't even fallen out tried to woo me with another dance and a drink. I was polite, but he wasn't at all the kind of person I was interested in. The party continued muchly thus, and I lamented the fact that I couldn't find many people who appealed to me at all.

The parties continued on through the spring when I finally got a short respite. A few weeks just after planting, many of the bigwigs needed to go over their numbers. Who had put what in the ground, how much, where, and what the general condition of the soil looked like? There would be a lot more breaks like this in autumn, but I'd take what I could get.

So I returned to school and my daily life.

One evening after all of our classes had finished, I came upon a group of circling, giggling fourth-years. Pinea was at their head, and upon seeing her I moved to her side.

"What's up?" I asked. She jumped a little and then pulled me into their little circle with an evil smile.

"Alana, you're here, I'm so glad, we were discussing setting up some orders." She spoke so low that we all had to lean close. "You see poor Menae here is getting married at the end of the year, and her future hus-band is . . ."

"He's nice, just kind of . . ." the girl in question said.

"Right, right, so we're going to get her some . . . helpers, from a shoe-maker in town. He uses wood and metal to make things she can use to push things along at night."

I wanted nothing to do with this order, but the way my friend had latched onto my arm, and the terrible mistakes I felt like they were about to make made me speak up.

"One, find somewhere more private to discuss this than the common room, good grief there are first-years around. Two, that sounds disgust-ing, wood and leather? It'll be almost impossible to clean. You need some-thing like metal or glass, and if you didn't mind using a bit of magic . . ." I then broke them down several basic designs that would be found in any number of locations on Earth.

I got a bevy of stunned looks. At some point, Kala had joined our little group and even she was wide-eyed. As they blinked a few more times, it was Pinea who pulled me over.

"I never knew, Alana. You must have spent some time on those designs. Why don't you sell a few, or at least the sequences? I'm sure we could get you a good price."

"I've never made such a thing in my life. If you want to use my suggestions, go ahead, but leave me out of it." I tried to pull away only to have Pinea hold me tight.

"Don't you at least have the sequences?" Pinea begged.

"No."

"Well . . . you are the best in our year. Could you write one for me?"

"Didn't I say leave me out of it?" I said as I glared at her.

"You know that favor you owe me, Alana, about the maid?" She could not seriously be trying to cash in a years old debt now. "I'd like to use it."

I gave her a deadpan look. "Fine."

It took me less than an hour to write up something that would fit in an apprentice-level core, along with a few design notes. About a week after passing those off to Pinea, I was gifted a small box and a dirty look by my erstwhile friend.

As I made my way through my final year of school, I felt terribly alone. Other than Pinea, who was a pain at the best of times, most of my close friends were now gone. Dras had graduated, Charles had never been one to go to our school, only appearing every now and then, but even he seemed to be absent a bit more in recent months, and Kala . . .

I cared for Kala, but there was still awkwardness there. We couldn't come to a good conclusion on how to speak to each other, how to deal with where we stood. There were attempts, to be sure, but neither of us could go back to how things had been, and we both knew it. Perhaps in some years things would work their way into a normal friendship again, I could hope at least.

I mused on this as I stood atop a tower at our school, looking out at the city below. The lights and sounds filtered up to me, hanging in the summer air. I had only one more season to go, only one last push until I reached the next stage. I didn't honestly look forward to it that much. I'd graduated high school once and knew that it didn't make anything better. I could feel the wind around me, pushing me gently forward to my next destination, and I faced it with a light melancholy.

Mid-autumn marked the beginning of our examinations. Most of these were much like one would expect from an Earth class, simple written tests on what we had learned. There were a few exceptions though, and these were of note.

There were also practical aspects in our classes that needed them. In Atali Dance, I had to perform a routine for Professor Etia; in my instrument classes, I needed to run through a piece of music. All of the spell-casting classes made us display some of what we'd learned, mostly small tricks here and there.

Magical Item Creation was a beast of an exam. After the written portion, we were given a full afternoon to create an item from scratch. We weren't told what it would need to be ahead of time, but instead given a small sheet of paper with instructions on what it needed to do. They were all fairly straightforward: a heater that responds to adjust, based on the ambient temperature and manual controls; a light with three methods of activation; or other such things. Mine was "a floating object that can support a person's weight." There was a list of how each needed to function, but nothing too grandiose. That was mostly because my classmates were almost all still stuck on the apprentice level of their core and couldn't make anything with too many lines of coding.

I pulled a face upon reading it; this was too easy. I designed a chair of one of the more magically reactive woods. They were all subpar, but there was a type of pine from the western coast that worked passably well if you didn't mind having to spend tons of mana on it. I could have used metal, but the downside would have been weight, requiring more mana as well, and being dangerous.

The tools for shaping it were already set out for us, and we'd worked with those for years, so making a basic wooden chair shape was simple enough, a few holes and cuts and I had something that would be functional, if a bit uncomfortable.

The sequence as well was simplistic, just an upward force if the bottom was less than three feet from the ground. I made it limit its power to only equal that that was being placed down upon it, but that was not too bad. As a fun add-on, I threw in an on/off switch and a limiter on speed to keep it from acting like a catapult if someone turned it on while sitting on it, and I was done.

My grade on that one was quite good. I saw a few others have some of their attempts not go quite as planned, but by the end of the day, everyone seemed to have a functional version of whatever they were given.

Along with the written exam on theory of war, Combat Spellcasting had a brief practical. Professor Endel met each of us in the arena at a specified time, and after showing him some of our spells, we had to engage in a short duel. None of us were expected to beat the old war-mage, but we had to show what we'd learned.

He and I faced off for one last time. I'd been informed that he was wearing armor that would protect him from any lighting, so I went hog wild. The arena was littered with illusions, fake footsteps to make it look like I'd gone invisible, swaths of melted sand, and the small sticks that represented sedatives.

I danced along the side of the arena throwing spell after spell at him from as many directions as I could manage. Each and every one seemed to bounce off of his shields and defenses as he responded with something that looked rather like one of those old bullet dodging arcade games. He couldn't find me, so his next best option was to fill the whole arena with projectiles and hope that one hit.

I launched a thunderbolt down from the sky only to see it absorbed by the bubble of magic protecting him. The arena shook as it turned into harmless light and sound. Since nothing else was working, I went back to basics. I was only one or two spells out from being spent and needed to strike something decisive, so I loosed my strongest scream on him.

It seemed he'd neglected his sonic protections, and while most of it was taken by his own aura, I got him to stumble, nearly falling to his knees. Sadly, he seemed to have accurately guessed my position and with one final push filled the whole area with magic, enough to break my own shielding and drop me, ending the fight.

I let myself lie there, chest heaving as my breath came in gasps. A brief look confirmed that Endel was much better off, if still tired, he huffed a bit as he walked over to where I lay.

"Good showing, full marks. I'll give you a recommendation to the army if you want. I still know a few people." He offered a hand which I gratefully took, letting myself be pulled back up.

"I'll pass. I've already taken a job in research sir."

"That is a shame, you'd do very well. Well then, I'll see you at graduation."

"Yes, sir, thank you, for everything." He gave me a smile as we walked out, patting my shoulder a bit as he saw me off.

CHAPTER 38

✦

LEAVING THE ACADEMY

I stood before my mirror in the clothes that would serve as my under layer before graduation. The black quilted cloth hugged my body tightly like a second skin, warming and comforting as I prepared for my big day.

"Nervous, Miss?" my maid asked, standing to the side.

"A bit if I'm honest, but nothing for it."

"That's the spirit, come now, let's get you ready." As she spoke, she pulled the first piece of armor off of its rack.

My armor was that which I'd been given years ago after the attacks that left me still a bit nervous during storms. There had been a few small changes for this occasion, but nothing that would disturb the enchantments. It now shone black, with a few decorations indicating my place and the like in my class, a deep green with small golden threading. Here and there were a few spots that had been scuffed and damaged over the years, but in this world that wasn't seen as a mark of shame, it merely showed that I'd seen combat. What armor would suit me better than that which had seen me through battle already and out whole to the other side?

Based on her expressions, I thought the girl dressing me was having a great time acting like a squire would for any knight. Save after the armor went on, she had to do up my hair in a severe updo to fit under my helmet, an item that I would carry until we reached the field.

Our class was small, well, compared to the graduating classes from years ago, we were larger, but I still compared this to my own high school from my past life. Here our numbers ranged in the hundreds, and not high in that. As I reached the staging location, it was easy to see and put a name to all of the faces, all of those who'd seen our way through this academy together.

Before long, we made our way to the arena, standing there in the bright winter sun. I hadn't noticed during Dras's graduation, but they must have used magic to both heat it and remove the snow that was beginning to fall at this time of year. While I remember the stands being a bit chilly, the area where we were was not so.

After a few short speeches and a handful of names, I was called to the front. My heart pounded as I took the stairs one by one to the podium where our dean stood. The smiling man reached out and tied a midnight black sash around my waist.

As he did so, I let my eyes move up a bit. I hadn't looked for my parents before, not wanting to fidget, but there they were, sitting right on the front row and smiling, my brother and his shit-eating grin right beside them. Directly above and behind, I saw Dras, Lucien, and Mystien, of course. They'd have to have pulled a lot of strings to get that many in, and thankfully they'd stood right in line with my family; someone had thought of the perfect positioning.

Before long, the ceremony was over, my family meeting me as we all left, walking along the path that led to our carriage.

"You look good in that armor, dear, it suits you well," Dad said as I approached him.

"Trying to recruit me to the army?" I raised an eyebrow as I walked up to give him a hug.

"Never. I don't want you to have to see battle again, not ever again. Though that capture unit you escaped has made offers . . ."

"I'll pass on that." I shook my head, the army wasn't a place I wanted to go, not now, not ever.

"Good, let's go to your party then." With that, we all piled into the carriage, one of the plainer ones, and it shot off down the road.

The ride seemed to go on and on, and I was getting a bit confused as we finally stopped. It shouldn't have been that far to go to one of the eateries in the upper city. When the doors finally opened, I understood. My family had guessed, and quite correctly, that I might enjoy a bit of a different party than some fancy ball, and they'd brought me to the perfect place.

The Starlit Sky stood there, as it always had, with one change. A small sign by the door indicated that the bar would be closed for the evening for a private event. I nearly ran up the stairs to my once home and flew inside to see the smiling faces of all of my friends. Some of them wouldn't have been comfortable in some elegant restaurant, but here they were spread out chatting.

The staff had gone above and beyond with the food. Between them and my parents, they knew all of my favorites, the soups and roasts that I liked best, a light herb salad, all ending with paw-paw ice cream. I was told the last bit was my brother's idea.

We sang and chatted, told stories, and as we did, I looked around. I couldn't help but notice a few of the changes. Everyone was decidedly older. I'd known some of the people here for most of my life; hairs had grayed, and skin had developed new wrinkles. Dras and Charles were both way different than they'd been as boys. If I wasn't mistaken, Lude, The Sky's cook had a bit of a bump. I suppose her marriage to Jackson was going well; so did a rather familiar-looking redhead who was hanging off of Mystien's arm. I'd have to figure out who she was later.

After a short time, Kala made her appearance. She'd had her own celebration to attend and looked a bit awkward joining mine, but we quickly pulled her in, letting her jump in on all of our fun. After a few strained moments, I pulled her to the side.

"I'm glad you came." I gave her a smile as she moved closer to me.

"Yeah . . . it's good to be here."

I had a few things I could have done. We could have had some mopey, sad talk, or perhaps made up and . . . No, both of us knew that in this society, at this time, there would be no long-term future, and there was no need to go through that pain again. I did still care for her though, so instead of bringing the mood down . . .

"Hey, I hear Pinea's throwing a party tonight, you coming?" I gave her my brightest, most inviting grin.

"Of course, who would miss that?"

With a few words, we gathered up our peers and headed upward into the city. I think my parents had known this would happen and prepped a carriage, because we had no issues on that front. The small black vehicle rolled and rolled, and eventually stopped in front of a massive house that was clearly our destination because of the many lights and loud music emanating from the structure.

I'd thrown a party, but Pinea, that night put on a rager that would have made the most debauched fraternity proud. She had learned from my good example at least, and a number of casters were periodically curing poison, particularly for those leaving the main room. No worries about roofies or anyone being too drunk here.

I crashed in one of her spare rooms, of which there were many. As I made my way out the next morning, I found that I was not the only one who'd failed to make it home. Sleeping and sleepy people were strewn about the first floor of her mansion, some stumbling out of rooms, some on couches or the floor.

Before long, a disheveled Kala made her way out of a nearby room, and not alone. As I went to see her, the young man she'd been in there with blushed and rushed off to busy himself. She was nearly laughing as she joined me.

"Have a good time?" Pinea said as she appeared beside us, pulling us in and making wiggly eyebrows at Kala.

"Yes, actually, I did," the priestess responded.

"Excellent! So, um . . . I may have underestimated one or two things, don't suppose I could ask for a bit of help?" she said as she looked at the mess of people.

"Sure." It was no skin off my back to cast a few spells.

"I suppose that's a reasonable request," Kala said, as she took in the chaos that surrounded them.

"You work on the hangovers while Pinea and I take care of breakfast?"

"Sounds good."

A few moments later, a small table of bread, cheese, jam, and lots and lots of water was set up, and people were slowly making their way over to nurse themselves before returning home.

A few days later, I reported to my first day working for Mystien. I still had to go through his insane security protocols, something that I was told would be run every day that I came in. The facility was too secure for all of that to be waved for any reason.

It had grown since I was last here, either that or I'd only been shown the barest amount of it before, I was unsure. We passed room after room with perhaps a dozen others working for the old mage working on various tasks.

"So . . . what am I doing exactly?" I asked as he led me to a smaller room with a desk and a number of tools.

"For now, I need you working on a few different tasks. They tell me you're good at rune sequences so I'd like you to go over a few that we're having issues with; those are nothing too major, but tools we think we'll need and need to be made on-site. Other than that, I need you to catch up with our current state of affairs."

Great, get out of school for more education and what sounded like apprentice work. I raised an eyebrow at him.

"So I'm just making items?"

"For now," he said, glaring. "What do you know of the mage Ristolian?"

"Not much, he was supposedly a genius wizard who did some really impressive magic, including . . . Am I allowed to talk about that here?" He was also probably from another world, just like me.

"You are, this facility deals with a number of things, but those gates are our biggest project. Everyone here knows, and is secure to know. Good on you for making sure. Yes, Emperor Durin's home was also built by him, as you might have guessed, and there were a number of things there that have been . . . mysterious, but useful. A lot of writings and important bits on rune sequences particularly."

"And I need to go through those, and I'm guessing some of your notes, to understand your work?"

"Correct. After that . . . well, some of the things we've found indicate that Ristolian didn't write everything down, particularly not some of the more important bits involving the Alcubierre Gates. He did, on the other hand, leave information about where he learned some of his secrets. The expedition isn't ready yet, won't be for another year or two, but I'll need people I can trust on that one. Are you interested?"

CHAPTER 39

✦

A DAY IN THE OFFICE

Jobs were . . . well, they were jobs. There was no getting around the fact that what I was doing wasn't particularly fun. It was informative, but not particularly fun. At the moment, the biggest push on my abilities was the studying of the current information.

From what the researchers could tell Ristolian had recovered information on how to make the gates from elsewhere, some ruins on the Elven continent. Part of the team was working on figuring out exactly which ones and where, but they were running into issues. The reports of the location was from diaries that were hundreds of years old. Add that to the fact that there were few maps of that continent, and what there were weren't really up-to-date or of a known accuracy and you find big problems.

They were quite unsure of anything more than the general area, one which accounted for several cities. The efforts to parse that down to something bit by bit were slow, but they were making some progress by guessing things based on his day-to-day experiences.

The maps were also a massive issue. There was nothing like GPS here, so mapping was . . . primitive; it depended on people who were not really that good at measuring distances between large areas and lines that were not always straight. This meant that two maps of a given area might agree for instance that one city was west of another, but they might not know how far that would be as a crow flies, or at what angle. There were implications that larger organizations or countries might have truly accurate ones, but those were considered close to a state secret.

My other duty, of examining tools and making sure they work was . . . quite frankly a bit easy. Sure I was supposed to go over a lot of the information that the researchers had, or that our historical benefactor had left, but most of it was just basic. With the "help" menu, I could find their flaws in almost record time, and while the ancient magus had no doubt known a lot, most of what they found educational wise was from the guide.

Literally, much of it was transcribed directly from the guide, Ristolian had added a few notes here and there, and his explanations were much better, but the biggest chunk of the information was straight out of the guide, he even used a lot of the same exercises. This man had done what I might otherwise have and made a basic textbook that went into a lot of the nuances of making the system work. He did leave out the explanation on the "help" menu though, as well as not saying where he got the information. I suspect that this was to hide some of the knowledge that he didn't want disseminated.

It seemed that my predecessor had wanted to open a school at some point, so he'd written down a lot of information on basic magic and education, as well as philosophy and governance. Most of the latter bared a strong resemblance to Earth ideals, as well as what Emperor Durin was trying to put forward. Some of it looked like it needed ironing out, and Ristolian hadn't actually ever opened his school, but it looked like he'd laid the groundwork well. I suspected that Lord Durin's home was supposed to be Ristolian's academy.

I inquired, but nobody knew what had happened to the ancient mage. There was also the possibility that they weren't telling me, or Emperor Durin hadn't told them. In the end, Ristolian was probably dead now, as it had been hundreds of years.

It was a few months in, and I was sitting at my desk designing a tool to measure heat to a fraction of a degree. My pen scratched out line after line as I consulted various reference books and our design specifications. This job wasn't anything complex but was needed for some experiment in the labs. Why the researchers in charge of it didn't have one already I didn't know, but as a trainee I was making one for them.

"What are you doing here?" A small hand reached over my shoulder to point at one section in the code.

"It's a read-out, the base design in our standard book one on page three hundred thirty-five."

My partner in training gave me a look, her frizzy brown hair bobbing around her waist as she turned to look at a page I already had open.

"It's surreal to me that you can work like that?"

"What?"

"You seem to rush through these like it's nothing, and it always works."

"Selene, I'm almost literally copying it verbatim from the books."

Selene pouted at me, crinkling up her nose. "Yeah, but yours always work. I can never get mine to work when I need a different layout or readout or whatever."

To be true I was using the "help" function to iron out a lot of bugs. I understood most of what I needed for them, but if I ran into something that I didn't, or couldn't figure out on my own after an hour or two, I just ran it through the menu to be done with it.

I shrugged. "I'm pretty sure this is all just busywork anyway."

"What?"

"Well, do you honestly think they don't have something that can give a readout like this? Perhaps they want one a little different for convenience, but they don't actually need it."

"Then why have us make all this crap?" She pointed at several of the bits and bobs all over our office room.

"Well, isn't that obvious? You're going on the same expedition as I am. What will we do if we end up out in the middle of nowhere and need some random tool? We'll have to be able to make it. Same reason they have us working on our Atali, or the other crap we get roped into." I pointed to the little pamphlets on Elven flora and fauna that were sitting nearby.

We'd been tested on some basic survival stuff, but nothing too intense. I wasn't sure but I thought that was partially because we were not in charge of that, and partially because from what I understood the Elven continent was just too different. It sounded tropical as opposed to our native land's almost far northern climate.

Selene looked at me with a frown. She was an interesting girl, a couple of years my senior and no slouch when it came to magic. The little wizard girl had gotten top marks, and much like me had few suitors, though for different reasons. While I rebuffed most of them, she didn't seem to get many.

She wasn't ugly, as such. Most of the people in this world were quite fit, and while there were some that didn't have great bone structure, that was rather odd. She just didn't really seem to care how she looked. Her hair was always left a mess, badly in need of a comb and cut, and she always had ink stains all over her hands and dresses. It was like she didn't really care. I had to respect that.

"It would be nice if they could just get us going already, I hate just waiting," Selene complained.

"Seconded, but I'd rather it be done right than rushed and waste a year or two roaming around in the jungle." It was also not going to be a small venture. My last count was somewhere around twenty people on three ships.

We worked through the afternoon until the time came to head home. There were no windows of course, and we only knew the time based on a number of clocks here and there, several of which I'd had a hand in building.

Our manager, Olnir, was there the next morning. He was a stereotypical middle-manager type, middle-aged and with a stick firmly up his rectum. While I still dealt with Mystien every now and then, this guy handled a lot of the day-to-day operations along with training. I could say without a doubt that he didn't like me at all; luckily, I was too competent for him to have any real complaints.

"Good morning, ladies," he sounded like the last word was some kind of poison, "Please join me, we've got some things to go over."

The two of us just shrugged as we looked at each other and followed the man down the hall. It wasn't often that we were given anything other than paperwork to go over, and frankly anything would be a nice break. It had only been a couple of months, and I was already hating doing this job, had I not been promised a big payout in the end, I'd walk right now.

We went deeper into the facility than we had ever gone before, passing labs here and there and finally coming to one that was absolutely massive. The size was probably because of the two gates at either end.

These looked almost like those that were used to get to and from Emperor Durin's home, with a few exceptions. They were smaller and of a slightly different color. They were also brand-new as opposed to the ancient structures that I knew worked.

"Wow," Selene said.

"We're running a test today. Please stay out of the way of the full researchers."

I could see a number of folks in robes going here and there, checking instruments and measurements. Mystien stood to the side, watching over all of it with critical eyes.

"Ready," he said, as he made a motion to a man at what appeared to be a control panel. At which point, several levers were pulled, and I could almost feel the mana in the room.

"No issues so far, sir, the mana is flowing just as it should," the man replied after a second or two.

"Good, connect." At his word, another lever was pulled, and it all went awry.

For the barest of seconds, there was a pushing and pulling around the portals, their insides flicking a crimson shade. A heartbeat later, they spat distortions into the air, space around each filling with motes of light and discharges of energy. As the item crashed, the mana violently ripped through the stone gateways, the rock they were composed of cracking like a gunshot as pieces shot outward.

As I saw the shards fly I tried to put up a barrier, only to find it pointless. One was already established around the items, keeping all the shrapnel contained in a small place. Several smoking chunks of rock bounced off of the protections and lay there, looking like meteorites within their little protective bubbles.

The leader of this brigade came to join us. He looked slightly displeased, but not terribly surprised. "Enjoy the show?"

"I'm sure you'll get it next time, sir," Olnir said.

"I doubt it. What about you two?" He similarly seemed unimpressed by the brown-nosing.

"It was . . . impressive, even if it didn't make a working gate."

"What were you trying to do?" I looked at the rubble as the wizards came to float the bits away for examination on nearby tables.

"Good question, our goal in this test was to try and have the insides of the gateways be defined as the same location. It's one of several methods we've tried, none of which have worked."

"How?" Selene cocked her head.

"Another good question. We know that the gates use a module, which is somehow adding another few runes to the sequences. We're unsure if we've managed that properly, though we think we have. If that is the case, then we need to figure out what those runes are doing, because whatever it is, is not known to us."

"What have you tried?" I asked, curious as to what they were doing.

"This test was trying to define the inside of the gates as the same place. We also made an attempt at having it defined as something entering one instantly exiting the other. That test worked much like this. We even tried to have them pull the insides of each other to their own inside. That was one of our more successful tests, in that rather than exploding they both shot across the room at high speed and collided."

I blinked; they hadn't even considered bending space. It wasn't that these men weren't smart, because they certainly were, and they also knew their craft. It was that nobody had made that logical leap. There was no paradigm shift into thinking of space as something that could bend and warp.

"Well, what's next, sir?" Olnir asked.

"Nothing, it takes too long to code these, and there's something missing. We'll fiddle with the connection magic to make sure we have something working, but until the expedition is over, we'll hold off on another attempt."

"But if you could . . ." Selene perked up.

"We have other projects, wasting funds and time when we have other ways forward is useless, which is why I'm hoping you lot succeed. Once we get a lead on what they're supposed to do, we can probably make real progress. Until then, I want you working on understanding the modules. The information on that cannot leave this room though. You'll also be doing exercises with some of your compatriots twice a week now that you're sufficiently ready."

After my teacher had turned and left, our manager looked at us. "I think it's too soon, but if he says so . . . There are a few things we'll need to go over." It took me half a beat to realize what he'd said as he was speaking Atali as he did so.

CHAPTER 40

✦

THE PRINCE'S GAMBITS

THE NORTHERN REACHES
OF THE EMPIRE OF SHADOWS

Men poured into the small facility. Days had passed as they'd pounded this hidden location with spell after spell of artillery. Once they'd finally breached the barrier, they'd been met with traps and a handful of golems. That paltry resistance had only delayed them for a few moments.

The Emperor of Shadow's soldiers passed hallway after hallway, each as empty as the last as they poured deeper and deeper. Before long, the lead of the group stopped, putting up a hand to motion the men following to stop.

"Something's not right. Where are they?" He paused for a moment to look to his sides; only more empty halls greeted him.

As if in response to his words, a single line of red glowing light flew down the ceiling and past, branching off into each hallway. As it spread, it sent itself into every room one by one. The men looked on in horror as the whole facility was overtaken.

"RUN!" their commander shouted, his final word.

Roughly halfway up a mountain on the other side of the valley, three men watched. The explosion was not big enough to make it rain debris, but it certainly sufficed to level their former home. As it moved, with charge after charge hitting the weakest points of the structure, it boomed.

"Well, that at least was a success," Lorrae said as he adjusted his clothes, looking more and more old and tired than he ever had before.

"Enough of one at least," his grandson agreed.

"No, that was a loss for us. They lost only a few men; we lost our only base of operations. It's clear who the winner of this engagement was." The prince, now fully a young man, frowned. "We'll have to split our forces now, keep a lower profile. I hate to emulate our enemy, but . . ."

"But it is likely the only way forward, my liege. Without cutting the head off of this snake, we'll never destroy it."

"I know, Lorrae. Come, let us go for now, there's much to do."

As a group, the three made their way into the caves. These mountains were riddled with holes and caverns, and this system could take them well to the other side of this peak without going above ground. They walked in silence, each man lost in his own thoughts, all too tired to share with his companions.

The bulk of their men had fallen back to some of the cities in the north. In particular one known as the free city of Ice's End, more commonly known as either Ice's End or the free city, depending on who you were. This metropolis was sizable and far flung from any other settlement.

The area around Ice's End was rather unusual. With a natural deep harbor going out to the Western Sea, it could both receive ships from the outside world and engage in fishing several cold-water species, which formed its primary industry. These fish would be salted and sold to any land a merchant could reach. Normally, salted fish would be a low-cost product but due to the influence of mana many of these cold-water species could be preserved for years with minimal effort and no flavor loss, making them an excellent commodity for the war-torn human lands.

While south of the city there was little other than frozen tundra for nearly a hundred miles, it sat upon a natural hot spring. This was the only reason the towering glaciers to its north hadn't overtaken the location, instead leaving it with incredibly strong natural barriers. If one wanted to invade, only the route by sea would work.

For these reasons, and several involving trade, almost nobody bothered to attempt to seize the city, at least they hadn't until now. Prince Lief had slowly moved his men and their families in, posing them as refugees had been difficult, as had hiding their mage status. He'd focused on physical magic users at first, since any of them could, with some training, pose as sailors of some skill.

As he exited the mountain cave, the prince looked toward the former dean. "Lorrae, are you ready?"

The old man nodded and began casting. This spell would speed them along much like the one he'd used to escape the capital, only at a much slower rate, and with far more stealth involved.

THREE WEEKS LATER

THE FREE CITY OF ICE'S END

LORD KNUD

Lord Knud looked out across his hall. For so many generations, his family had ruled this city, passing lordship from father to son down through the line. All the way to himself, where he feared it must end.

Knud was not a small man by any definition nor a young one; he had ruled for nearly forty years, and taken three wives in defiance of tradition, but only out of desperation. He'd loved his first wife, to be true. That woman had made his youth a joy, and when she failed to give him a child, he had felt wounded.

Though it bucked tradition, after many years, his first wife had encouraged him to take a second. She feared that her failure to produce an heir would sink her family. The lord had hesitated at first, but only at first, and he'd soon taken a second wife, a young girl whose beauty was renowned. Perhaps lust had gotten the better of him.

Sadly, with his second wife he'd failed as well to produce an heir. This was a stab to his own pride as a man, for clearly it was not any doing of his wives, but his own failing that kept him from continuing the family. After several years without so much as a pregnancy, he took a third wife, much to the chagrin of his first two.

While he'd held little hope at the time, eventually his third wife had felt her belly grow. The man had been a wreck for the entirety of her pregnancy, knowing that this might be his only chance. While he'd desired a son to continue his lineage, when he'd been handed his little Astrid, he could feel nothing but love for the small girl.

Now his eyes settled onto her once again. She'd grown so, from the small child into a beautiful young woman. At fifteen years of age, her platinum hair and brilliant blue eyes struck all who saw her. Her lithe grace opposed her father's bulk, but in their eyes, their noses, and their auras, they matched.

Lord Knud's reverie was interrupted by a servant. "My lord, another ship arrived with more refugees. You wished to be informed before they were let off?"

"Hmm," the man grunted, "How many? And their makeup?"

"Only five, my lord. Two cousins and their grandfather, the older cousin seems to have a wife and daughter with him."

As the ruler considered, a small voice chimed nearby. "Father, doesn't their respect in bringing their elder rather than abandoning him deserve some reward?"

Astrid knew her father was frustrated by the number of men coming to their city. They got few on a normal year, but recently the influx had been much larger. She understood his considerations; many men coming all at once could upset things, particularly if they were without families. That said, she also felt that they should give some kindness to those flee-ing this Lord of Shadows, a man who certainly sounded evil to her ears.

The Lord of Ice's End had always had a soft spot for his daughter, and to an extent she wasn't wrong. "Allow them to enter the city, but make it clear that they'll need to see to their own arrangements." At his words, the servant retreated, and the girl gave him her most radiant smile.

The elder went back to the paperwork that he must complete to keep his city running as his child began working on a new piece of embroi-dery. He didn't know of the potent forces he'd just invited into his home, or of their enemy in any meaningful way. He knew not that his decision would change the future of his people or of his lands. Knud's thoughts were focused on other things: the fishing industry's recent successes, the new public works that must be built, and his family's future.

CHAPTER 41

◆

ONWARD AND OUTWARD

I stirred as the sun made its way upward, shining bright light through my nearby curtains. Slipping out of bed, I looked to the bright day outside and stretched, feeling the bones in my spine pop one by one. It was a truly glorious feeling and today was a good day for it.

Today was the first day of spring. As always, I still wasn't sure about my exact birthday, but I was decidedly now twenty, at least for this world. Could I then consider this day my birthday? Well, not really, but I was celebrating anyway, for other reasons.

I walked over to the clothes I'd lain out the night before and began to dress, finally putting on a particular necklace I'd made recently. The small silver pendant hung perfectly and went well with the otherwise rather practical outfit.

Now properly ready, I turned to see the rest of my room. There were a few bags that the family servants would be carrying down to the carriage when I called, but otherwise it was fairly stark. All of my things had been packed and were either coming with me, or being stored for the duration of my trip. I preferred it that way, since I didn't really care much for most of my belongings and those few that I did would be coming with me, except for one.

As I came downstairs, I was met by my parents. Dad looked proud while Mom just seemed worried. My mother and I had never seen eye-to-eye on too many things, and this was one that we wouldn't this time either. She fretted about my desire to go and see things that I'd never seen and to be places I'd never been. And while I understood, I would never see things her way.

"You don't have to go if you don't want to," she said as I came down the stairs to meet her in the dining room.

"I do want to go, Mother."

She sighed, looking at my dad, but I knew she'd get no help there as he gave her a sort of apologetic smile.

"Just . . . be careful, and come back to us."

"That's the plan, Mom; it's not like I'm going alone. Oh, Dad, make sure to keep your pendant close. I don't think it'll be important, but you know, just in case."

He nodded. "I know, Alana."

"Oh, and, Mom . . ." When she looked up at me I pulled out a small package. "Keep this for me while I'm gone. I'd hate to lose it over in the Atali lands."

With trembling hands, she opened the little cloth bundle to reveal my spindle. It was the one she'd given me all those years before, that I'd always kept as a memento of home. I didn't spin much anymore, but even then it was still well worn.

As she took it out, her eyes teared up and she reached over to hug me. "I will, I will," she whispered as she wrapped me up in her arms.

I had already said my goodbyes to my small friend group, though I couldn't tell them exactly when or to where I was leaving. The staff at Lucien's had been supportive, if a bit of a pain. Charles had given me sort of a sad smile but wished me well. I think he rather fancied me, but nothing had ever really come of it. Pinea had suggested a party, an idea that I'd had to decline.

I'd told Kala over tea with her and her current squeeze, a nice girl with pitch-black hair. She'd been going through partners quite hurriedly as of late, and I think she was still trying to figure everything out. As a parting gift, I left her a big jar of sugar, since I knew she liked it and the temple wouldn't really approve of her spending her own money on it.

As I finished up my breakfast and rose, my father waved me off, wrapping my mother in one arm so that she couldn't follow me all the way out. "We'll leave it to you then, sweetheart, take care."

"All right, love you, bye." Dad wasn't much for long goodbyes, having seen plenty himself. I wasn't much for them either.

The ride to our meeting place wasn't much different than my normal commute to work, save for the pair of massive luggage crates that was sharing the vehicle with me. I looked almost wistfully out the window as the streets of Lithere passed me by. I'd left the city a few times in recent years, but there was no arguing that this place had been my home for what seemed like most of my life. I started counting up years on one hand but quickly abandoned that. It didn't really matter, since it was home now.

Soon enough, we pulled in. Rather than the lab, we were meeting at a separate locale, well, several separate locales. My group was forming up at a local inn, warded for our meeting today. Our researchers and assistants arrived one by one. It had been decided that the best way to make sure that anyone watching didn't realize what was up until it was too late was for us to all travel in our own groups, all under different names, at least until we made it to our ships.

My group consisted of various individuals from all across our labs. Olnir was, of course, the marginal leader of the group, much to our collective dismay. Selene joined with me as well, both of us worked well together, and we'd been through enough training with each other that we could work quite effectively as a team. For physical protection, we were joined by one of the current knights, Glen, a short and stocky fellow who I'd met some years ago during one of our training exercises. He wasn't fast as such, but I remembered him hitting like a freight train and being durable as granite, so that was good. The unknown part of our team were a pair I hadn't met, but who could only be brother and sister; their dirty blond hair matched perfectly, and they looked like gender-swapped versions of each other.

As I hopped down to join the group, our last member pulled in. Dras had grown up well from the reedy youth I'd met so long ago. Now, his dark brown hair fell a bit over his eyes, and he even had the beginnings of a closely cropped beard. I was fairly sure that Mystien had him join our group as a favor to me, and I wasn't about to question it. He'd become quite competent and I knew I could trust him.

"Now that we're all here," Olnir began, "we'll be going over our route. Our group is heading through the northern gate and turning to exit through the city of High Rock. From there, we'll head slightly north before turning west. Our eventual destination is here"—he pointed to a section of the map— "at the port city of Silverstone. Any questions?"

"How much does everyone know about our mission?" I asked the three members of the team I didn't often work with.

"Everyone knows what they need to, and not more." His message was clear, at least some of our members didn't know all the details about the gates, and there might well be some things I wasn't informed of.

"Our schedule?" Dras asked from the side.

"We'll make High Rock tonight. We'll stay at an inn when we get there and continue from that point. Our route should take us no more than fifteen days to make it to the port. The crossing can take anywhere between two and a half and three months, depending on conditions."

With no more questions, we all piled into a pair of carriages more suited to long-term travel and set off. When I saw the gate to the city through the small window as we were passing by, I could feel my heart pound in my chest. This was it; this was my chance to go on a grand adventure. Today was the day that it all started, and we could find our way to something finally major and world-changing. I wasn't sure I was really ready, but there was no point in second-guessing anything at this point.

The day's travel was rather uneventful. This close to the city and the former Central Duchies, the roads were good and everything was still in a sharp order. In the past, it would have been because of the king wanting to display how the area near his home was so much better, but now I suspected that the areas around all major cities were getting some benefits.

Dras, Selene, and I shared a carriage, and we had a few moments of light chatting throughout the day. Dras, in particular, had barely ever left Lithere in his life and had no idea how to deal with the countryside at all. He kept his face nearly pinned to the side by the window as we passed through fields and small groupings of trees.

"You know, I went out for a few of the school projects, but I never got the chance to just take it all in. The fields are so big, and there are so many more trees." He just couldn't seem to get over how much land we were covering.

"Dras, we're not even really out of the urban area proper. This is all cultivated, and rather densely; once we get out into the real countryside, there will be open land for miles."

"I know, it's just . . . It's one thing to know about it and another to actually see it."

"Wait till we get to the ocean; that'll be the real treat." With that, I leaned back and tried to take a brief nap.

When we arrived at High Rock, the sun was just starting to sink into the horizon. The sky taking on its deep red hues as the light began to slowly fade. This, of course, was a strong cue for us to very quickly find an inn for the night, because I doubted anyone wanted to sleep in these carriages when there were so many beds about.

It didn't take long for us to find somewhere with rooms open. The inn, called The Mermaid's Rock, was middling in how fancy it was. It wasn't cheap by any means, but was not super-expensive either. The building seemed to be going through some expansions, particularly recently, but it had all we needed. The room we girls shared even had a tub.

I quickly learned that the pair I didn't know were named Robert and Leah, and they were indeed twins. From what I could gather, they specialized in healing magic, flora, and fauna, respectively. There were no priests on this trip as they wouldn't be able to join us without forfeiting any claim to neutrality, so these two were, much like myself, bards.

"So you're here to help us manage with any plants or animals?" I asked Leah as we settled in.

"Well, I'm mostly here to see if there's anything useful that needs to be made note of. There aren't many trips going over to the Elven lands you know? This is a really big chance for me to get deep in there and learn about things I might never get to see otherwise."

"Oh."

"Yeah, so I'm supposed to help you lot with whatever it is you're doing while I look into new potential sources of wealth. Don't worry too much. I've studied all the documents, and even had a book of plant samples that one of my grandfathers bought some years ago. There are some insanely cool flowers that grow over there. Did you know that there's this one that you can use in medicine to . . ." She kept on for a while as I slowly lost concentration and drifted off to sleep.

There is only so much that one can look out onto the countryside and feel wonder. Turns out it's about three days, with a few punctuations for each new big thing like seeing mountains in the distance, or large forests. That was how long it took for Dras to stop being wowed by the landscape and start to get bored.

It had been fourteen days at this point, and we were all thoroughly tired of sitting in carriages as they rolled down the road. Our horses had been changed out a number of times, as had our drivers, and this was pretty normal from my understanding. The animals got tired, and the men just didn't know the roads nearly well enough. The new drivers were all military, so there wasn't much a reason to worry about them, and the roads were fairly clear.

There was still sporadic bandit activity, but even during the kingdom's years, it had been present only when things were really bad. With the new government being much more effective and far, far better at patrolling, we hadn't run into any issues. Most wouldn't attack carriages anyway, and even if they had, with the pure quantity of magical might housed in our little rolling boxes, we could have turned them into a thick paste.

In an unusual change, our vehicles rolled to a stop, and I tiredly blinked at the door. There were no sounds of a city nearby so I was a bit on edge until I heard the knock.

"I thought you might enjoy seeing this, so I asked the drivers to stop." Olnir's voice filtered through the wood, and after putting up a basic shield, I opened the door.

The late afternoon sun shone down upon us as we left our carriage, looking around. The man in question normally annoyed me to no end but today he had a bright smile on his face.

"What's going on?" I looked at him and where we were.

"This is the best place for a view—it's stunning" was his answer. If I had to judge by looks, I wasn't the only one a bit irritated by it.

The man himself didn't answer but rather turned to walk up a nearby hill. Selene gave me a quirked eye to which I could only shrug.

"If nothing else it's a good chance to stretch our legs. Let's go see what it's all about."

"What's that smell?" Dras asked from behind me.

I sniffed the wind briefly and thought I knew what we were in for. "Oh, I think we'll see in a moment."

As we crested the hill, the salt air blew over us, the scent of seawater and sand harsh but refreshing. From this little hill, we could see the town of Silverstone, and I instantly understood its name.

Two huge cliffs jutted out from the sides around the harbor, creating a natural and perfect place for ships to dock. They lived up to the name, for as the sun hit them, they sparkled silver in the light; some mineral in them must have shone, and it dazzled as we looked down on the fair-sized city. To me that was striking, but the others in our group just reacted to the ocean.

"It's so big," Dras said.

"I've never seen that much water in my life," Selene agreed.

The rolling ocean spread out behind the town, sending gentle waves to splash against its many docks. The blue-green water went on and on, seemingly endless as it stretched on to the horizon. We all took a long while to enjoy the scenery and compliment Olnir on his choice of attraction. This was followed by a brief and slightly foolish picnic where we watched the sun set over the horizon. It was a chance just too good for us to pass up, and we were a bit ahead of schedule anyway.

ABOUT THE AUTHOR

Wandering Agent is the North Carolina–based author of the Melody of Mana series as well as other fantasy and isekai stories.